RAYS OF HOPE · BOOK ONE

STAY WITH ME

MARIA LOEWEN FRIESEN

*To my husband, my parents, my brother, and
sister-in-law, thank you for your continuous support.
Without you this book would not have been possible.*

To my children, my inspiration.

CHAPTER ONE

Some moments you know you're going to remember forever; this was one of them. If she could, she would erase it from her memory. No one wanted to remember the night they killed their father.

Olivia's wet clothes clung to her skin. Her cold finger-tips held on-to her dad's jacket. Puddles covered the Stormont Vail Hospital parking lot. The biting Kansas wind pierced through her T-shirt. In mid-September, the weather should have been warmer.

She lifted the jacket and pushed it against her stomach. Two hours later, the storm was over. She could have waited two hours. She could have told Dad to stay at the office. They could have celebrated another day. She shifted her gaze to the parking lot cement. Her throat hurt. She inhaled deeply, forcing her lungs to work. She shook her head, closing her eyes, replaying the night's scenes in her mind.

"Looks like we'll have to cancel our plans. Even if I could make it home, it wouldn't be safe to risk it. We'll celebrate your birthday tomorrow."

"Dad, tomorrow isn't my birthday. It'll be too late then. It won't be the same." Olivia stood in front of the window, watching the wind bend the trees.

"Olivia," Mom looked up from the TV, "your dad will come home when it's safe to drive. Let him be."

"Oh, it's not that bad." The porch chair flew over the rails, onto the lawn. Water flowed over the rain gutters, and gushed out of the tube, creating a lake on the front lawn.

"Your mom's right, Olivia," Dad paused, "I'll tell you what, I'll keep an eye on the storm, and if it looks like it's calming down, I'll come home."

She sighed. "All right. Not the fourteenth birthday I had in mind."

"I promise I'll be home as soon as I can."

She hung up the phone and waited, standing at the living room window. In the background Reba played on TV. Mom crunched on the salted popcorn Olivia popped that afternoon.

For forty minutes the rain pelted down. The wind whistled, blowing around the corners of the house, mocking her. Then, like a hushed pack of howling wolves, it ceased. The rain stopped, and the tree branches lifted back to their normal height.

She glanced at her vibrating phone. "I'm about to leave. Be home in a few minutes."

The fire-fighters said he crashed into an oncoming vehicle. Both drivers were killed instantly. She knew why Dad drove, but why had the other? They should have known the storm would pick up again. They often did.

Olivia squeezed the tears behind her eyelids. She should have told him. Told him to stay home. She bit her jaw. Someone touched her shoulder and peeled Dad's jacket away.

"Leave," she said, opening her eyes.

"Let's go home."

"I'm not going anywhere. I deserve to be in there." Olivia titled her head toward the hospital. "I deserve to be dead." The volume of her voice raised; her words turned into weeping. "I want to be dead, Mom." She turned to face her. "I need to be, instead of him, he needs to be with you!"

Mom stood, staring at her, shaking her head. Olivia opened her mouth; the salty tears dribbling onto her inner lip. "I'm sorry."

Here stood a woman whose partner had been taken away. Mom was a widow because of her. Olivia shook her head vigorously. "I'm so sorry, Mom. Dad never would have left the office if it wasn't for me."

Mom stared at her. Olivia closed her lips. What was she thinking? Mom believed her. It was her fault.

"Mom?" she cried. "It's my fault." The words sounded like a question.

Mom lowered her gaze, cradling the jacket in her arms. Her boney shoulders sagging. She stepped around Olivia.

"Mom!" she cried, wanting the woman to stop. To comfort her. To tell her it wasn't her fault.

Mom's head tilted forward. Her back curved over the jacket. Her feet slushed through the puddles, as she walked across the parking lot.

Olivia straightened her chest, the crisp air drying the tears in her eyes. Her empty hands hung beside her hips. She breathed heavily, in and out. Mom blamed her.

Mom climbed into the Yukon. She closed the door, the taillights shimmering against the wet concrete. Would she ever forgive her?

The funeral came three days later. Friends and family swarmed from their vehicles dressed in black, dark purple, or dark blue. Olivia accepted their hugs. When they said "sorry for your loss," she nodded. Some were eager to get the politeness over with; while others continued comforting as they walked away, smiling over their shoulders. But all gathered in groups, shaking their heads and *tsking*, nodding and agreeing, glancing in Olivia's direction, then at Mom's.

"It's devastating … the poor girls, what will they do now?" Olivia imagined them saying.

The day after the accident people started stopping at their house. They gave casseroles and cookies; some brought soup. By the second day they'd collected so much, Dad's parents and sister came over to help them eat.

Mom invited the visitors in for coffee and served the cookies they had brought or the ones that a previous visitor had dropped off. Each time Olivia hid, anywhere but in the living room, pretending a chore or her homework desperately needed to get done. She kept unfolded laundry in baskets for moments like those. Most of the time she stayed close enough to listen in on the conversations, yet far enough away that no one would bother speaking to her.

The visitors would offer their sympathies. Some told jokes that no one laughed at. Some pitied Mom to the point where Olivia wanted to march in and make it stop. She hadn't meant to. She'd never meant for Dad to get killed. When the conversations ran dry, which they often did, they asked about Olivia. How was she doing? She and Erick were always so close, they'd say.

Olivia folded her T-shirts, listening like an old playlist she'd heard a hundred times.

They'd stop coming after the funeral. They'd return to their normal life. Would they invite them to join their parties and barbeques, or would they hesitate? Thinking, *maybe it was too soon for Mrs. Crandell and her daughter to return to normal life.*

Life would never return to normal. They'd eat quietly across from each other while desperate flies buzzed around the light bulbs. They'd fearfully glance at the head of the table, then shuffle the food around in their plate. Just like they had the last two times they'd eaten dinner alone.

Other people could talk about healing, how things would get better, but it was easy for them when they weren't the ones needing the healing. They weren't the ones who would have to face the coming years without their father. She would never heal.

"Olivia," a tall man appeared at the corner of her eye, "I noticed your solemn expression during the service." The pastor smiled pitifully, "I don't know what you're thinking right now, but I hope you know that the Lord will bring joy into your life again, if you let Him."

The pastor kept his posture straight, like a speaking doll strung around a pole in a plastic box. His hands hung in front of him, neatly folded. His smile never wavered and his eyes remained fixed on Olivia. She watched this man every Sunday and each time he looked the same. Neatly combed and properly clothed.

She faced him and said, "I know, but I don't intend on letting Him. I don't deserve joy. God can keep my dose for His God-fearing, righteous-living Christians. I'm sure the church could use the extra amount."

She glanced at the people sitting in a group talking. Probably about the same thing they'd talked about all afternoon. Those head-shaking, tongue-clicking, sympathy-offering, caring hypocrites could have all her joy. She didn't need it.

"Olivia, everyone deserves happiness. What happened to your dad, will happen to all of us one day. No one stays alive forever, it's part of living. Your dad's time came, and all of ours will too."

She stared at the pastor. Fury raised up her chest. She clenched her jaw and then relaxed it. Pity for the clueless man mixed in with her fury. How could someone have the nerve to speak like that to a person who'd barely lost a loved one? Did he not know better?

She stepped aside and walked away, needing to be alone. The thought of loneliness provided comfort for the first time in three days. She wanted nothing more than to be alone.

She kept her head low, hoping people would take the hint and not want to speak to her. Two feet away from the door, she heard Mom's silent sniffles. She was crying, again. Olivia searched the room for Mom's voice. She sat on a bench wiping her eyes, nodding as women stroked her arms, doing their best to comfort her. Surely, Mom's closest friends would provide some comfort. Hopefully they reminded her she hadn't lost everything. Only her partner, the one she shared her life with, the one who made her whole.

Olivia lifted her eyes to the door-frame she stood under and pressed her hand against the knob.

Mom lost her husband; she lost her father; they both lost their best friend. All because she insisted that he come home for her birthday.

Olivia unlatched the door. The wind yanked it open. She pushed it shut and stood beside it. The wind tousled her hair, flapping her skirt against her legs. The cold raised the hair on her arms. She lowered her head and allowed the tears to warm her face. She inhaled deeply and closed her eyes.

CHAPTER TWO

wo years and seven months later, she faced the church she
sat in on her father's funeral. The church she attended every
Sunday. She'd seen it many times throughout her childhood.
Every Sunday when her father took them to church. Every
day during Bible school and occasionally on a Wednesday
after she turned thirteen, until her father passed. She never
went to youth group after that. She never wanted to go. Dad
used to force her, saying she needed friends her own age.

The church's wooden double doors stood ten feet tall,
short compared to the height of the bell tower overhead.
Over the brown bricks stuck bronze letters spelling out the
church name. A demanding—perhaps welcoming to some—
building drawing attention to everyone who lived in or vis-
ited the suburb it stood in. Not every suburb in Topeka had
a church. Dad always said they were blessed to have one.

As a five-year-old, she agreed. Olivia proudly walked
through the giant dark stained doors into a room with
benches reaching to the very front of the soft red carpet-
runner. She held her head high as she nestled her bum into

the edge of the cushioned seat, resting her back against the bench. She always sat beside her dad, while Mom sat on the other side of him. He once said he felt like a kindergartener sitting between the prettiest girls in class.

At sixteen the building didn't hold any charm. The brown bricks seemed darker, the stained windows seemed dirty, the doors peeled and the knobs wiggled if you turned them just right. The rusty bell chimed unevenly over the cemetery.

Yet she attended church service every Sunday morning. Because Dad would want her to. He had never cared as much about youth group; therefore, she neglected it. Either way, her former job at the restaurant wouldn't have given her the time to go.

Olivia breathed in.

She often wished she could undo what she did that night. The night's scenes replayed in her dreams; in her thoughts. She wondered what their life would be like if her father had lived. The reason for his death was never lost on her. Her mother's continuous desire to push her away didn't help.

She sighed, lowering her neck.

Olivia checked the lavender colored dress she wore. She smoothed the skirt, turned in her flats and lifted her face to the parking lot, spotting the groom. He walked toward the building, patting his suite pockets. Surely, he hadn't lost the rings. Shouldn't he be inside, standing in front of a mirror, practicing his vows? The ceremony would begin soon. The groom disappeared through the side door of the building.

Olivia straightened her posture and forced her eyes to smile. If not for the crowd, but for the woman who deserved happiness more than anyone else. She inhaled deeply, relaxing her muscles as she exhaled. She closed her eyes. *It's time.*

She stepped around the open wooden door, into the church. Everyone stared at her. She should have taken the back door. With her face a respectable shade of red, she walked into the back room where Mom stood waiting. Mom had asked Olivia to be the maid of honor. Probably because it would've looked bad if she hadn't, but either way, Olivia accepted. She would stand beside her mom, the one woman in their household who had moved on from the past.

With her arms stretched out Mom turned a full circle. Unlike the night at the hospital, Mom looked young. Her cheeks lifted from smiling. Her straight, blond hair was freshly highlighted, reaching the top of her shoulders.

The love shone on her face when she spoke of her fiancé. Her face lit up like it used to when she spoke of Dad. Mom deserved to be loved, but how she found love in anyone else than Dad, Olivia would never understand. The thought of Mom loving another man seemed utterly wrong. But she hid her misunderstanding. It was Mom's big day—second big day.

"You look stunning." Olivia smiled and gave Mom a lose hug. "It'll be a spring wedding no one will forget."

Mom squeaked, like a teenage girl. She squeezed Mom's forearms and asked, "Are you nervous?"

"You have no idea." Mom's smiling eyes panicked. "What if I trip?"

"You'll be fine. You've done this before, remember?"

Mom nodded, her face sobering. Had she said the wrong thing? Was it inappropriate to speak of one's first wedding on the second?

Mom's hazel eyes met Olivia's. "Some people never find love their whole life; others are lucky enough to find it twice. Your father was amazing; I would go through it all again," Mom paused, her eyes bore into Olivia's, "for him." Then she lowered her gaze, like scrolling through flashing memories. "Everything," she muffled.

Voices crowded in the neighboring hall. Through the thin walls she could hear ushers directing people, babies crying, men greeting each other. The large front doors shutting, vibrating the standing mirror in the corner.

"Mom?" Olivia lowered her eyes, willing her mom to look at her.

She did. Her expression solemn. Olivia waited.

"Dave is wonderful, and I love him very much."

"I know you do." Olivia pressed her lips together, smiling the best she could. She held her mom's gaze, released her forearms, and stepped back. "This is your big day. Enjoy every bit of it."

Mom nodded. She looked herself over in the mirror and said, "It's time to get married."

And that's what she did. On Saturday, April twenty-fifth, at four o'clock, Mom said "I do" for the second time. Olivia hoped it would be the last time.

The reception followed the ceremony. People danced and laughed, celebrating in true fashion. When Mom cut the four-tiered cake she smiled and giggled the way Olivia imagined she had at her first wedding. Dave looked at Mom, completely captivated by her. Everyone could tell how he loved her. He smiled the way a fifteen-year-old boy smiled at his high school sweetheart. Thirty-nine-year-old Dave probably didn't know such love existed, considering he'd never married before.

Olivia stood in the corner, closing her water bottle. A medium size, blonde haired girl approached her. Olivia placed both hands on the bottle, smiling a hello, waiting for the girl to speak.

"So, you're Dave's stepdaughter." The girl paused, when Olivia didn't respond she continued. "I'm Samantha Hendrix, Dave's niece. But call me Sam, everyone does. I guess that makes us step cousins. I'm glad to finally have a cousin. My brother and I are the only children in the whole family."

Oliva smiled. So, this was Sam. Dave spoke of her once. He said the girl could talk for days and still wouldn't have said everything on her mind. Olivia hadn't thought much of it, not realizing she would be the one hanging out with her at family gatherings.

The more Sam talked, the less she would have to.

"Not that my brother could be considered a child, the

man's twenty-one years old. At that age you'd think he'd have a girlfriend. I don't see much of him anymore. We used to be close, then he turned eighteen and fool-headed." Sam moved her head and gestured her hands as she spoke. The ice tea in her cup nearly swirling over.

"Moved in with Nate when he was twenty. Nate bought a house, and he charged Wyatt, my brother, a healthy rental fee. Later Josh moved in. Nate's the smartest one of them all. But my brother and Josh moved out about a month ago."

Sam sipped her tea and swallowed. Her eyes fixed on Olivia while her head teeter-tottered, switching rhythms when she spoke. "Nate works on Dave's farm. I see him around when I clean Dave's house. He's the most good-looking guy you will ever see." Sam rolled her eyes.

"But I guess he has a very big temper and probably a lot of stubborn pride. Him and the boys got into a big fight and Nate kicked everyone out. I don't know whose fault it really was, of course my brother won't admit he had any fault in it. Probably didn't, I don't know." Sam shrugged. "My best guess, all three men are equally to blame."

Olivia breathed in, for Sam's sake. Sam sipped her tea, lightly smacking her lips, like a food critique evaluating wine. She lowered the cup, tilting her head, focusing on Olivia.

"So, when are you moving to the farm?" she asked.

Olivia sank her shoulders, releasing her breath. Dave's farm.

The place she was to call home for the next two years and four months. The place she would come home to for

Thanksgiving, Christmas, summer breaks. Three hundred-fifty miles west, across the state.

"When Mom and I are done packing. Mom and Dave rented a cabin for the weekend, they should be back Tuesday afternoon." She set her gaze on Sam. "I'm guessing we'll leave next Tuesday."

One week later, Olivia taped the last box in her room. She stacked it on top of the others that needed to go into the rental truck. The mattress that laid on the carpet was to be loaded the next morning. Her sleeping bag laid stretched out on the mattress with a pillow at the end. She surveyed the four walls, plastered with white and purple wallpaper. The white trim shined after the scrubbing they received. A chain dangled from the lightbulb in the walk-in closet. Olivia sat up and yanked the chain, turning the light off.

The empty house—the empty home—should have affected her. Where laughter once echoed, where warm food once steamed on the table, while three hands joined in prayer. But the house lost its nostalgic qualities over the years. The family photos hung on the wall, but the frames locked the reveries inside. The growth marks on the kitchen entry frame, visible, but isolated, nearly cold to the touch. The back-yard displayed the once loved yard games that now sat untouched.

The house had become simply a stop in their routine.

Olivia picked up the box and walked downstairs. To the left of the stairs, the door to Mom's room stood open. The same room Mom cried in the night Dad passed. A lot happened since that night. Mom remarried. Olivia discovered hard work. She'd gotten her license. But that only scratched the surface.

She remembered that night all too well.

"It's not my fault" she'd repeated, fighting her conscience. But the truth wouldn't leave. It snuck under her covers, into her mind, until her scattered heart sobbed, and her body weighed down, making every move nearly impossible.

She'd gripped the railing, taking one step at a time down the stairs. Mom's sobs drifted up the stairs, stabbing Olivia. Fearfully, she'd taken the last steps. The rest of the house was dark, not another soul in a three thousand square-foot home. Olivia opened the cracked door, softly calling out, "Mom."

Aching sobs cried out.

Again, Olivia called, "Mom." All the while, asking herself why she still stood there. The Mom she remembered never comforted her, she wouldn't start now.

But Olivia called again. Mom, lifting her head, aimed her swollen eyes at her daughter. She yelled, "Get out."

Olivia stood frozen, willing Mom to take back her words. *No, no,* she'd thought. *She didn't mean it.*

Mom's scratchy voice broke through her sobs; she began to whimper. Quietly she said, "go."

Olivia stared at her mom. Her open palms hanging beside her hips, her eyelids dampening, waiting.

She clogged her aching throat, and turned away. *One step, three step. Five, seven, nine* ... she leaped up the second floor, leaned against the hallway wall and slid down. She hugged her knees, rocking.

Her own mother hated her. She was the one who begged Dad to leave the office in the storm. He would have never left had she not asked him to. Mom blamed her. Olivia lowered her head to her knees and slowed her rocking. Afraid and alone, like she deserved.

The sound of Mom's footsteps jerked Olivia back to the present. Mom shuffled through her wallet, selecting dollar bills, setting them on the counter. "Could you pick up dinner? I ordered it half an hour ago," Mom looked at Olivia, "by the time you get there it should be ready."

Olivia set the box down and walked toward Mom. She grabbed the money, stuffing it inside her pocket, and lifted the keys off the counter.

"Anything else?"

Mom clasped the wallet shut. "No." She looked up, smiling. "Thank you." She strode past Olivia toward the box beside the staircase.

Nestled into the Yukon, Olivia slid the keys in and turned the ignition. She backed out of the driveway, deciding to make one last stop.

At the cemetery, irises bloomed underneath bare tree branches. The birds sung over the freshly mowed grass. In the distance automatic sprinklers hissed and popped out of the ground. Strands of hair played around her face in the light early evening breeze. She hugged her elbows, wishing she'd brought a sweater. She gripped the keys in her right hand, stepping to the foot of Dad's grave.

She read the words she had read every week for nearly three years. *Erick Crandell… Born 1982-Died 2018… beloved Son, Husband, and Father…* Olivia bent forward, crossing her legs as she sat down.

Thirty-six years of life.

A tear rolled down Olivia's face. She dropped her eyelids, remembering everything about that night. Her woolen socks rubbing the thick carpet. The sound of Dad's clear, heavy voice over the phone.

The sticky black screen still felt glued to her ear.

Wind sweeping the furniture off the porch, rain streaming down the street, full-grown tree branches dipping into the lake on the front lawn. Rain clattering against the living room window. Loud. Like rioters bellowing on the streets.

Olivia wrinkled her lips. She pressed them together until they hurt.

It was the worst storm in four years. Yet, she begged Dad to drive home. She *begged* him. *She* did it. A tear trickled down.

Olivia inhaled, deeply, resisting the urge to sob without end. She needed to do what she came to do. She opened her eyes.

"I'm leaving, Dad," she paused, staring at the stone, half waiting for a reply.

She shook her head.

"Mom has met someone new. He's a farmer. Can you believe it? Mom being a farmer's wife. What your Lord thought when He put those two together, I have no idea."

She studied the stone in front of her.

"A lot of the things your Lord does don't make sense to me," she paused. "You won't see me graduate. You and Mom won't be able to spoil your grandkids. You won't be able to sit at the kitchen table" a chuckle swelled up in her throat, "and lecture me about not coming home often enough."

She smiled at the thought of Dad sitting on the floor playing with grandchildren. Then she sighed and wiped her eyes. "But that won't happen. You're gone. Mom has married another man, another man she sleeps with, laughs with, a man she shares everything with."

Olivia ripped a grass leaf apart. "But I won't ever find another dad. I'm sixteen now. You and Mom raised me, and that's enough for me."

Sounds of the suburbs played in the background. A vehicle door closed on the church parking lot. Birds flapped overhead, calling to one another. Minute after minute, she gazed at the stone. Finally, she looked up. The sun would set soon. She needed to pick up dinner. She stood up, brushed the grass off her jeans and stepped closer to the headstone.

It was all too real. A chapter in a book that could never be torn out. No matter how hard one pulled, the pages could never be removed. Guilt dug into her soul. She would never move on. Couldn't.

Olivia bit her lip. She'd made her bed; she would lie in it.

Her focus lowered to the headstone.

"This is it."

She placed a hand on the stone. "I'll take care of her. I promise." She squeezed the rock. What she wouldn't do to hug Dad's shoulders.

"I'm sorry, Dad."

"Thank you, for caring enough about me to risk your life. But I wish you hadn't. I should have never asked you to come home." She squeezed the tomb, until the edge jabbed her hand. "I'm sorry, Dad."

Olivia removed her hand from the tomb and straightened her back. "Goodbye."

Her throat swelled, she breathed heavily. After a second, she bolted.

Maybe she felt more sorry for herself. Dad was dead. He didn't feel pain, but she was alive. A beating heart that felt every ounce of pain the so-called loving Lord laid on it.

CHAPTER THREE

I t looked okay.

White stucco was peeling off the two-story house. At one time the red shingles could have looked nice. The faded red shutters around the windows added a bit of flare. The pear tree shaded half of the house. The porch railing looked freshly painted. It matched the white porch swing hanging in front of the window. Oil stains surrounded the welcome mat. Two dog bowls and a food container stood in the corner.

It was a downgrade from their home in Topeka. Even the grass seemed of lesser value. The yard looked bare—almost vacant. A clothes-line stood beside the house, a pear tree stood in front of the house and a Locust tree stood behind the house. This was a bachelor pad. But Olivia had to admit, the farm echoed with life.

The cow mooed, the calf cried, horses nickered, chickens clucked. The sound of a power tool drifted out of the round-top; something clunked against its concrete floor.

Olivia scanned the lawn. The further away they'd driven from Topeka, the shorter the grass, the shallower the river, the fewer the lakes and the fewer the trees. But *no* trees? Two didn't count. She could hear her dad now, if he saw what she saw, "God must have run short on supplies when he created Southwest Kansas." Her thoughts exactly.

The rental truck door shut behind her. Footsteps crushed the gravel. Olivia stood, arms dangling from her shoulders, staring at the house that would be her home. Mom stepped to her right; Dave stepped to her left.

Olivia heard Mom mutter, "Oh, boy."

She smiled to herself. How would Mom fare under these new conditions? Mom was a city girl, who now lived fifteen miles from the nearest Starbucks—if Shallow River even had one.

"Well," Dave looked at Mom, then at Olivia, "let's go inside."

Olivia stepped forward, her flipflops scraping the concrete sidewalk. The warm early May breeze curved around the corner of the house, lightly swinging the porch swing. She'd love to be the one swinging the swing. Maybe when Mom didn't need her, she'd sneak down for a few minutes.

She stepped over the doorframe and walked toward the dining area. Dave glared at her, glancing at her feet, then at her face. Olivia looked at her feet.

Oh.

She slipped off her flipflops, then looked at Dave. He nodded. He turned to his left, into the living room. Mom's shoes were neatly placed against the wall by the door. She followed her husband. *Strange man,* Olivia thought.

One sofa, one love seat, one coffee table, and one side table stood neatly in the middle of the room, facing the square box TV. The early nineties TV stood against the sage green wall. Dave had most likely purchased his furniture in the early 2000's and had never updated. Olivia scanned the room. Neat, but not nice. Not good looking. The scratched wood floor poked her bare feet. Olivia clasped her hands together behind her back and bit the inside of her cheek. Not nice.

In front of Olivia stood an oak stair frame with white painted railing on the right side. Dave noticed Olivia examining it. He nodded toward the stairs. "Up there is your room." He turned toward the stairs. "I'll show it to you." The three of them walked up the stairs, Dave leading, Mom in the middle and Olivia last.

They walked along a narrow hallway. The floor was lined with short wool carpet, and the walls were covered with striped wallpaper. The upstairs consisted of one bathroom and two bedrooms. Both bedrooms were completely empty. The bathroom had the essentials, but didn't look like anyone ever used it.

"Our bedroom is downstairs, behind the living room," Mom said, smiling. "You'll have the whole upstairs to yourself."

Olivia nodded. After several silent seconds, she turned around and headed downstairs, her mom and stepdad following. "I'm going to move in then."

She slipped on her flipflops and walked out the door to the loaded rental truck. A tall guy with long curly hair walked toward the house, coming from the round-top. He wore a white T-shirt and blue jeans that flared out over his cowboy boots. Dave's hired hand? A handsome man. *Very* handsome.

He smiled when he saw her. Olivia attempted to smile, dipped her head, and strode to the back of the rental truck. She pushed the door up. Boxes were stacked from the floor to the ceiling. She huffed, stepping onto the bumper, using the vehicle frame to help herself up. She stretched her arm and wiggled the top box loose.

"Let me help." The man's voice spoke.

A hand removed the box from her reach. The creases in his hand were stained with oil. Dirt circled his short finger-nails. Olivia looked down. He set the box on the gravel. His T-shirt slid forward, showing his lower back. He straightened. Olivia lifted her eyes to the boxes and reached for another one.

"Let me do it." He leaped up, removed the box, and set it on the ground. He wiped the oil off on his hip and reached a hand up toward Olivia. She placed her palm in his and wrapped her fingers around his hand. His skin felt like sandpaper.

"Thank you," she said.

"You're welcome." He dipped his chin, smiling.

She felt the warmth of his hand against hers. She'd for-gotten that she was holding it. She let go of his hand and slipped her fingers into her jean pocket.

"I'm Nate Johnson."

"Olivia Crandell."

"Nice to meet you, Olivia."

She smiled, lowering her eyes to the boxes. Her name sounded better when he said it. She rarely talked to anyone, especially not cute guys. Nate looked like he was in his twenties. How old did he think she was?

Wanting to fill the silence, she said, "We should bring the boxes inside."

"I'll follow you."

Nate followed her into the house. Mom and Dave stood in the middle of the room. To the right of the front door stood a round wooden dining table and one buffet table. Nate set the box on the dining table, wiped his hands on his jeans and greeted Mom. Nate's hospitality pleased Mom. Olivia could tell by the silly smile on her face.

"I'm sorry I couldn't make it to the wedding," Nate said, "unfortunately the farm keeps me pretty busy."

"It's all right, someone had to watch over things while Dave was gone." Mom smiled at Dave like a love-struck sixteen-year-old girl.

Dave focused his attention on Nate. "How is everything?"

"The 8430 broke. It'll set corn planting back a week."

"Let's take a look."

Nate nodded and walked out the door.

Dave looked at his wife. "I'll see you at supper. Do with the house whatever you want." Dave kissed Mom's cheek and walked out the door.

Dave loved his farm. She could tell.

For two days Olivia and Mom unpacked and broke down boxes. Mom stood over the couches and said, "good thing we kept our couches." Dave's couches had to go. They set his couches on the front lawn, vacuumed the floor, and replaced Dave's couches with Mom's brown leather couches.

They slid the square TV down the porch steps and threw the cord onto the lawn. Then they carried their twenty-inch flat screen TV out of the rental truck and set it where the old one had stood. Their side tables and coffee table hadn't fit in the rental truck, so Dave's would have to do until Mom had the chance to purchase new ones.

Olivia scooted her bed from one wall to the other. Exhausted, she told herself it was good enough. She set her homework desk in front of the window. The tree blocked her view, but it would have to do. She grabbed her books and set them against the wall. There wasn't much to see any-ways. She mounted posters and pictures on the wallpapered wall and hung up or folded all the clothes she owned. She stepped out of the closet and nodded. Good.

She scanned the room and caught a glimpse of her dad in a photo. Melancholy shadowed her thoughts. Nearly three years later, the pain of her father's death continued to change into a pain she couldn't identify, a deep feeling that brought sadness beyond explanation.

If her father was here, she wouldn't have this pain. If she hadn't begged Dad to come home that night, Dad would be here. They'd still live in Topeka and she would still have a parent that loved her. The truth about her life never left her.

Now that Mom remarried, she kept away from Olivia even more. Thinking back on her childhood, did Mom ever want her around? Mom never took her shopping. Olivia's clothes just appeared in her closet. Not until she was able to drive by herself had she picked out her own clothes. Although Olivia never minded that part, thankfully Mom had good taste.

She picked up the broken-down boxes and walked down the stairs.

"You must deep clean." Sam kicked off her shoes and marched to the kitchen bar table. She smacked her hand onto the white Formica countertop. "When Dave's grandma comes over, she'll waddle through the house and examine every nook and cranny. She's seen this house hundreds of times, but now that you're living here, she'll expect you to do all the cleaning. I did it until now, but she won't have it. She'll say, "Dave's wife's *ne fulle!* Her walls were covered in fly poop. I thought my Dave knew better than to marry a lazy wife," she'll say to my grandma. Then she'll tsk her tongue and say, "Those lazy Englishers."

Olivia and Mom stood in the kitchen, eating breakfast, staring at Sam.

"Because of Dave's wedding I didn't get the chance to do it this year, so now you have to. But I'll help you since it's your first time, we just won't mention that to Great Grandma. Next week you'll invite Great Grandma, Grandma, and your sister-in-law—my mom and me for *vaspa*. Coffee and sweets at four," Sam explained. "Then she'll look at your spotless house and nod, saying, "*soa goot*." That's what you want her to say, you want her to say it's *really good*. That's why I'm going to help you. You say you've deep cleaned before, but your deep cleaning isn't up to a Russian Mennonite's standards. I know because I've cleaned Englisher's houses after they say they've deep cleaned, but it's never really clean."

That day, Sam poured steaming hot water into three buckets, scented with Fabuloso and dish soap. She handed them each a mop, a rag, and a toothbrush. Mom reluctantly obeyed Sam's orders and listened to Sam point out Mom's cleaning flaws. Olivia knew her mom well enough to know she did it because she wanted to please Dave's family.

Sam over-emphasized the need for a spotless house. Their house in Topeka always smelled and looked clean. Sam spoke as though they had been pigs.

Together they went room by room, scrubbing the ceilings and walls with wet rags. They dusted the fans, lights, and every item in each room. Stripped and washed every linen in sight, then hung them outside to dry in the warm spring air. They moved the newly situated furniture, then swept or vacuumed, whichever worked best. After that they shampooed the carpets. On the wood floors, they rinsed their rags and wiped every floor corner. When the rags couldn't reach, they used their toothbrushes.

After three days, they reached the kitchen.

"Oh," Sam sighed, "the kitchen. Good thing Dave doesn't have a lot of cookware."

"I brought all of mine," Mom said.

"And they're all in there?" Sam's eyes widened.

Mom nodded.

Sam tilted her head. "Do you cook a lot?"

"I love it. I bake when there is nothing to cook."

"That's why Dave married you. You warmed your way to his heart through his belly. He loves to eat. Wouldn't guess it though, by the way he looks, would you?"

Sam scanned Mom up and down. "You two make a good pair."

Mom stared at Sam, obviously annoyed, but Sam didn't seem to notice. She strode into the kitchen, plopped down in front of a cabinet and began emptying it out.

Two days later Olivia dumped the last bucket of tan colored water out the back door. She wiped out the bucket, then threw the rag into the hamper. Mom dumped the last set of curtains onto the dining table and set the whicker laundry basket on a chair. Olivia sat down and watched her sort through the fabric.

Mom looked out the window, watching Sam climb into her blue convertible Jeep. She shook her head. "I don't know about that girl."

Olivia watched Sam drive off. "I wonder if she drinks coffee?"

Mom laughed. "Goodness, any girl with that much energy shouldn't be allowed in the coffee aisle." Mom picked up the basket and walked into the laundry room, then back into the dining room.

"I'll hang up the curtains if you want to go outside." Mom bunched the curtains together in her arms. "You haven't seen much of the farm yet."

"Fresh air would be nice. Are you coming?"

"No, I have some things I'd like to get done."

Olivia nodded, then walked out the door, barefooted. She rubbed her shoulders. She'd never been this tired in her whole life. A twelve-hour shift at the restaurant couldn't compare to this. How could Mom still want to work?

Olivia shrugged. Let her work.

CHAPTER FOUR

On Monday morning at eight o'clock on the dot, Olivia walked into the round-top for the first time. The air smelled of motor oil. Hundreds of stains and a fresh layer of dirt covered the concrete floor. Multiple tools that Olivia couldn't tell apart hung on pegboards. Toolboxes lined the left side; in front of the toolboxes stood a big wooden table. Against the far end wall, plastic jugs were neatly lined on wooden shelves. Three four-wheelers stood in front of the jugs; beside the four-wheelers, pushed into the corner, stood a blue 60's model pickup. Beside the pickup, against the long rectangular wall hung shovels, brooms, ropes, chains and other things Olivia couldn't identify.

What caused Dave to think she could work on a farm? What caused her to say she could? She could tell the difference between a Phillips and flathead screw driver. Only because of furniture assembly instruction manuals.

The door opened behind her, sending in a nippy morning drift. "Good morning," Nate said, the door shutting.

Olivia turned around. "Good morning."

He stood in front of the door, coffee cup in hand. His blond hair curled around the edges of his cap. He looked cuter than she remembered.

He set his coffee cup on the wooden table and sat down in one of the lawn chairs.

"Are you gonna sit all day?"

Nate chuckled. Why? It wasn't funny. Wasn't there work to be done? "We have to wait for Dave."

Oh. Olivia breathed. She turned her eyes on Nate, hoping he'd stay busy on his phone. She didn't remember ever meeting someone so attractive. Sam's opinion matched her own exactly, "most good-looking man you'll ever see."

She rolled her eyes to the floor. She needed to control her thoughts. Nothing good would come from admiring her co-worker. Only distraction, which would surely lead to unemployment.

Two minutes later, Dave walked into the shop and told them his plans for the day. After Nate left to continue with the corn planting, Dave turned his attention on Olivia. He adjusted his cap and said, "Well, well, well."

He looked at her. "Follow me."

He walked out of the shop. Olivia followed him across the gravel and onto the grass to the front of the barn door. He pushed the sliding door open and out came two black cats. She followed him into a room filled with ropes, brushes, saddles, garden tools and other things Olivia couldn't identify.

Dave pulled the light bulb string. The bulb swung from

the ceiling, above Dave. The wooden floor creaked as Dave walked over to the garden tools. Four-inch holes dotted the walls and floors. The place was clean of spider webs and dust, yet Olivia shuddered, thinking of all the mice and snakes behind and underneath the wooden plants.

When she asked Dave about it, he handed her a rake and said, "That's what the cats are for."

"What am I supposed to do with this?" Olivia held the rake in front of her.

"Clean." Dave handed her a shovel. "Wheelbarrow is around the door. The cow's stall and the chicken coop need to be mucked. The barn needs to be thoroughly raked. Cats poop everywhere. By then it'll be lunch time. After that, you can till a patch of dirt for your mom's garden."

Dave patted her on the shoulder. "You'll be all right." Then he left.

Since when did Mom garden? Mom had never grown a plant in her life, other than maintaining a few rose bushes, boxwoods and the lawn.

Olivia drove the wheelbarrow a few feet forward to what she guessed was the cow's stall. Inside the stall, a sliding door accessed the outdoor cow pens. The two open doors allowed plenty of fresh morning air to flow through the barn. The fresh morning smell almost did enough to mask the manure odor—almost.

Olivia carefully kept her feet away from the patty clumps, not wanting to ruin her sneakers. She extended the rake as far as possible, gathering all the clumps into one pile. Why let the cow inside at all? Couldn't it just stay out, like the cattle did on the pasture ground? And why only have one cow at the farm? Why not have it with the other cattle?

Olivia focused on the ground, scooping the manure onto the shovel. A giant nose nuzzled the inside of her knee. Olivia squealed and turned around. A golden calf with big brown eyes looked at her. With its nose pointed up, the calf stared at Olivia's face.

"Aw, where'd you come from?"

A cow.

Olivia looked up. A calf came from a cow, so surely the cow was close by.

Olivia's eyes widened. A full-grown golden momma cow stood underneath the door frame. She planted her front legs firmly against the compact dirt floor, while her hind legs stood out in the sunshine. Olivia picked up the rake and held it out in front of her. She pointed the rake to the cow, nearly hitting the calf.

"Stay away." Olivia waved the rake in the air.

The rake hit the calf's forehead. The calf jumped sideways toward its momma.

The momma lowered her head and charged forward. She punched Olivia above the knees, sending her to the ground and the rake flying. Olivia scrambled to balance herself on her palms and scooted backward against the wall. The cow threw her head, aiming for the girl threating her calf. Olivia threw herself to the side, dodging another blow. She crawled out of the stall on her belly, jumped up and shut the gate.

Olivia rubbed her legs. The bruises would show yet. She looked around. The cats sat on the hay bales, staring at her. After a few seconds they resumed with their "paw-licking."

Olivia sighed and focused her attention on the tools inside the stall. The half-finished job needed to be completed, otherwise Dave would ask about it and she'd have to tell him about the incident.

The cow stepped out of the stall. *There!* She opened the gate and tiptoed behind the calf. Once the cow and calf rounded the corner, she ran to the door and quickly slid it shut. She stood, her back to the door, taking a moment to relax.

Olivia finished raking the stall. After she safely placed the tools outside of the stall, she opened the sliding-door and ran to the gate before the cow came for another visit.

She wheeled the wheelbarrow to the chicken coop and began scraping poop off the concrete floor. She dumped shovel after shovel into the wheelbarrow, creating a mountain. She used the shovel to punch it down, wanting to make room for the remaining residue.

The wheelbarrow began to sway. Olivia rushed to balance it, but gravity took control, dumping the pile of animal poop onto her sneakers. Animal waste reached to the bottom half of her calves.

Olivia shook her head and breathed deeply. She stepped out of the pile and shook the remains off her feet. Small clumps stuck to the cracks of her sneakers. She wasn't about to remove the clumps with her fingers. She looked at the mountain laying on the chicken coop floor. She grabbed the shovel and began the task all over again.

Around five o'clock, Olivia stood in the freshly plowed garden. Her shoulders ached, her hands shook and moist dirt stained her sneakers. She placed her hands above her hips and glared at the tiller. Her legs ached at the thought of pushing it into the round-top. Dave and Mom stood beside her. Their casual chatter echoing throughout the farm.

"Tomatoes too," Dave said, "homegrown tomatoes taste better than anything you can buy in the store."

Olivia faced them.

"Yeah." Mom stared at the patch of dirt, nodding.

One of the black cats brushed against Mom's bare legs. The cat scratched its face and looked up, mewing.

Dave laughed. "I think he likes you."

Mom smiled and picked up the cat. "You'll help me garden, won't you?"

"You'll do great. It'll be nice to have someone growing vegetables on our own property instead of my sister always bringing them to me."

Dave and Mom walked off the patch of dirt, continuing their conversation. The two looked naturally happy together. Olivia lowered her eyes. Would she ever find that again? Happiness. She'd forgotten how it felt. To be happy.

Olivia walked up the steps to the mudroom door. The sun hovered over wheat fields, winding down the farm. She set the bucket of eggs on the concrete steps; holding the door open with her back, she lifted the egg bucket and stepped into the mudroom. She set the milk pail and the egg bucket onto the wooden countertop beside the clay sink, in front of the window.

She'd remain forever grateful to Dave for milking the cow. Removing hens from their nests without getting pecked proved challenging enough. Squeezing milk out of a cow … She preferred not to think about it. Dave could do it. She slid off her sneakers, grimacing at the smell of sweat, dirt, and manure. She'd probably never smelled worse.

An aroma of seasoned meat and fresh evening air filled the kitchen. Steam rose from the simmering pot on the propane oven, drifting out through the open window above the kitchen sink. Underneath the cooktop, the oven light shone, displaying a cast iron pan filled with corn bread dough.

Something about the small, open floor plan felt inviting, welcoming. If she listened closely, she could probably hear the animals chewing, and the chickens scratching the dirt. A peaceful kind of quiet.

Nate walked up the front porch steps and smiled at Olivia.

He should go home.

The moon hovered over the farm, softly lighting the white

barn and galvanized round-top. It was late, but Olivia on the porch swing was an invitation he couldn't resist.

"I see you're enjoying the night air." Nate stood in front of the swing. "You mind if I sit?"

Olivia shook her head.

The swing creaked when Nate sat down. He stretched one arm along the back and the other on the arm rest, examining the swing to check for cracking. *It would hold.* His gaze landed on Olivia. The porch light glimmered on her black hair and her lightly tanned cheeks. Nate cleared his throat and looked away.

"It's nice out here," she said. "We didn't get nights like these in Topeka."

"The city. It hides God's beauty."

"With man's eagerness to build." Olivia looked ahead, as if too captivated by the scene to look away.

"Exactly." Nate glanced at her, not allowing himself to linger in her beauty.

"You worked late." She looked at him.

"Corn needs to be in the ground. We're already two weeks behind everyone else."

In the distance coyotes howled, owls hooted, and crickets chirped. The farm animals slept in the corrals. The equipment was parked on the side of the round-top. Yellow light shined through the windows of the house.

The song of the country, the painting of the American dream.

A thought he often repeated to himself. He would work

and enjoy this land until his skin wrinkled, his hair turned gray, and his joints gave out.

Nate turned to face Olivia. Her eyes carried something he hadn't seen in other girls. Eyes that always hurt, carrying a knowledge, a truth, an understanding of reality.

"Does your dad still live in Topeka?"

She continued to swing, eyes pointed ahead, her hands folded in her lap. But her muscles tensed; for a second her face fell like an athlete who suffered a blow.

"I'm sorry." He forced his eyes away, focusing on the railing. "I didn't mean to pry."

"My dad died in a car crash almost three years ago."

He jerked his head to face her. "I'm so sorry, I just assumed ... I didn't know." He lowered his eyes to his knees. Dave never mentioned his fiancée's widowhood. Or her former husband. Nate always assumed she was divorced. But he should have known better. Dave also came from a Mennonite background. Mennonites didn't believe in remarrying unless their former partner was deceased.

"It's okay."

"How did he die?" Nate looked up.

Olivia's jaw clenched, her eyes lowered to the railing, her swinging slowed.

"I shouldn't have asked." Nate lifted his hands. "I'll stop now."

He studied her. His heart somewhat heavy. "I didn't mean to hurt you."

She lowered her head and placed a hand on the arm rest. "You didn't, I did." Olivia stood up.

She did what? Nate's eyes followed her, until she stepped into the house. Part of him wanted to run into the house and force her to explain.

He'd upset her, hadn't he? He'd said things he shouldn't have.

He sat in silence, as the mosquitos flew around the porch light, wondering if he'd messed up. The girl that filled his thoughts since he'd met her left in the middle of a conversation. He ran his fingers through his hair. Yup, he'd messed up.

CHAPTER FIVE

The day came when Mom invited Great-Grandma, Grandma, Aunt Mary, and Sam for *vaspa*. That morning, Mom baked a coffee cake, key lime cupcakes, and cinnamon rolls. She set out homemade bread, freshly baked from the day before, and two different types of jam. She lifted the lid off the butter tray and debated if she wanted to serve her first attempt at homemade butter. She shook her head and set the tray back into the fridge.

Olivia scooped six tablespoons of ground coffee into the coffee maker and poured in six cups of water. One for each person.

"Oh no, Olivia." Mom took the coffee jar from Olivia's hands, and began scooping more coffee into the paper filter. "More coffee." Mom shoved the jar into Olivia's hands and turned around. "The bread." She lifted the loaf out of the oven. "I needed to reheat it, not bake it again."

Olivia set the coffee maker to brew and focused on her mother. "Calm down, these people are your relatives. This is not the last time you'll get a chance to impress them."

Mom shook her head, and sat down on a highchair by the bar table. "I don't want to impress them. I just want to do it right." She sagged her shoulders.

"Dave didn't marry you because you're just like his sister, his mother or his grandma, he married you because you're you."

Mom nodded. She winced and squeezed her arms against her stomach. Olivia rushed to her side.

"Are you okay? What's wrong?"

Mom relaxed, lifting her head, taking a deep breath. "It's gone now."

"Do you have those pains often?" Olivia asked.

"Someti—" Someone knocked on the front door.

They heard speaking and looked at each other. Sam's voice. A joyful noise that made your head hurt but brought a smile to your lips. Mom walked to the door and welcomed them in.

Great-grandma waddled through the door, behind the rest of them. Mom closed the door and offered them a seat around the dining table.

"I love what you've done with the place. It never looked this good when it was just Dave living here." Mary said as she sat down. "Oh, Dave kept it neat and clean, with Sam's help. But he never did make it feel cozy. It always felt like a house, never like a home. Now," Mary nodded, "the minute you walk through the door, it feels homey."

"Yes, that's what I thought too," Sam said.

"Thank you. I did my best."

"Maybe later we could look at your garden. Or have you not planted anything yet?"

Mary, a few years older than Dave, spoke the entire time the coffee brewed. She wore a sky-blue T-shirt with a white maxi skirt. Her blond hair was pulled up in a loose bun, curls framing her face. Except for his darker hair color, Dave looked like his sister. Growing up with Mary, Dave probably never had the chance to talk. It would explain his quietness.

Grandma and Great-Grandma wore their black head covering. Olivia saw them wear it at the wedding. Grandma, with a few less wrinkles than Great-Grandma, wore a homemade dark purple dress. The fabric looked like something you could buy at Hobby-Lobby, but all together, the dress was not pretty. Her caring eyes and loving smile covered her clothing style and made her beautiful.

Great-Grandma wore a multi-colored dress, made of the same kind of fabric Olivia had seen her wear at the wedding. She wore a bigger head covering, one that covered almost her entire head. Her thick layer of gray hair peaked through the front of the covering and draped down her forehead. If she smiled, she might have looked sweet. But Olivia had never seen her smile or heard her speak. But because of Sam's warnings, Olivia expected a tongue lashing about something. Sometime before the end of "vaspa."

When the jam was brought onto the table and the store-bought butter was set in front of Great-Grandma's eyes, the tongue lashing began. The cupcakes were light and fluffy, and the cake was flavored with the perfect amount of coffee and vanilla. The cinnamon rolls looked Pinterest worthy and tasted better than any professional chef's rolls. But Great-Grandma focused on the jam and butter.

Great-Grandma spoke with a thick German accent. "Dis jam es not good. Vhy not make homemade jam, from real strawberries? Dis butter, did Dave not teach you how to make butter from de cow?"

Mom swallowed and set her coffee cup down. "I've made butter, but I didn't serve it, afraid it wouldn't taste good."

"You haf to eat de butter to know if it tastes good or bad. Bring it to me."

Mom got up and brought Great-Grandma the butter tray. Olivia stared at "Granny." Anyone who judged Mom so harshly didn't deserve a luxury treat like homemade butter. But Granny slathered a thick layer on the corner of a slice of bread. She shoved the corner into her mouth and clasped her teeth together, tearing the bread apart. She scraped the inside of her mouth with her tongue and started to nod.

"Dis es good."

Mom's smile resembled a kindergartener after her teacher stuck a gold star on her coloring page. "You think so?" Mom asked.

"Yes." Granny wiped her mouth with the back of her hand. "Do not be scared to bring dis butter on de table." Granny set the bread slice on the bread-and-butter plate in front of her. "Vin de strawberries are on sale I vill teach you how to make jam."

Mom forced a smile, doing her best to hide the panic in her eyes.

"We'll do it at our house," Mary said.

Mom relaxed and offered a real smile.

Josh turned onto Dave's driveway, gravel crushing underneath the pickup tires. He parked in front of the shop, puckered his lips around his cigarette, then dropped it out of the window. He shut the engine off, opened the door and jumped out of the pickup. He rubbed the cigarette against the gravel with the bottom of his boot.

A young woman washed the square windows on the walk-in shop door. She scrubbed each little window, moving her body in a circular motion. She dropped the scrubber into a bucket and bent down to rinse a rag.

She wore light blue skinny jeans that stopped halfway down her calves, displaying her stained sneakers. A gray T-shirt hugged itself around her upper body. Strands of hair poked out of the short black braid that hung along the back of her neck. Walking up to her, Josh held in a whistle.

"The windows are just going to get dirty again." He kept his hands in his pockets, smiling. When the girl continued wiping the door, he leaned forward a bit and said, "Miss."

The girl turned, a shocked expression on her face. Unlike other girls, she didn't scream. She removed a headphone from her ear and let it dangle against her toned stomach. "I'm sorry, I didn't hear you drive up."

Josh smiled looking at her. Beautiful. Her eyes the perfect shade of blue; black strands of hair flapped against her lightly tanned cheeks. His eyes trailed to her neckline. Tan lines countered her shoulders, sporting a farmer's tan.

"What do you want?"

Josh cleared his throat, surprised the sharp sound had come from her mouth.

"I'm here to drop off an engine. Don't usually make house calls like this, but Nate asked if I would. He says he's busy, not that we aren't."

"Do you need help unloading it?"

Josh swallowed a chuckle. She'd never seen an irrigation engine if she thought she could unload it.

"I'll wait for Nate or Dave. They'll have better instructions on where to leave it."

The girl said nothing.

Josh gestured to the bucket. "Do you work here?"

"Yes, I live here. I'm Dave's step-daughter." Josh's eyes shot up. He'd heard Dave was getting married, but Nate never told him Dave's fiancée had a daughter.

Nate came around the corner of the round-top, wiping his hands as he crossed the slap in front of the hydraulic shop door. He stood beside the girl. Close enough to show Josh he was comfortable around her. They worked together. Lucky Nate.

"Where do you want the engine?" Josh asked.

Nate nodded toward where he came from. He turned and said, "This way."

Josh looked at the girl, smiled and said, "Nice to meet you."

She nodded, her eyes following him to his pickup. He pretended not to notice, hiding his smile. He hoped her taking a second look meant what he thought it meant. When he sat down on the driver's seat, she'd already began wiping the door. Josh turned the ignition and backed to the side of the round-top. He would learn more about her, starting with her name.

Lindy stood behind the dining room window, studying Nate and the other boy's expressions. She knew what they were thinking. Olivia was a beautiful girl. Her dad would be proud of the woman she'd grown into. Lindy couldn't say she'd helped with that. After Erick passed, Olivia grew up on her own.

She blamed herself. Olivia did. Erick's mom once told Lindy to forgive the child. At the time she considered it. Only five months after her husband's death, the need to blame someone had been too strong.

Living with the one who brought her "other half" to his death-bed—seeing her every day, expected to care for her, raise her, love her—proved to be more than she could handle. Inwardly disappointing the one she loved—still loved at the time—knowing the pain he'd feel if he knew, hadn't helped.

She'd considered it. Forgiveness. Thought maybe it would make things easier.

Had she forgiven Olivia? Not officially. Perhaps she never would. It would be easier now that she was happily married again.

An upper hand had played out Erick's death. Truly, Olivia couldn't be blamed. Lindy's life events had brought her here. With Dave. To a home. A family that wanted her around. A family that accepted her. Something she'd lived without since the summer before college. When she lost both her parents in a plane crash.

She knew the truth, yet she couldn't help her thoughts. Olivia looked so much like *her*. Not like Lindy and Erick. *She'd* caught everyone's eye. No one passed *her* without taking a second look. Lindy remembered *her* well. Thought of *her* whenever she made strawberry shortcake.

She should leave those thoughts behind. Along with the few things she kept in a shoebox. They were mostly things from her and Erick's time together. Maybe then she could look at Olivia, without thinking of *her*. Maybe then she could forget the past. Forgive the person who'd made her a mom. Love Olivia the way she deserved.

Yet, how could she? When the biggest reminder of her past called her *Mom*.

The washing machine buzzed, removing Lindy's thoughts. She stared at nothing. No one stood in front of the round-top.

Only the dog, Cash, slept on the concrete slab in front of the round-top. Lindy breathed, turning her body.

She should water the garden.

CHAPTER SIX

The end-of-May sun heated Olivia's neck as she stepped down the stairs in front of the church. A steady breeze played with her mid-calf skirt, forcing her to bunch the fabric in her fist. She'd no desire to expose her bottom half to curious thirteen-year-old male eyes. Her sandals clopped against the wooden stairs, following Mom and Dave to the front of the gravel parking lot.

Over the last four Sundays, Olivia had begun to memorize the details of this country church. She knew which boards squeaked when the pastor stepped on them, she knew which benches sat lumpy, and where to sit so the pastor wouldn't look at her. He never looked at the person sitting in the back row corner, her preferred seat.

Of course, Dave did not know about her preferred seat. Therefore, she spent most of her church attendings counting floor boards, or studying the mahogany trim around the windows. Occasionally, she'd tune in on the sermon. It was nearly impossible not to listen to his sermons.

She had watched him from the back corner before. He'd

stride past the podium, from one side to the other. Bible in hand, pumping out the words as if he'd seen Jesus speak them. Then he'd lay his Bible down on the podium, rest his arms, and scan the congregation, breathing in the words like oxygen. Silently pleading everyone to open their hearts. Then he'd conclude his sermon with a peaceful ending.

An ending meant to seal Jesus' words into your heart. To make you think twice about your life, if nothing else.

Olivia wanted to stomp on the pastor's words. His peaceful ending.

To wring them. Then *Stomp, stomp, stomp…* on every one of them, until the floor boards broke. Until every emotion drained from her bones, and leave them on the cracked floor boards. Rubble with rubble. Instead, she twisted her fingers, rubbing her thumbs against her palms until they turned purple.

What would happen if her eyes met the pastor's? Would she shout and pound her fist on the wooden bench frames, or would she sink into the cushions, as her limbs and nerves went numb, unable to feel the tears on her cheeks? What would happen then?

She didn't want to know.

Olivia sighed.

The eighty-year-old white, one-room church nested in the dirt claiming its spot in the middle of the ankle-high corn field. Surrounded with gravel and two dozen vehicles, whose owners called this church "their church." They were the children who had played around it, grew up, found Jesus, got married, and took their children to this church every Sunday. Every man sported a forehead tan line, separating the sunburned skin from the natural skin, because no one wore their caps.

Olivia stared at the building. She lowered her eyes to the children playing around their parents. A sharp realization pierced her lungs. She breathed deeply, straightening her chest. She wanted to be a little girl. To play carefree, to be protected around her parents, to have someone say, "It's okay," while they stroked her shoulder and held her.

A part of her wanted to blend in with the church members, to step closer to the building, walk into the church. To find something. Something she'd lost. Or never had.

She should stop going. Mom wouldn't care.

"Olivia, you're a hard worker."

Olivia jerked her attention to the elderly lady standing in the circle Dave and Mom had created. Olivia stepped into the circle, closer to earshot.

"Dave's had nothing but good things to say about you, not that he says much at all." The lady waved a hand and smiled. "Maybe you could help at the air show? We would just love it if you'd help us. My husband and I dread doing it ourselves again, with our age increasing, it just gets harder and harder."

"We would tell you exactly what needed to be done. And it would only be for one day," the husband said.

The couple's anxious faces made her chest tighten. The

gray-haired woman batted her eyelashes, clinging to her hand-bag, as if it kept her round spine from toppling over. The white-whiskered man's sandpapered lips pierced shut, his eyes pointed at Olivia, waiting. His arms dangling from his shoulders, like a scale keeping him balanced.

"I'd be happy to help." Olivia smiled.

Anything to keep her mind busy.

The first car pulled in around ten o'clock on Saturday morn-ing. Olivia stood at the airport gate and accepted their pay-ment. She pointed at the grass parking area, smiled at the driver, and told him to have fun. She repeated this process for twenty other cars. When the cash in her butter container overflowed, she switched to her ice cream container. After forty cars, Olivia handed the ice cream bucket to an older lady and thanked her for taking her place.

She walked the long driveway to the airport buildings, her flipflops flopping against the asphalt that sparkled in the late morning sunshine. Classic and modern show cars stood on the neatly trimmed buffalo grass all along the driveway. Kids and adults awed at the machines as own-ers watched carefully, making sure not one scratch would mark their vehicle.

Tents were set up in front of the runway, providing con-vertible seating for the airshow later. Around the corner stood the shops, food stands and a few games. Citizens of the town crowded the concrete slabs, livening the buildings that sat bare for the rest of the year.

Dad would have loved this.

She could see him marveling at the 1980 Pontiac Firebird, bending over it, hands behind his back, pointing and rambling on. Olivia slowed, facing the row of cars. She wanted to take a closer look. To look through the driver window and scan the leather seats. To imagine her dad standing beside her, speaking to her.

She turned her head, swallowing.

She picked up the pace and rounded the corner to Mr. and Mrs. Bell's food stand.

"Oh good, you're here. I don't know why someone else couldn't watch the gate, we could've used your help hours ago," Mrs. Bell said as she set drinks on the buffet table.

"I'm here now."

Mrs. Bell sighed and sagged her shoulders. "Yes, you are." She tapped Olivia's shoulder as she walked by. "Thank the Lord for you."

Olivia got to work, rearranging the buffet, and hanging up menu signs. Minutes later she began filling plates with barbeque beans, hamburgers, pasta salad and potato chips. Mr. Bell added up the cost and placed their pay in the wooden box that acted as the register. Mrs. Bell grilled patties and dumped them into the plugged-in roaster oven. Olivia smiled at every costumer, gladly serving each one. She recognized some of them from church and some of them from town.

"A little bit of everything, please."

Olivia focused on the burger she was making. "Do you want mayo and lettuce as well?" Olivia looked up and felt her stomach tingle. It was him.

The guy looked her in the eyes, smiled and said, "everything you got."

Olivia nodded. She squirted ketchup, mayo, and mustard on the buns and laid lettuce slices on the patty. She reached for the tomatoes and hit the edge of the plate. The tomato slices flew off the plate and landed on the asphalt. The plate balanced on her foot. The man leaned forward, eyeing the mess behind the table.

Olivia squatted in front of the tomatoes and scraped them together. Mrs. Bell turned around and urged her to stand up.

"Here," she handed Olivia a plate of cut tomato slices, "we'll clean it up later."

Olivia set the plate on the table and finished preparing the burger. She busied herself by ladling a pile of beans onto his plate and dropping a handful of chips beside the beans.

Olivia looked up, her heart still barely beating. Was her face as red as it felt? She handed him his plate. "Here you go."

She needed him to leave, before her heart stopped completely.

The boy's entire face smiled. He lifted his plate, looking into her eyes, "Maybe I'll see you around some time?" he asked.

She'd like that. Olivia lowered her eyes, unable to hide

her smile, stirring the barbeque beans inside the roaster oven. She should say something. Suddenly her words tied. She looked up, trying to untangle the knot. Her lips parted, but nothing came out.

"Maybe?" he asked again.

Olivia nodded.

His smile broadened, making him look even cuter than before. He grabbed a drink, looking at her, he said, "Talk to you later Olivia," then he turned toward Mr. Bell and paid his meal.

He knew her name. How? She wanted to yell after him to ask for his name. She bit her tongue to make sure she wouldn't.

What a sight. Everything about him made her want to look twice. His brown wavy hair covered the back of his neck, edging the neckline of his red T-shirt. It highlighted his broad shoulders, flowing loosely beneath his chest. He swayed his feet as he walked, his head held high. Like every concrete square was laid out for him.

Who was he?

"Olivia," Mrs. Bell pointed at the line waiting to be served, "we have customers."

"Yes," she shook her head, "sorry."

After the lines cleared and the food was nearly gone, Mrs. Bell helped Olivia clean the tomatoes off the asphalt. She scooped the dirt covered slices into the trash can. "Stay away from Josh." Olivia figured Mrs. Bell was talking about the guy who caused her to drop the tomatoes. "A boy with eyes and a smile like his, he'll swindle you into blind a relationship."

Mrs. Bell stood up, and set the trash can straight, unfazed by the words she'd said. They didn't stand out to her, like they did to Olivia.

Olivia stood up, brushing the rocks off her hands. "I'll probably never see him again."

"Better that way."

Olivia watched Mrs. Bell from the back. She wanted to ask why, but Mrs. Bell had sunk into her own zone, cleaning up her work space.

It shouldn't bother her. She didn't know the guy, and probably would never see him again. But she wanted to. She wanted to be the one he spent his time with, the one he called just for fun.

Olivia caught her thoughts. She shook them out of her head. She'd gone too far.

By the time the air and car show ended, the day had turned from a perfect spring morning to a hot afternoon. Still people sat around talking, eating, playing, and *ooh*ing at cars for a good three hours. Then they slowly packed up their chairs, blankets, and whatever else they brought. They gathered their children, offered to help clean up but looked relieved when the committee assured them that they had it under control.

Olivia politely asked Mr. and Mrs. Bell if there was anything else they needed help with, when they said no, she hid her relief, smiled, and wished them a good rest of their day.

It was hot. She wanted to air out her toes on the cool wood floor, pour sweet tea over ice into a quart size mason jar and sink into the coach. Maybe take a nap. Away from people, away from memories. Memories that rarely brought comfort.

Everywhere she had looked, the event had reminded her of her dad. She saw him in the crowds. She saw herself as a child. She saw her dad the way he looked before he passed, playing games, and buying cotton candy. She had stood by herself, occasionally drifting off, thinking that when the air-show would begin, they would walk to the runway and watch the stunt flyer swirl down together.

Every time she caught herself doing this, she forced herself to believe reality. Each time she had realized the truth, the grief hit harder.

Sometimes she wondered if she would always feel like this.

She drove the twenty miles to the farm. Over the hills and through the valleys. Cattle grazed the pastures, corn stood ankle high, waving in the afternoon breeze. It shriveled into cone shaped leaves, showing its dark, musky green colors. Olivia empathized with the miserable crop. The corn could wait for rain, but what could she wait for?

She could weep, if she had anything left within her. *You brought your dad to his death.* The voices echoed in her mind. *Remember what you did?*

Of course, she remembered. How could she forget?

Her shoulders flexed against the seat. Her feet pulsed, rubbing on the gas pedal. Heavy, like cinder-blocks that hovered over the ground.

How could she ever not remember that point, that

decision. Reba's voice over the TV, her mom shifting on the couch, glancing at Olivia. The dimness of the living room, the TV show's scenes reflecting against the walls, the shadows in the porch light. Her father driving home. What had he thought when the storm picked up? What would he have said to her, had she been there?

Would he have eyed her? Shown the blame in his eyes. Olivia could see it. His big, draining eyes, his mouth half open, parched, gasping for air. She envisioned herself beside him, sensing every word she knew his eyes would have said. *You did it.* Big, round green irises, never blinking. *You're the reason.*

Olivia gasped for air. She licked her lips and breathed heavily. A tool rattled on the passenger side floor. She flinched, tightened the grip on the steering wheel.

She knew better, but she couldn't shake the odd feeling that someone sat behind her. glaring at her. Olivia scratched her cheek with her shoulder. She turned her head, only to confirm the back windshield inches from her face, on the single cab truck. A toolbox on the bed, blocking her view.

Eight miles later, she notched the gears in park and leaned her head against the seat, closing her eyes. Three years. After three years she still felt like this. The hot afternoon sun glared through the pickup window, onto her legs. She placed a hand on her warm leg and let the sun burn her skin. Tears rolled down her cheeks and off her face.

How could she ever justify her wrong? No court would sentence her to juvie for begging her father to come home in a rain-storm. They would call her insane if she said she'd killed her father. But she *had*. She was the reason. How could she ever make things right?

She stared at the floorboard. *Get out. Rest. Move your limbs,* she told herself. Like a stuffed doll, with flat stitched knees, her legs hung like rags. She had too. Who else would do it for her? How could she help Mom if she couldn't help herself?

Inside the house, Olivia sat down at the kitchen bar-table, laid her head on her elbow, and let the A.C. dry her sweaty skin.

The front screen door swung open. *Maybe it's him.* Olivia's heart beat faster at the thought of Josh walking through the door.

"It's a hundred degrees out there." Sam's voice made Olivia's head hurt. Olivia hid her whimper in her elbow. "At the end of May. It's gonna be a hot one. Mom picked a wrong time to get pregnant. That poor lady's skin is gonna burst like a cherry tomato, she won't be able to walk from the house to the car without running out of breath. But I'll help her. It'll be fun to have a little sibling I suppose." Sam huffed and plopped down on a dining room chair. "Who would have thought that my mom, at forty-three years old, would get pregnant?"

Olivia lifted her head and slid around on the stool, toward Sam. Mary pregnant, huh? She should be happy for Sam, right? Olivia could picture her bouncing a baby on her knee, while she rambled on about everything from the baby's frequent diaper changes to college funds. A baby would be good for that family.

Fear shot through Olivia like electricity. Would Mom get pregnant? No! Oh, she hoped not.

"I've heard it gets harder for women to deliver a baby the older they get. I'll pray for her." Sam paused and stared into the kitchen. Olivia looked into the kitchen. Was she praying right now?

"Probably until the baby's out of the house. Kids can be a handful and raising a teenager at fifty won't be easy. Not that I'm a handful. I'd say I don't bring my parent's much worry. I don't go out much. Pretty much stay with my own crowd."

Sam looked around the house. "Where's your mom?"

Olivia shook her head. "I don't know." She stood up and walked to the screen door, where her sneakers sat against the wall. "I have to feed the animals." Olivia slid on her sneakers and walked out the door.

"I'll help you." Sam ran down the porch steps, after Olivia.

I'd prefer you didn't. But Olivia didn't say it. What was Sam doing here anyways? Had she barged in, visiting the farm this often before her and her mom moved in?

It was near dinner time. Nate wasn't there, Dave wasn't there, and why had Mom not come to the airshow? And where was Sam when Olivia had stood alone by the fence, while the people around her laughed and talked to their family and friends, enjoying this blazing hot Southwest Kansas day?

Sam wanted to help, but Olivia didn't need her now. Sam raised her voice behind Olivia, "You forgot the milk bucket."

Olivia bit her lip and breathed heavily. She pushed the barn door open with extreme force and watched it hit the end of the railing. The dirt barn floor rattled in front of her. Olivia looked down and held her breath. Not good. An obese light brown snake with dark spots curled its end half on the floor like a sausage roll, tapping its rattles against the compact dirt.

Its upper end stood up like a spring; its flat head faced the stall door. The dog barked, his tale between his legs, backed into a corner. *Not good.*

The barn door slid passed Olivia, blocking her vision of the dog. Olivia faced a white tin door for one second, then turned toward Sam. "The dog! He'll get bitten."

"We'll get bitten," Sam yelled. Sam looked around the farm. "Where's the garden hoe?"

"In the barn!"

Sam ran to the round-top and opened Dave's pickup door. Olivia stepped closer to the barn door, slid it slightly open to peek at the dog. How far could snakes pounce? Would fifteen feet be far enough away from the dog? Even if it was, the snake could slither closer to the dog.

Footsteps ran up to the barn. Olivia looked away from the dog and slid the door closed.

Sam stood in front of the door, with a gun barrel pointed up in her left hand. Her wide-open eyes, full of fear, focused on Olivia. Her right arm hung beside her hip; her hand balled into a fist; her lips in a straight line.

Olivia held the same expression as she looked at the gun, then at Sam. "You're gonna shoot it?"

Sam nodded. Olivia waited for Sam to load the gun and set up her aim. Sam stared at Olivia, holding the gun in the air.

"Well, are you gonna shoot?"

"Open the door."

Olivia pushed the door hard, then backed up. Olivia looked at Sam. She held the gun against her shoulder and squinted along the barrel. Olivia glanced at the snake. It turned its head and sizzled its tongue at the girls.

"Shoot!" Olivia yelled.

"I can't," Sam cried.

"Do it Sam! Do it, now!"

The snake's head lifted. It was gonna pounce. Olivia nudged closer to Sam, placed one hand on the barrel and a finger on Sam's index finger, ready to press the trigger.

"Shoot!' Olivia yelled.

"You shoot."

Olivia pushed Sam's finger against the trigger; the gun went off with a *bang* and kicked the girls backward. They stumbled to gain their balance. Olivia's ears rang immensely. She searched the barn floor for the snake, unsure of where the bullet went.

"Where'd it go?" Sam asked, rubbing her shoulder.

The whimpering dog ran to the girls. He jumped from

one girl to the other, rubbing his head against their legs, showing his thanks.

"I don't know." Olivia walked closer. She felt a soft cushion under her sneaker. She stepped back, examining the grass. A four-inch piece of snake flesh, covered in blood stuck to the bottom of her shoe. "Ewww!" Olivia felt vomit rise up her throat.

"Gross!" Sam covered her mouth. "Scrape your shoe against the grass." Sam pointed to the ground.

Pieces of snake flesh stuck to the barn door and walls, they laid on the floor and the ground. Sam bent over and eyed something on the grass. Olivia watched, horrified as Sam reached down to pick it up. Sam straightened her back and faced Olivia. She dangled the rattles in front of her face.

"I'm keeping these."

CHAPTER SEVEN

Josh lifted his face to the sky and inhaled the dusty air. Specks of green peeked up from the clay fields around Nate's house. A dust devil whirled along the dirt road, across the fields and onto Nate's driveway. Dust settled on his skin. He licked his lips and spat onto the gravel. Even if Nate hadn't kicked him out, he would have moved out sooner or later. It was lonely out here. The dust storms came out of nowhere—some years were worse than other years—and when it rained the tire ruts were nearly too deep for your truck to drive through.

Josh walked toward the front door and up the concrete steps. He knocked on the glass screen door, then stared at the grass that crept up the tan colored siding. The door swung open, nearly pushing Josh off the steps.

"You need to mow." Josh nodded toward the grass.

"What do you want?" Nate stood underneath the doorway, holding the door open.

"My video game." Josh pushed Nate aside and walked into the doublewide trailer home.

"It's not here." The screen door slammed shut.

"Sure, it is." Josh searched the makeshift living room. "I left it here when I moved out. Now I want it back." Josh lifted the couch cushions, moved the lawn chair away from the corner. He bent over to search the TV stand, that Nate had dragged home from a garage sale.

"I want you to leave. You've been smoking."

"No, I just need my video game then I'll be on my way." Josh smiled at Nate. He read each CD case, then threw them on the floor. "What's Olivia doing today?" he asked.

"How would I know."

Josh shrugged, scanning a CD case. "You work with her." He picked up another case, scanning the cover. "Here it is." He waved the case, then stood up.

"I was thinking, maybe you could give me her phone number?"

Nate glared at him, his jaw set firmly, like the arms that hung from his shoulders. His *I'm serious* look. "You can't have it."

Josh nodded his head in Nate's direction. "You two already got something going on?"

"No, I—"

"Then she's single? Give me her phone number."

"I don't want you talking to her." Nate stepped aside, opening a path to the door. "I want you to leave my house and leave Olivia alone."

Josh opened his palms, lifting his shoulders. "C'mon,

you're making me sound worse than a crook. I never did anything that affected you. Never even gave you a reason to kick me out."

Nate stared at Josh, giving him a look that said, *"Are you kidding me."* His lips opened, against his will, it seemed. Like the need to explain angered him. "I wasn't about to have my mom come over," he raised his voice, "and find pot in my kitchen cabinets. Either the drugs quit or you move out." His voice calmed as he added, "You made your choice."

"You kicked me out before I had a chance to make a choice."

They had fought a lot over the years. When Nate knocked down Josh's sand garage and stole his toy cars; when Josh released earth warms in Nancy's backpack and told her Nate did it; when they both ended up in jail because Kevin convinced them to spray paint the sheriff's car. Every fight had lasted a day at the most. But this one, they couldn't get past.

"What I do on my own time is up to me," Josh said.

"And who I let in my house is up to me," Nate said.

They looked at each other for two seconds. Josh lowered his eyes. They might never get past this one. He shook his head, "And who I see or don't see is up to me."

He needed to go. Nate wouldn't get past this. He would forever see him as his loser used-to-be-friend.

He walked toward the door, pausing when he lined up with Nate. He faced him, feeling dizzy. "I would never purposely hurt a girl; you should know that."

Nate glared at the wall. He didn't believe him.

"I'm not who you think I am."

Nate jerked his face toward Josh. "You don't know who you are."

Josh lowered his eyes to the doorknob. Silence filled the room.

"I'm keeping this." He waved the game, then walked out the door, counting the steps as he walked down them, careful not to fall.

Did he know who he was, walking like an old drunkard? Josh climbed into his pickup and slammed the door against the pickup frame. He situated himself on the seat and threw the CD case on the passenger seat. What would his sister say if she saw him like this?

His mom would drop her head into her hand, *tsk* and grumble, while she shook her head and shoulders. A son smoking weed would surely damage her reputation. At that point his dad would make a few phone calls, his mom would pack Josh's bags and off to a recovery home he would go. If dropping out of college hadn't done it, this would.

He started the engine and hit the gas pedal. His tires spun off Nate's driveway and drifted onto the dirt road. He laughed and nestled in the seat. He'd make it a good weekend.

And it was. Josh, Wyatt, Kevin and Blake played every video game in Josh and Wyatt's house. Outside, the wind blew. It pushed the neighbor kid's tricycles across the street. The recently set-up swimming pool tarps flapped in the wind. Mrs. Ham's freshly planted flowers shriveled, the drying heat soaking all the moisture out of the plant. The boys joked, drank beer, and vigorously moved their thumbs on the remote controls.

Josh leaned back against the couch cushions, stretched out his legs and balanced the beer bottle on his stomach. "Where's Nate? He not coming?" asked Wyatt. Josh shook his head and took a sip of his beer. Unless Kevin or Blake had told him, Nate didn't know where they were. He wouldn't have come. Not after everything that had happened.

"What happened to him? He's been acting strange lately?" Kevin asked.

Blake focused on the TV, doing his best to beat Wyatt. "Ever since you and Wyatt moved out, he's been acting weird."

Josh stared at a living room corner and took another sip of his beer. "Probably thinks he's too good for us."

Josh scanned the room, while the boys focused on the TV. They didn't need to know why Nate avoided them. They didn't need to know why Josh moved out. Josh tilted the bottle up and drank the last bit of the beer. He didn't need the rest of the guys looking at him like Nate did; losing his closest friend was enough.

Josh stood up and walked to the kitchen to get another beer from the fridge. He twisted the top off and threw it at the trashcan, cheering himself on when it landed in the middle. "Nothin' but net," he said as he walked back into the living room.

Josh caught a whiff of odor. He lowered his nose to the neckline of his T-shirt and sniffed. Yuck! He cringed and shook his head. He walked to the end of the kitchen bar table and threw the box of beer bottles into the trashcan. If he'd known the housework involved in living on his own, he would've begged to stay in college.

His growling stomach nearly matched the volume of the train horn that woke him every night. He shuffled leftovers around in the fridge and found a box of cold pizza. He slid the cold cardboard across the ceramic counter-top, grabbing the neck of a soda bottle. He popped it open and walked to the bar table.

Inside the cardboard to-go box eight pizza slices laid spread out, two of which had mold growing on top. Ugh! Josh examined the slices, determining which ones were edible.

It wasn't a Michelin star meal, but it was better than Nate's cereal. His mother's cooking, now *that* had been some fine dining. The best Josh's mom could do was order take out from Black Heifer's. He'd eat delivery meals with his family any day, if they'd ask. Everyone knew Josh couldn't afford to order from Black Heifer's. He knew his family wouldn't appreciate anything less.

The front door swung open. Josh looked up, one hand resting around the coke bottle on the counter top and the other holding a pizza slice in the air. His fifteen-year-old sister stepped onto the living room floor.

Josh scraped the pizza off the box and brought the box to

the trashcan. He rounded it out, with hopes it would hide the beer bottles.

"Did mom bring you?" Josh straightened his back.

"No, I drove." Veronica plumped her school bag on the counter and sat down on the opposite side of Josh, on a wooden barstool.

Josh smiled. "You know you're not supposed to drive by yourself."

"Mom and Dad took the Escalade to Mr. and Mrs. Davis's place."

Josh smiled to himself, as he grabbed his half-eaten pizza slice. Mrs. Davis hosted a women's book club every month, while Mr. Davis and the husbands shot golf balls off their deck. The Davis's backyard stretched onto the golf course, making it easy for the young employee to go around the next day and collect every golf ball, then return them to Mr. Davis for a small fee.

Young teen boys would do anything for a bit of extra money—if they had none. Fortunately for Josh, he always had money. And never had to work for it, until he moved back home.

Josh nodded toward the pizza slices spread over the counter. "Want some? I have soda in the fridge."

Veronica shook her head. "It would taste better if you heated it up."

Josh shrugged. He'd rather eat it cold than soggy. "I'm going to go change and then we'll go eat." In truth, Josh needed a reason to change before his sister smelled the smoke and alcohol stench on his clothes.

By the time he walked down the hall, into the kitchen, wearing a fresh pair of cargo pants and an army green T-shirt, Veronica had laid out her school work on the counter. She'd shoved the pizza in the trash and set out her reusable pink water bottle. Obviously, she hadn't come here to simply hang out. Not this time.

"I have one more test this week before school's out and I *cannot* fail unless I want to continue the class after school lets out." Veronica's eyes followed Josh to where his soda bottle stood. "Jackie's hosting a pool party at her parent's house the first weekend of June and if I don't ace this test, I'll have to miss it. Jackie's friends have a lot of stuff planned for this summer. I've been listening to them talk about it all spring. So, if I go to her pool party then maybe I can go to all the other stuff too."

Woof! Josh shook his head and stretched his eyelids. *Teenage girls.* Veronica's first summer as a high school student. Now was the time to get to know all the right people—ideally, she should have been doing that over the winter. According to her invitation, she had been.

He remembered his high school days. Filled with sports, whatever bit of learning the teachers crammed into him, parties, and girls.

Josh's eyes widened. He set his soda down and focused on Veronica. "Jackie and these girls, they hang out with boys … your age?" Josh lifted his soda, appearing calm about hormonal teenage boys.

Veronica shrugged. "Yeah."

Josh tensed up and stretched his body out nearly an inch.

Veronica giggled. "Chill. They're not going to hurt you." Veronica arranged her notebooks.

No, but they'll hurt you. That's what teenage boys do. He relaxed and prepared to give Veronica the speech that his parents should have given her.

"Sis," Josh breathed in, "watch out who you hang out with." He breathed out. "Not everyone is worth your time. High school is filled with senseless kids who don't give their actions a second thought. Most of the stuff will leave you bruised emotionally and physically, some of it will get you arrested, and a few things will leave you changed for life. Be careful."

Josh felt like he had made his point. But Veronica kept her focus on Josh, like she expected more, so he added, "High school is one level, college is another."

Veronica held his gaze for a while, as if taking in what he had told her. "Is that why you dropped out of college?"

His perfect big-brother wisdom punched him in the gut. He lowered his gaze, gestured with his soda bottle, and drank two gulps. He sat the bottle down and nodded, "Yeah."

It wasn't a total lie.

Josh wiped the corner of his mouth, walked around the bar table, scooted his stool further from hers and sat down.

"What do you need help with?"

Veronica stopped playing with the pencil in her hand and glared at the text book. She nodded. "I'll be careful, Josh."

She looked up at him and suddenly he felt responsible for every little thing this kid did. No one could see it, but Josh felt a ton of bricks dump onto his shoulders. Nonetheless, her innocence and honor made him smile.

"Good." He focused on the books. "Let's get started, so we can finish and go get some real food."

On Monday morning, fog hovered over the farm. It allowed the morning dew to rest on the buildings, leaving drops of water on the grass blades. Olivia brought the first basket of laundry to the clothesline at eight-thirty. Dave assured them the fog would lift and the sun would shine by mid-morning. Olivia didn't trust the weather. Especially not after the stories she'd heard. But Dave knew this land better than she did. If he said the sun would dry the kitchen towels, then it most likely would.

She flapped the tea towels, hung them over the line and pinned two pins on each towel to hold it in place. She moved down the line until half the line displayed aprons, kitchen towels, and bar towels. Birds chirped in the grass, they pushed their feet off the ground, flapping their wings. They flew above the clothesline and landed by the baby watermelon plants.

The dog jumped up from behind the house, and ran to the garden. He halted instantly when the birds flew up, wagging his tail. After several seconds, he glanced at Olivia for approval, then trotted proudly toward the clothesline. "Good job Cash." She praised the dog with cuddles and behind-the-ear scratches.

Mom stepped out the mudroom door, which stood on the side of the house, with a bucket of scraps from the morning. She dumped the scraps underneath the chicken-coop-tree, rinsed the gunk off the rim and began walking toward the clothesline. The chickens raced to the scraps, pecking the peels vigorously.

Mom looked as though she'd lived here her entire life. Her skin was tan from work in the garden, her blond hair was discolored from weeks of not visiting the salon. The hair that had always hung neatly above her shoulders was tied up in a bun. And her perfectly rounded nails had chipped from whatever else Mom did all day. Mom smiled at Cash and showed him a little love.

"Beautiful day, isn't it?" She looked up at Olivia, while she straightened her back. "Crazy how hot and windy it was over the weekend and today it's like this." Mom shook her head. "Crazy."

"It is." Olivia smiled at Mom. "Maybe it'll rain." It hadn't rained the entire month they had lived here.

"Dave says it won't."

Dave made Mom happy. Something Olivia had never been able to do.

The Dave Olivia knew was a kind, content, quiet man.

According to his sister, he'd been lonely, praying for a wife the last twelve years. He wanted a housewife who would support his farm, help him manage it, and stand by him when his crops didn't grow. He wouldn't settle for just any woman. She had to be a woman who could handle his lifestyle.

Here she was, a middle aged, city widow who had never milked a cow or held a chicken. She hadn't known the difference between a silage cutter and a combine, probably still didn't. How Dave had chosen her, she didn't understand. Maybe it was God's direction—after all of Dave's praying. Or maybe it was a trial run that wouldn't work. They'd get divorced and she and Mom would move back to Topeka.

"I better go mix the bread dough so it can rise." Mom walked toward the mudroom door and into the house.

Olivia set the clothespin basket into the laundry basket and began to follow Mom.

Dave walked up to Olivia with a pair of boots. He scratched his neck, like he didn't know how to say what he wanted to. "I realized you didn't have any boots." He gestured toward her feet. "Those sneakers, they're not suited for farm work. And Sam, blabber-mouth she is, came up to me yesterday after Sunday dinner and told me you shot a rattler."

It was Sam's idea. If it hadn't been for her, she probably would have left the door open, stupidly standing, thinking, until the snake bit her or Cash.

Dave held the boots in front of her. "Here, you've earned 'em."

She opened her mouth to protest. Instead, she closed it, setting the baskets down. She grabbed the boots and examined them. The shaft was white, with a pink trim. The bottom part was made of light brown leather and heavy-duty stitching like the ones Nate wore. For shooting a snake?

She looked up at Dave, feeling like a thirteen-year-old getting her first phone. Smiling, she said, "Thank you."

Brand new boots. She'd always gotten new shoes when she needed them. She'd grown up wealthy, so why did this feel special?

Olivia shoved the thought away, aware of the silence.

She threw the boots up and down in her palms. "When did you get these?"

"Yesterday. Your mom and I drove to town after church for Sunday dinner with Mary and John and well, figured you needed a good pair o' boots."

Oliva nodded, smiling, afraid to say thank you again. Dave returned her smile, nodded and walked to the barn.

Olivia was still smiling when she placed her boots in the laundry basket and walked into the mudroom. She set the baskets on the counter and switched out her sneakers for her new boots. She walked around in the mudroom, testing them out.

Mom and Dave ate out yesterday? Maybe she should've went to church after all. Any restaurant food sounded better than the pizza rolls she had.

Olivia lifted the bottom of her sneakers, crinkling her

nose at the sight of blood stains. She walked to the nearest outdoor faucet and rinsed the sneakers thoroughly, then she set them on the concrete steps in front of the mudroom door. The sun would dry them—she looked at the overcast sky—eventually.

She unlocked her phone, checking the time. Eight-fifty. The morning had gotten away from her. She slid her phone back into her jean pocket. If this weather held on, they might not do much. Either way, she needed to do her morning chores.

After she raked the cat poop off the barn floor, Olivia dumped the leftover water out of the troughs, rinsed and scraped whatever gunk might have piled up on the bottom, then refilled each trough with clear water. A light drizzle dampening her T-shirt.

Footsteps came from the round-top, brushing the grass in front of the corrals. Nate stopped and watched her work, waiting. She kinked the garden hose, crawled through the panels, dragging the hose behind her. She straightened, facing Nate. Surely, he hadn't watched her the whole time. Perhaps she should have walked through the gate.

"I wanna teach you how to run the swather. The hay needs to be cut soon and Dave wants you to cut it." Nate began walking toward the concrete slab in front of the round-top, where the faded green and yellow machine stood.

Steady rain drops landed on Olivia's head, one after the other until they became a heavy stream, soaking her shoulders.

She dropped the garden hose and ran to the clothesline. "The towels," she yelled.

Olivia removed the pins, stuffed them in one hand and flung the towels over her arm. Bath towels hung on the second line, still wet from the washing machine. She removed them from the line, one by one. The line began to bounce up and down. Nate stood at the other end of the line, yanking towels off and crunching them together in his hand. He jogged toward Olivia and placed a hand on her back, urging her to the house.

They stomped off any mud on the rug, then laid the towels on the dryer, beside the baskets.

"They would've been fine. The rain will stop soon." Nate looked at Olivia, standing inches away from her left arm.

"It might not."

He tilted his head in agreement. He slid off his grass covered boots, walked to the window, and watched the rain. Olivia took off her boots and threw the towels in the dryer. She set their shoes beside the door and flipped the light switch. A dim yellow light lit the room.

She joined Nate, watching the rain dripple down behind the window screen. Light, steady rain drops knocked on the glass. It showered over the farm, cleansing it from the dirt that had built up from Sunday's windstorm. The dog, already soaked, ran to the front porch for cover. *A little late Cash*, Olivia thought.

CHAPTER EIGHT

Everything looked fine from afar. When the light shone in the perfect angle and he stood a foot away from the pickup, he could see the hail damage.

He wanted to kick the tire, punch the hail dents. Had he known the day's drizzle would turn into an evening thunderstorm, he would have parked his pickup inside. Not that he could've. It didn't fit in the garage; Wyatt's new pickup took up every square foot. If it wasn't for the neighbor's house standing six feet away from the garage, he would gouge through the brick wall and add a second garage door.

Josh examined the rejoicing neighborhood. The sun glared against the water flowing down the street. Birds bathed in the temporary city streams, chirping from one flowerbed to the other. Open windows released the echoes of family dinners and blaring TVs.

He looked up at the sky. The empty storm clouds hovered above Shallow River. They'd finished what they came to do.

The clouds crossed over the sun and the dark evening light returned.

"Beautiful rain we got, huh?" Wyatt walked up to Josh and eyed the sky, "You think it'll rain some more?"

Josh lowered his head, biting his teeth. "I don't know. It better not hail."

"Oh, a little bit of hail doesn't hurt. We need the rain."

Josh eyed Wyatt. "You wouldn't say that if your pickup looked like this." He nodded toward the Dodge standing in front of him.

Wyatt nodded, examining the pickup. He shook his head, "Sorry man."

Wyatt shrugged his shoulders. His clueless friend didn't care that he'd selfishly hogged the garage space. Thunder rolled in behind the red brick three-bedroom house. Josh walked to the driver door of his truck, opened it, and hopped inside. A few sprinkles popped on his windshield. He started the engine, turned on his wipers, and put the transmission in reverse.

On days like today he wished he still had access to Nate's metal shop. His doublewide trailer and hobby shop weren't much, but the place had housed three men and protected four vehicles. And the car Nate should have brought to the junk yard years ago, but he planned to restore it one day.

They would stand around the car, beer bottle or cigarette in hand, and talk about their "one days." When money wasn't tight and they didn't live in a fifteen-year-old doublewide. He had moved out, but besides that, nothing had changed.

Josh caught his thoughts; no need to lie to himself. He

switched his left signal light on and waited for a car to pass before he crossed and drove onto the liquor store gravel parking lot. The day he walked into Nate's shop, and stupidly offered Nate a share of the pot, he'd changed their friendship.

If he could go back, would he change it?

To change where his choices lead him, he'd have to go further back. His first semester of college would be a good place to start over. If he could rewind time, he'd save himself from getting kicked out of college; he would finish all four years and earn his degree. In two years, he would get a job. Most likely anyplace but Shallow River. He'd walk into the bank, in his slacks and dress shirt, with a low-fat latte into his own office. For lunch he'd walk to his go-to restaurant and order his usual. Or did bankers bring lunch to work?

Life could've been different. It still could; he could go to a community college. Live the same life his parents had planned out for him years ago. Would they celebrate—happily pay for community college—or had they given up on him completely?

Josh climbed the wooden steps to the glass door. The bells shingled above as he stepped into the cooled one room liquor store. He wiped the mud off his spitfire Ariat boots and walked across the room to the beer refrigerators. He set the six pack on the glazed wood countertop and waited for the cashier to turn around. A broad, shriveled woman turned around and looked down at Josh.

Oh no, her.

She scanned Josh up and down. "ID."

Josh tapped his pant pockets, pretending to search for his wallet. He tilted his head and cringed. "I forgot my wallet." He shook his head. He smiled his smoothest smile. "Could you put it on my friend's account today? I'm sure he won't mind."

The woman weighed down on her palms, forcing weight on the edge of the counter. "You're not leaving with this beer unless you show me an ID."

Josh *tsk*ed and looked at the six pack of Coors. He stretched his lips and lifted his head. "Well, I guess today isn't my lucky day. I dropped an irrigation motor this morning. You bet the customer gave me a good tongue lashing when he came to pick it up this afternoon. My boss wasn't in a good mood."

Josh widened his eyes, looked directly at the woman, and shook his head. "Guess it's the weather, those clouds can really dampen someone's day. Or it was because I backed into his work pickup." Josh smacked the countertop and stepped back. "Oh well, all I wanted was to relax and wind down with a cold beer, but," he shrugged, "I guess today just isn't my day."

The woman focused on Josh, her expression cold and stiff. She looked the same way she always did.

"You're not getting any beer kid. You're not any older than you were last week when you came in." The woman lifted her head toward the door. "Come back when you're twenty-one."

Josh smiled, nodded, and walked out the door. He should

borrow that ladies work schedule. If he knew when her shift started and ended, he could schedule his shopping to make sure he only came in when Ralf worked behind the counter.

He hadn't lied to the woman. Sure, he hoped she would feel sorry for him and sell him the beer, but this time his story wasn't a lie. His day really couldn't have gone worse. He would punch his anger onto his steering wheel if he had the energy. But hitting objects wouldn't justify his terrible day. He needed something to calm him down. Anything to relieve the stress, anything.

He searched through his pickup, nothing. Had he used it all already?

Shoot! He slammed the glove compartment shut. Well, he'd have to get more. He pushed the gear stick into drive and turned onto Shallow River's main highway. He drove to the outskirts of town, to a medium sized house with minimal amount of clutter. The buffalo grass neatly trimmed around every piece of metal that laid on the property.

If Keith removed the clutter from the yard, he would have less work to do.

That was the thing with Keith, one wouldn't label him as a drug dealer if he didn't know him. Maybe a busy factory employee who couldn't bear to part with his junk, but not a drug dealer. The man didn't think other people needed to know his business; he liked to keep to himself.

Josh parked under the Locust tree in front of the garage, behind Keith's suburban. He jumped out of the pickup and lit a cigarette. He slid the lighter into his front jean pocket, and removed the cigarette from his lips, releasing the smoke in his mouth.

The clouds continued to gather, nearly as thick as they'd been before the storm. The dark gray and blue globs showed no sign of green. The hail was most likely over. It was too late to care; his pickup would never be the same.

The dense, wet breeze picked up Josh's hair, cooling his forehead. Keith stepped out the garage walk-in-door and met Josh on the concrete slab.

He swung out his hand and clapped it against Josh's palm, forming one big hand shake. "What can I do for you man?" He lifted his pants further up, straightened his back, then folded his arms across his chest.

"The usual."

"That the only reason you come out here?" Keith chuckled. "Here I thought this might be a social call." He finished his chuckle, shaking his head. "Come with me, I got some in here." He turned around, leading Josh through the garage door.

In the garage, Keith lifted the lid off the hamper that stood between the dryer and the kitchen door. He threw Josh a firm white package and leaned against the dryer. "Listen man," Keith scratched his neck, "I need someone to, uh, run errands for me." He waved his hand as he talked. "I'm thinking you might be the perfect guy for the job."

"What kind of errands are we talking?"

"Business. I get my orders, ah ..." He lowered his head,

studying the concrete floor. He glanced up at Josh, then shrugged off whatever worry he had. "From a few towns west—Colorado. There aren't enough hours in the day for me to drive everywhere I need to go."

Keith focused on Josh. "I'd do all the dealing—set everything up and do the talking, all you'd have to do is drive." He paused, tilting his head. "Are you up for it?"

"Would I be doing this for free?"

"Nah," Keith swayed his head, then focused on Josh, "you'd get a decent cut."

He could use the money. With more cash he could save up to buy a house. His current income would never give him that extra money. His boss was probably planning the perfect moment to fire him. After he'd backed into his pickup and dropped an expensive irrigation motor, Josh wouldn't blame him.

He breathed heavily, slowly breathing out. His life wasn't going anywhere any time soon. With extra money, he could open his own business, of some kind. He had his sister to think of. But she wouldn't have to be involved. He could quit whenever he wanted. No one would ever have to know.

Josh looked at Keith. "You pay for the fuel and you got a deal."

On Tuesday, after his eight-hour work-day, Josh set out for his first one-hour drive to Walsh, Colorado. He hoped to drive there, pick up the order, and drive back before anyone had a chance to miss him. But first, he needed dinner. He drove onto Casey's parking lot and parked in front of the red rectangular building.

As he stepped out of his pickup, moist, cold air swept through his T-shirt; light rain dampening his hair. Two days of cloudy, rainy weather. The sun peaked through occasionally, glistening on the wet concrete. Then it slid behind the clouds for five hours or more.

Josh opened the glass door, allowing customers to walk out. A familiar voice came from the counter. Olivia.

She stepped toward the door, stuffing a receipt in her phone case wallet. Josh avoided the urge to hurry the last customer through the door. He dashed behind the person, through the door and let it shut before Olivia had a chance to walk out. He halted in front of her, smiling.

She shook her arms and dropped her phone.

"I'm sorry," Josh bent down to pick it up, "I didn't mean to scare you."

The doorbell tinkled beside them. People walked in and out. Josh placed a hand on Olivia's arm and ushered her away from the door out of people's way. She slid her phone in her back pocket and stepped further away from him.

"It's all right," she said.

Her hair hung freely, brushing her shoulders. He liked it open better than in a braid. But even in a sack cloth with her hair chopped unevenly, she'd look beautiful. Simply standing beside her made his heart happy. Something he'd never felt before. The prettiest lips he'd ever seen smiled at him. He fought the surprising urge to kiss her.

She glanced past his shoulder, out the windows. Her smile fading.

He needed to say something.

He cleared his empty throat, searching for words. She watched him awkwardly slide his hands in his pockets. He shook his head, gaining a smile. *Think. Be yourself.*

His shoulders relaxed easing the tension in his spine. "Would you want to go see a movie with me this Friday?"

She blinked, lowering her focus away from him. Obviously, second guessing her answer. What did she want to say? She straightened her back and opened her mouth to speak.

"We don't have to see a movie if you don't want to," Josh said, "we could go mini golfing too. Whatever you want, really."

Please don't say no.

He searched her expression, watched her lips. What was she thinking? He wanted her to say yes more than he first realized.

"What movie did you have in mind?"

"The town's playing Jumanji at the community park Friday, I thought we could go there." He wanted to asked if she liked adventure movies. Did she like movies?

She looked at him, meeting his eyes. A sigh released her lips when she smiled. "That sounds like fun."

Relief flooded his mind. He felt his feet on the hard floor, he heard the shoppers around him. He released a breath he didn't know he'd been holding. He smiled, releasing a happiness that nearly turned into a chuckle. "I'll pick you up at eight. The movie starts at eight thirty."

She nodded once. "Okay."

"I'll see you then." He wanted to hug her, squeeze her hand—something—before he left. But he kept his hands in his pockets. She stared at him, smiling, waiting for something. He smiled back.

"Well, I got to get going." She ducked her head; stepping to the side.

"Yes," he needed to go. "I do too, I got to get going." He pointed to his chest.

He needed to go before he made a bigger fool out of himself. "I'll see you Friday." He tipped his head and waved as he walked away.

He glanced at his waving hand. *Stupid.* He tucked his hand into his pocket, shaking his head.

The bell shingled above him as he walked out the door, his stomach growling as thunder rolled. He forgot to get food. That'd have to be okay, he wasn't going back in there now. Letting her know that he forgot what he came to get would be embarrassing.

He watched the door, but she wasn't leaving. He looked at the time on the radio, then at the door again. Fully prepared to duck if she came out of the gas station. He didn't need to seem like a stalker. But she stayed in the building.

He had to go if he wanted to get home at a decent hour. He placed the gear stick in reverse, looked over his shoulder, smiling to himself and backed up. He couldn't believe she said yes.

His smile faded. What if she went out with him and she decided she didn't like him? Why had she taken so long to answer him?

CHAPTER NINE

Wednesday morning, Nate, with his head ducked, opened the round-top walk-in door. He brushed his hands through his hair, doing his best to dry it out. Olivia sat in a lawn chair by the work table, in front of the tool boxes, watching him from where he couldn't see her. He really was a good-looking guy. She could watch him work all day.

Sudden gratefulness rushed through her. She was the one who worked with him every day. Not Sam or any of the other girls Nate probably hung out with. The girls he partied with on the weekends got to know a bit of Nate, but she was the one who got to know his work habits, the things that made him mad; the things that made him appreciate his job. The work he did so well.

Olivia brushed her legs with her fingers, then pulled her sleeves below her wrist. Who was Nate on the weekends? She'd never seen that side of him. She looked up, spotting the holes in his jeans. She wanted to find out.

She lowered her eyes when Nate walked toward her, stomping the mud off his boots. Clumps of clay dirt marked his trail.

"You better sweep that up before Dave comes in," Olivia said.

"It's a mud pit out there. Can't be helped." Nate plopped down in a lawn chair across from her. "We'll clean when the weather clears up."

Nate chuckled and slouched in his chair. "Dave and I were wrong about the weather. Three days later and it's still raining."

"Rain is a good thing, right?"

"Gave you a chance to finish your school work, didn't it?"

"Yeah." Her heart warmed knowing Nate thought about what she did when she wasn't working on the farm.

He looked at her, his eyes full of warmth and sincerity. "Good," he said.

"This rain." Dave's voice drifted in from the doorway. He stomped his foot on the rug. "The hay needs to be cut. With four inches of rain, we won't be able to cut until mid-June. The alfalfa will start blooming," Dave said, looking through the big shop door windows.

He sagged his shoulders. "The Lord's blessing us with much needed rain-fall and here I am complaining." He turned around and walked toward them, hands in his pockets. He looked up and lifted his shoulders. "What should we do today?"

"This will really help the dry land corn; it might even give the wheat an extra boost and the hay," Nate paused, "it'll get cut." He scanned over Dave and Olivia. "Everything'll be fine."

Dave nodded. "We should be glad the hail didn't hit us

worse than it did Monday." Dave shuffled around on the work table.

The steady rain bounced on the slab. It shined the gravel, soaking into the earth. Dave and Nate had repeated those words throughout the last few days. It calmed the urge to work outdoors, on the fields, in the sunshine. At dinner all three of them ate their food, looking out the window. At breakfast they took turns standing in front of the window, sipping their coffee while the puddles widened. The dog laid on the front porch, resting his chin on his paws, waiting for it to stop.

The rain fall sounded heavier in the tin-covered building. She liked rain splattering against her bedroom window. It brought her to sleep. She wanted to cozy up on the couch with a warm knit blanket and a steaming cup of coffee while rain-drops pelted against the house's windows. After her last sip of coffee, she would nest her back against the couch cushions, pull her blanket above her shoulders and fall into a deep sound sleep.

Olivia fought off a yawn.

Josh. Her sleep vanished, remembering yesterday. What happened?

He'd asked her out. Her, Olivia Crandell. The coolest guy she'd ever met wanted to spend time with her.

Why? Why would a guy like Josh want to date her?

What if he got to know her and hated what he found out? Or what if he only wanted to go out once? Maybe she should have said no. What if Mrs. Bell was right about him? Olivia didn't know him or what kind of date he had in mind.

She never said yes to a date before. What if she didn't know how to act? What if he tried to kiss her? She'd been kissed once, in eighth grade at a classmate's party. A short, barely-lip-touching kiss in front of everyone.

The thought of it still embarrassed her.

If she wouldn't have walked out on Nate the night they sat on the porch swing, things could have worked out differently. If she would've told him about her dad, if they would've connected more. That little spark she thought they felt when they met could've turned into something.

She could've rejected Josh if she really liked Nate. She could've chosen to wait around for him. Olivia glanced at him. He never showed interest. Not like Josh. He probably never liked her in the first place.

"Well," Dave stood up straight, "Olivia, service the mowers. Clean the deck and replace the knives. You said they're leaving streaks, so now's a good time to fix that. The knives are in a box on the loft." Dave looked at the makeshift loft at the other end of the round-top.

"Nate, fix that clunker in the corner." Dave nodded toward the blue 60's model Ford pickup in the corner, where it stood without a layer of dust. The area around it was neatly swept like the rest of the shop. "You won't get it done, but you can start. Olivia needs a farm pickup."

That was going to be her farm vehicle? She didn't think

she needed one, she'd hardly gone anywhere in the month she'd worked here. Except to church several times and a few errands Mom had sent her on.

Olivia helped Nate push the pickup away from the corner. He told her to pop the hood open, then he examined the engine. He grabbed tools from the toolboxes and set them on the edge of the pickup's frame. He attached a socket onto a wrench and smiled at Olivia. "Can you drive a manual?" he asked.

She blinked, and stared at him. A what?

Nate chuckled, beginning to unbolt *things* underneath the hood. "A common vehicle will have either an automatic transmission or a manual transmission. This pickup has a manual transmission, so it operates differently than your mom's Yukon, which has an automatic transmission."

"I'll learn," she said.

Nate smiled. "I'm sure you will. I'm gonna teach you."

The *knickity-knick-knick* of the ratchet wrench, the rain on the tin roof and Dave's shuffling in the background were the only sounds in the round-top. Familiar sounds. The sounds of a home.

The rainy days ceased Thursday morning. Water puddles shimmered under the sunlight. The damp grass, the silver round-top, the green and red equipment sparkled, like a freshly deep cleaned kitchen. Olivia inhaled deeply. She stretched and yawned as she looked out the window above her desk. A verse Dad used to say came to mind.

"God's promises are new every morning."

She didn't remember which verse he said it was, but she didn't want to remember either. Her dad, faithful and honest in his love for Christ. He led his family in the way of the Lord, just like Paster Matthew preached about in church. She confidently followed, protected by Dad and his faith.

Until he died. What did that say about her?

Olivia flung the blanket off her legs with such force it nearly hit the floor. She hated moments like these. She walked to her dresser and chose her clothes for the day. She hated when the memory of her past crept up from within. Never knowing when the pain would sting and ruin the present. She hated them, yet she accepted them.

It was always there. The aching memory, the reality of her decision, the constant desire to honor her mother. The woman whose world she had broken. It had all become part of her being. It rested deep within her. Sometimes, out of nowhere, it peaked up and made Olivia wish *she* was dead.

A dead body couldn't feel. It didn't dream. It didn't *remember.*

Olivia stood in front of the full-length mirror in her room. She didn't look like she did at fourteen. Her hips were bigger, her hair was shorter, her face looked older. But underneath it she saw the same fourteen-year-old girl. Could others tell? Did they see the despair, the longing? The girl who rejected

Christ, the girl who killed her father, the girl who pathetically yearns for her mother's love.

She lowered her eyes, dipping her chin and pulling her T-shirt over her jeans. Breakfast would be ready.

Olivia jogged downstairs, turned left to walk through the living room, into the dining and kitchen area. The house smelled of coffee, bacon, and fresh morning air. Through the open window, Olivia heard the birds sing their "good mornings."

On the propane cookstove, eggs sizzled in the cast iron pan. She went to the coffee maker and poured herself a mug full of steaming coffee. She scanned the area, sipping her coffee. Where was Mom? Olivia grabbed the spatula and slid the frying eggs onto the plate beside the stove and turned the heat off.

Dave walked into the dining room from the master bedroom. "Good morning."

"Morning. Where's Mom?"

Dave set the serving dish of bacon and eggs on the bar table. He sighed. "She's having stomach pains. Says she's gonna rest for a bit."

Dave looked at Olivia and smiled, obviously trying to shoo away the worry in her eyes. "She'll be fine."

He gripped the rim of the counter and slid onto the barstool. He loaded his plate heavily, to the point where Olivia thought he would eat everyone's serving. He looked at his plate and shook his head, dumping half of the food back into the serving dish. He closed his eyes, set his elbows on the counter, and rested his chin on his intertwined fingers. Olivia glanced into her coffee mug. She didn't remember the last time she prayed.

Dave gripped the fork that sat beside his plate and slowly, like a weary miner holds the last shovel of dirt, he began eating. Forgetting his usual morning coffee.

Olivia tore her attention off Dave, lifted the mug to her mouth and watched the coffee tilt toward her lips. Obviously, Dave doubted his own words.

That evening, Nate cranked the blue pickup's engine. The setting sun lit the farm with its orange and yellow glow. A few birds chirped their goodnights. The dog stretched out on the gravel in front of the yard, settling in for the night.

Olivia held the driver's door open, naturally happy for Nate's success. He'd worked every possible hour on this pickup since Wednesday. He said he needed to fix it before the ground dried out and he'd have to work on the fields. Nine o'clock in the evening, after Dave and Mom retired for the day, he laid away the final tool and closed the hood. Now, parked on the slab in front of the round-top, Nate woohooed and clapped his hands, celebrating his victory,

"Should have fixed this clunker a long time ago. Wasn't nearly as hard as we expected." He looked at Olivia. "Get in." Nate shook his head toward the passenger seat. But before

Olivia could move, he slid across the seat and slapped the driver's seat. "If this is going to be yours then you're gonna need to learn how to drive it."

Olivia smiled, shyly. She sat down and closed the door, adjusting herself on the seat, while holding the steering wheel. "What do I do?" She examined the few gauges behind the steering wheel.

"Press the clutch in, then shift into reverse."

Olivia studied the stick shift. "Where is it?" Faded lines and numbers covered the nub.

Nate explained the gears and Olivia did as she was told. She revved the engine as she released the clutch. The pickup bounced backward then halted instantly, causing Nate to knock his head against the dash.

He rubbed his forehead, eyed Olivia, and said, "You killed it. Try again." She started the engine and slowly released the clutch, pressing the pedal. The pickup backed off the slab.

With Nate's instruction, Olivia drove circles around the farm equipment. She smiled like a kid on a tricycle. "I'm doing it," she said. With her bottom on the edge of the seat, her head held high, one hand on the wheel and the other on the stick shift. This was her pickup.

Nate told her to park beside the slab, in front of the round-top. Olivia held the clutch in and hit the brakes, their heads bobbled. She put it in neutral, shut the engine and slid back into her seat.

"You did it," he smiled.

"Yeah," Olivia nodded. "I did."

"You did good. I wouldn't recommend you drive in town right away though."

Olivia nodded.

He cleared his throat and rubbed his palm against his leg. "Listen, there's a movie showing tomorrow night at the city park. I was wondering if you'd like to go with me?"

Olivia looked at the silver ribbed tin on the round-top. *Uh-oh.* She wanted to say yes. She lowered her eyes to the dash board. "I'm sorry, I have plans."

She gripped the bottom of the steering wheel with both hands, sensing Nate looking at her. She wanted to read his expression. Did he look disappointed? Out of the corner of her eye she saw Nate lower his attention to the rubber carpeted floor.

Olivia dropped her hands into her lap and studied Nate's expression. Twilight dimmed the cab's interior. Nate's overgrown curls stretched over his ear, covering his neck. Olivia wanted to reach her arm between the seat and his upper back, run her fingers through his hair, and stroke his shoulders. As if the dim light would forgive the shameful act.

"I probably shouldn't have asked. We're co-workers, I should've thought of that. Can't risk it not working out between us."

"Why wouldn't it work out?"

He glanced at her, leaned back against the seat, reaching for the grease rag that laid between them. Large, rough hands, covered in grease stains. He rubbed the rag against his fingers, shrugging.

"Would you want it to work out?"

Olivia's eyes widened. *Yes.* Whiskers countered his jawline, in the fading light his eyes sparkled. She wanted their relationship to last. She wanted him to stick around.

"We'd need it to."

He studied her expression. "Yes," his eyes trailed to her lips, then up to her eyes, "we would."

He held her gaze. Olivia's emotions bubbled up, nearly boiling over. She looked at the seat, scraping her fingers along the cover, waiting to feel like her normal self.

"What do you have planned for tomorrow?" Nate asked, holding the door handle.

She straightened, reaching for the door. They stepped out, looking at each other over the hood. The light nearly faded by now. She turned toward the round-top, stepping away from the pickup.

"I better go inside before Mom and Dave get ideas."

Nate stepped up beside her, and looked down at her. "You don't want to tell me?"

"No, I don't." It felt wrong to tell him. Especially after their time in the pickup. It would ruin whatever they'd felt. It could hurt him.

His sparkling eyes turned hard. His head looked higher. His chest looked bigger. "You have a date with Josh."

She stared at him. How did he know?

He stepped back. "You could've told me." The further he stepped back, the less she could tell the disappointment on his face. "It's no wonder, the guy's crazy about you."

Really? Olivia's heart beat quickened. What had he said about her? What made Nate think he liked her?

Nate's boots scraping against the concrete jerked Olivia out of her reverie. He watched her, parted his lips, like he wanted to say something. It made his eyelids heavy. His cheeks sagged with the words in his mouth.

Olivia stepped forward. "What?"

He needed to say it. He wanted to. She could tell. What balanced on the edge of his lips? That he was crazy about her. That she should go out with him and not with Josh.

"You can tell me." She reached out her hands, but stopped before they found his. She couldn't. She slid her hands in her front pockets to keep from holding his.

He shook his head, turned around and walked toward his pickup. The engine started; the red taillights lit the gravel. Olivia looked down. She heard the pickup drive off. After it passed her, she looked up at the empty parking spot.

CHAPTER TEN

Friday evening was the night Olivia would go on her first date. She smoothed out her dress, looking in the mirror. Was a dress over the top? She'd bought this long blue and white maxi dress with shoulder straps last year for casual summer outings. But was it casual enough? What did people wear on first dates? She scanned the clothes in her open closet. She fussed with her hair, bringing it over her shoulders.

She looked at her dirty toe-nails and curled them against her tan sandals. Maybe she should ask Mom? She would know what was appropriate.

Olivia walked to the stairs, and yelled for her mom. She came to the stairway and asked, "What?"

"Does this look okay for a first date?"

Mom's expression became sober, almost distant as she examined Olivia. "You look great." She headed to where she came from. "Have fun tonight."

Any other Mom might have freaked, asked about her plans, and told her how pretty she was. Or would have sat her down and talked about what to do and what not to do with a boy, then tell her to wear something that she thought was appropriate. But not her mom.

Oh, well, Olivia guessed she looked good enough. She walked into her room. What was Mom doing anyways? Wasn't she curious who was taking her daughter out? Didn't she know this was her daughter's first date—ever?

A Dodge pickup drove onto the yard and parked in front of the house. Olivia stepped closer to the window. Dave walked from the barn to the driver's side of the pickup, holding a bucket of fresh milk. "Oh no."

Olivia grabbed her phone, scrambled around in her purse searching for a couple of dollars and her ID. She stuffed them in her phone case and ran out of her bedroom. How often did Josh show up to his date's house with the stepfather, dirty as could be, holding a bucket full of milk? Not often, most likely.

Olivia slowed her pace and walked out the front door toward Josh's pickup. Butterflies couldn't define the uncomfortable feeling in her stomach. She shouldn't be this nervous. She stood beside Dave and smiled her hello, not wanting to interrupt their conversation. Josh soon switched his attention to Olivia, obviously happy to see her, he said, "Ready to go?"

She nodded and walked to the passenger door. She climbed in and looked at Dave, who still stood by the driver's side window. "You kids have fun. Have her back by eleven." Dave focused on Josh. "I know how long movies are."

Olivia wanted to hide her head between her knees and never look up. *Leave, Dave, leave.* But Olivia watched him slowly turn around. He walked around the house to the mudroom door, his bucket of milk nearly sloshing over. Josh looked at Olivia. "Let's go?"

"Yes," she said, relieved Dave was gone. Josh put the pickup in drive and drove off the farm, onto the black top.

Half-way through the evening, Olivia wondered if girls were supposed to feel this way on their first date. She sat on a quilt Josh probably stole from his mom's linen closet, her legs crisscrossed, drinking the bottle of Coke Josh bought from the beverage stand. An oversized bowl of extremely buttered popcorn balanced between them on the lumpy, blanket-covered grass. Every time their fingers touched in the bowl butterflies brushed the inside of her stomach. A part of her wanted to yank her hand away, while a larger part of her wanted Josh to take it.

She pretended to watch the movie playing on the white sheet, laughing when everyone else laughed, but every thought focused on what Josh would do next. What she wished he would do and what she was afraid he'd try to do.

Her heart beat faster, her breathing enhanced; what if he tried to kiss her when he dropped her off? Or before that? She thought of it before, but now, on their first date, it all seemed too real.

Olivia glanced at Josh and smiled to herself. This was real. She was here, on a date with a guy like Josh. If he kissed her—she imagined his lips on hers—she would like it. Very much. She brought the rim of the bottle to her lips, sipping Coke, while the street-lights turned on.

She could sit with Josh anytime, anywhere. He made her feel comfortable, safe. Whatever Mrs. Bell thought about him wasn't true. He made her heart happy. He *wanted* to be here with her. She repeated those words to herself. Hardly believing them.

She grabbed popcorn from the bowl, eating one kernel at a time, hoping this evening would never end. She wanted to stay with him forever.

Josh parked a ways away from the house. Out of eyeshot from any windows. That way Dave or Mom couldn't sneak glances at them. Not that Mom would care. Olivia could show her a positive pregnancy test and Mom would shrug, and get back to work. What would she do if her teenage daughter started showing?

Mom and Dad got pregnant before their wedding. She'd been nearly a year old before they finally got married. Olivia knew better. She remembered the few youth Bible studies she'd attended. But she'd love to see if Mom would give her a second thought then.

Josh shut the pickup engine off and looked at Olivia. "I had fun tonight." He smiled.

She forgot how to speak; all she could do was smile.

He lifted the middle seat and said, "You can sit here, if you want."

Awkwardly, she scooted next to him and fussed with her dress. She felt Josh look at her. "Can we do this again?"

Olivia lifted her head, nearly hitting Josh's chin. Their noses nearly touched. Olivia wondered if she should move, maybe she was too close. But every ounce of her being wanted to stay exactly where she was.

Josh brushed a strand of hair behind her ear. His breath tickled her cheeks—she wanted him to kiss her. Their eyes met and they held each other's gaze. Her eyes trailed to his lips as he leaned back, further away, dropping his hand into his lap.

"You're beautiful."

She glanced at the floor board, blushing. "Thank you."

"When can I see you again?"

Olivia looked at him, parting her lips, thinking.

Josh chuckled. "I'm getting a little nervous," he chuckled again, "thinking maybe you're not telling me something."

"Oh! No, I'm sorry." Olivia glanced at her lap. "I was just … I don't know, I can't believe that someone like you would want to spend time with someone like me."

Fear shot through Olivia's body, wishing she could take back her words. She didn't dare herself to look at Josh. She just ruined any chance she had with him—she knew it. Why had she said something so pathetic? To Josh, of all people.

"Hey." Josh squeezed her arm, then slid his hand down to her hand and held it firmly. "Hey," he placed his fingers on her jaw and turned her attention back to him, "I want to see you again." He smiled. "Do you want to see me again?" Josh squeezed her hand.

Olivia smiled. "Yes."

"Okay," relief shadowed Josh's face, "is Sunday to soon?"

Sunday sounded great. The sooner the better. "No."

"I'll pick you up at six."

Olivia nodded. "I had a good time tonight."

Josh held her gaze. What was he thinking? Was he wondering what she was thinking?

"So did I." Josh squeezed her hand a final time then reached for the door handle. "Dave is gonna come out here if I don't leave." He opened the door and jumped out, then helped her down.

Standing behind the driver's side door, inches away from Josh, Olivia waited. She lingered, knowing she should walk into the house. After a minute, she realized he wasn't going to make a move. Olivia stood up on her tip-toes, leaned in and kissed his cheek. Specks of pokey beard hair reminded her what she was doing. She jerked back and said, "goodnight," then jogged up the porch steps, through the door, the living room and up the stairs to her bedroom.

She walked to the window, then scanned over the farm. There he was. The pickup's taillights shone onto the gravel driveway. She felt like such an idiot. She should have waited for him to make a move—if he had even wanted to. He was being the perfect gentleman and there she went acting like an inexperienced child.

Olivia plopped on the mattress and slid off her sandals. At least Nate would never know about this. If he knew—she'd simply fall over and die. She should have talked more too. *Why hadn't she said more of what she was thinking?* Sam would never have that problem. As pretty as she was, she probably had a lot of experience with boys. Maybe she'd talk to Sam about this. Before Sunday, preferably. She needed to talk to someone, because she was obviously not doing it right.

The day came when Granny insisted every woman in the family come to her and Grandma's house to make "real" strawberry jam. Lindy needed to learn, she said. Mom and Olivia were the first ones there. At nine a.m. Mom knocked on the white door, and took a few steps back, holding a laundry basket full of kitchen stuff she thought they might need.

Mom had pulled her hair back into a ponytail. A short blond bundle of hair flopped above her neck. A simple T-shirt slid over her long maxi skirt, instead of the shorts she usually wore at home. Who was this woman? She jumped at every opportunity to please her in-laws, yet she wouldn't give her daughter a second thought. The distance between Olivia and her mom suddenly didn't seem far enough.

Olivia was like a sore in her mom's arm-pit. An annoying, uncomfortable blob that no one wanted and where no one wanted to be.

Why wasn't she curious where her daughter had been Sunday? If Olivia came home at midnight, would Mom even notice? Dave would. Her stepfather, who'd been her supposedly "new parent" for not even two months, cared more about her than her birth mother. She had known it would take time for Mom to heal after Dad's death. It would be a while before she would be her old self again. Not that her "old self" had cared much about her daughter. Although, it had been better than this.

But her time was up. She'd gotten remarried after all. What changed so much, that Mom couldn't love her own daughter? Did she truly blame her for her first husband's death? Olivia knew she was the one who'd asked Dad to drive home in the storm. But wasn't God the one who controlled life or death?

"Good morning, come in." Grandma Margaret's voice interrupted Olivia's thoughts. Probably for the better. She'd spent enough time trying to talk to Mom on the way here. She didn't need to fry her brain with thoughts about a woman who didn't care whether she existed.

Granny peaked around the left-hand corner, most likely coming from the kitchen, and waddled a few steps closer. "Goodness, you're here. Well come on in," she turned toward the kitchen, waving them forward, "You can start washing strawberries. Lindy, you cut them up. Margaret can cook and smash them." Granny walked past the strawberries and nestled into a rocking chair beside the phone table. "I'll supervise."

Olivia smiled to herself. *Cute little lady,* she thought. She would be cuter yet without that black scarf tied around her head. *Why did she wear it?*

An hour later, Mary and Sam walked into the kitchen. Mary was pale and glossy from sweat. Granny and Grandma fussed, telling Mary it was the morning sickness. Mom and Mary smiled at each other. They knew how pregnancy worked, they'd both done it before. Then they shook their heads, admitting it usually wasn't this bad. After an hour discussion, the four moms decided Mary better see a doctor.

Olivia snuck a glance at Mom, shaking a colander full of strawberries. If she was sick, would Mom fuss over her like this? She dumped the strawberries into a large bowl, lowering her stare.

After five hours of washing, cutting, simmering, smashing, ladling, and boiling, Sam and Olivia stood in the kitchen, washing dishes and wiping counters. While the four ladies sat in the living room. Olivia heard them laugh, swap birthing stories—everyone except Mom, who didn't talk about Olivia's birth. In between their birthing stories, they *ooh*ed and *aah*ed at what the neighbors had done. The ladies called it resting, but Olivia called it "old lady talk."

Olivia glanced at Sam. Now would be the perfect time to talk about Josh. Mom barely muttered a few "ohs" when Olivia talked about boys on their way to Granny and Grandma's house. Sam would at least care. If she stopped talking long enough to listen.

Last night had been the same as their first date. Awkward.

If Olivia kept it up, Josh might end it after their third date. He asked if Wednesday would work; she'd nearly said yes before he finished asking. The simple thought of it excited her. She could not afford to mess it up.

She laid the towel on the counter, beside the clean dishes.

"Sam," she stopped talking and looked at her, "I have a date for this Wednesday."

"This Wednesday, coming up? Like the Wednesday that will be here the day after tomorrow?" Olivia focused on the dishes in the sink. "Wow, on a Wednesday, huh? I mean my mom grew up hanging out on Wednesdays and Sundays, and only on Wednesdays and Sundays. So did Dave, Grandma, Granny every German Mennonite, really. Now they just hang out whenever they want—most of them do, anyways."

"Yes, so we've gone on two dates already, but—"

"Two dates? Who is he? Do you like him? You must if you're going on a third date."

"His name is Josh and yes, I do. That's the—"

"Josh as in the guy Nate kicked out?"

"I don't know." Maybe Nate had had several different roommates.

"Oh, I'd be careful if it is him. I don't know him, but if Nate kicked him out then there must be something going on with him."

He also kicked your brother out. But Sam wouldn't want to hear that.

"Nate wouldn't kick someone out for no reason."

"No, he wouldn't." Olivia picked up the towel and continued drying dishes.

"Nate's a nice guy. Wish I saw him more. Now that I don't clean the house anymore, I hardly ever go to the farm. When I do, Nate's never around."

Olivia glanced at Sam. *That's why she pops up out of the blue.*

"I don't even know what he thinks of me. Probably hardly knows I exist. We're from different Mennonite churches. His parents wouldn't approve of my church anyways. But, they might, if they liked me enough …" Sam blabbered on about Nate, but Olivia didn't pay her any mind. She knew Nate wasn't interested in Sam.

This conversation hadn't helped her at all. Mom helped her more than Sam had. At least Mom hadn't accused Josh of anything. What made Josh the bad guy? Three guys had lived in that house, anyone could have caused the fight.

CHAPTER ELEVEN

Memories, that's all they were. She could burn the box, but the memories would never leave. Maybe she should burn the box. Lindy scanned one photo at a time, emptying the stack in her right hand, piling them on the floor.

A smile spread over her lips. Erick. On his twenty-fourth birthday. With cake smeared on his face, after he had tried to smear frosting on her cheek. A chuckle built up in her throat. She could still hear their laughter. She slid the photo off the pile with her thumb.

Her breath caught in her lungs. Erick and Olivia.

Olivia looked beyond fragile. For the first month, Lindy only held her when she had to. Her eyes bore into the photo. She could hear Olivia's fading cry, Erick's soothing voice; she could see Erick bouncing, cuddling Olivia in his arms. Like a movie displaying on paper.

A tear rolled down her cheek. She rubbed the ink with her thumb. She'd taken this photo three days after. A photo of a three-day-old baby and a new college senior father, who relied on her for help. She could still feel her heart melting, watching the man she thought she'd love forever, hold his daughter.

Lindy laid the photos in the box. Olivia didn't look like that now. Like her father.

The bracelets she had made with her mom nested in the corner of the box. She slid them onto her wrist, smiling, remembering the days of fourth grade. After she finished her after-school snack, they would sit around the table, making bracelets. She loved those memories. Warm, comforting, like the snacks she'd eaten after school.

A photo peeked through at the bottom of the box. Curious, Lindy gripped the edge with her fingertips, sliding the keepsakes off the photo.

Her. Deceit stabbed her back. Why had she kept this? A picture of a woman who had caused the most chaos she had ever experienced. Her perfect wavy hair, framing her flawless features.

Lindy stuffed the picture through the rummage until her fingers hit the bottom.

She felt open, vulnerable. Every sight of that woman made her hurt. She reminded her of her past, of her present. Of the empty prayers she said in front of Dave, the routine church services she went to. Everything. That woman reminded her of everything she didn't want to remember.

She needed, she needed … Lindy rested her head in her palms, straightening her back. Her cool fingers rubbing her forehead. *What did she need?*

"Mom?" Olivia yelled from in the living room.

Lindy dried her eyes, turning her face toward her bedroom door. "What?"

"Can you come out here? I need your opinion on my outfit."

Olivia's third date. Ever. Lindy sighed. "I'm sure you look fine."

The house fell quiet. Lindy's ears focused on the door, listening for footsteps. "You don't want to keep your date waiting."

"He's here," she yelled.

Footsteps ran the other way. Lindy sagged her shoulders, turning her attention toward the scattered stuff on the floor. She tapped the photos against the wooden planks and set them inside the box. She latched the dusty wooden lid and heaved herself up, placing the box on the top closet shelf. In the corner, out of easy reach. The double closet doors clicked onto the magnet. Lindy strode out of their bedroom into the dining room, stopping in front of the window.

A Dodge pickup drove out of sight.

She knew Olivia had looked beautifully appropriate. She always did. Maybe she should have told her.

The laundry room faucet squeaked. Water poured against the sink. Dave, washing his oil-stained hands one last time before he would settle in for the evening. They had the house to themselves. A newly wedded couple in their honeymoon phase. A happily married woman, deeply in love.

Why did she feel like she was missing something? Lindy

stared past the porch railing, past the Locust tree, past the equipment, to nothing. Everything merged. Something. She needed something.

"There she goes."

Lindy jerked her shoulders up, turning her head. Dave stepped closer, against her back. He looked over her head, out the window.

Lindy turned her head, focusing on the driveway. "Yeah, there she goes."

Dave brushed his hands around her ribs, pulling her closer, wrapping his arms around her waist. He rested his chin on her shoulder. "Our daughter's first boyfriend."

Our daughter.

Dave nuzzled her neck. "Right? This is her first boyfriend?" Lindy felt him turn his chin toward the window.

She wrapped her arms over his, gripping his fingers. "Yes." She breathed deeply. "Do you think they'll last?"

Dave leaned sideways to glance at her. "It's too early to tell, don't you think?"

"Do you think she'd be happy? Live a good life?"

Dave loosened his hold, leaning back to study her.

Would Olivia ever forgive herself? Let go of her mistakes? She deserved to live a better life than she allowed herself.

"I don't know. It'd depend on their relationship." Dave studied her, watching her stare at nothing.

He snuggled his chest against her back, resting his cheek on her head. Lindy closed her eyes. Tears flowed to the surface.

He can't know. I can't explain. She squeezed her eyes, forcing the tears back, gripping Dave's hand. She couldn't lose him. Not again.

Every now and then you meet people who rejoice in all their decisions. You think, "They know what they're doing." Unfortunately, Josh was not one of them. Otherwise, he would be headed to Mr. and Mrs. Williams's new house warming party with the rest of his family.

His phone vibrated on the passenger seat. He reached over and pushed the phone around. The phone slid to the far end of the seat. Josh glanced to the side, he stretched out, moving the steering wheel with him. He clutched the phone and looked up. *Shoot!* He jerked the steering wheel to the left, preventing a near glide into Shade's Cafe.

The phone rang again. He hadn't realized it stopped ringing. He answered, "Hey, sis?"

"When are you going to be here?" Veronica asked.

"I'm not coming. Other plans came up." Josh signaled onto the main highway.

In the background of the phone call, girls giggled and boys shouted, blocking out Veronica's voice. Her voice sounded distant when she laughed, yelling, "if Thomas does five headstand pushups, I'll jump in the pool."

Josh pressed the phone closer to his ear. "I thought you were at the Williams's with parents?"

"We're at Jackie's. Turns out all the kids were going here tonight anyways. So, it's just the parents at the Williams's."

Josh opened his mouth to speak. But Veronica's distant voice sounded over the speaker. "He's doing it? Oh, no," Veronica laughed. Her laughter became louder as Josh pictured her bringing the phone to her cheek. "All right Josh, I'll talk to you later."

He heard bits and pieces of conversation over conversation, then the phone call ended. He checked the screen to assure himself. He shook his head and slid it into the cup holder. He set his jaw, pushing his back against the seat.

Where did Jackie live? He glanced at the neighborhood to his left. Most likely somewhere in there. If he drove down every block, soon enough he'd hear teens laughing and screaming. One house passed, then another. If he wanted to go, he had to make up his mind.

How mad would Keith be if he didn't drive to Walsh tonight? He would rather meet three angry men after an hour drive than spend the evening with drunk high school kids. He'd been to high school; he'd done all that.

Veronica's voice echoed through his mind. *If Thomas does five head-stand pushups, I'll jump in the pool.* Why had she not jumped in the pool in the first place?

Josh stared at the corner of the dashboard. His eyelids sagged; his fingers, like heavy springs, curled around the steering wheel. He jerked his head up, glanced in the door mirror and yanked the pickup left, nearly hitting the right curb.

He rolled the windows down, driving past every house, until he heard girls screaming. The boys chased them around in the backyard, pointing water guns at them. Josh parked behind one of the many vehicles around the house.

He let out a deep breath. Three years ago, he would've enjoyed this. Three years ago, he hadn't stepped foot inside a drug dealer's storage shop. He hadn't gone to college.

He lowered the sun visor and lifted the mirror lid. No one would see the wrinkle beneath his eye. He shrugged, slapping the visor up. Twenty looked good on him.

His sister ran out from behind the house, laughing, with wet clothes and hair flinging everywhere. A boy, a lot taller than Veronica, caught up to her, placed his hands on her waist and twirled her around. Their laughter subsided. They began talking in sweet, smiley tones.

Josh looked away; his eyes wide open. He grabbed his phone from the cup holder and jumped out of his pickup. He slid the flat screen into his back pocket and strode toward the back yard. A couple snuggled against a driver's door, whispering things Josh didn't want to imagine.

Any other day this would not have worked out. The parents would have complained, or they would have stood on their front porches, making sure the kids wouldn't make any trouble. But today, the whole neighborhood gathered at the Williams's, leaving the kids free to do what they wanted; as loud as they wanted. The parents knew exactly what their kids were doing: they were teenagers once. He could see them, standing on the deck, drinking cocktails, pouring whisky into glasses, joking about *"their days."*

"Hey man," a young boy slapped Josh's shoulder, "the elders are gathered at the Williams's today. I can tell you how to get there, if you'd like?"

One half of Josh's lips smiled. He squared his shoulders and lifted his body to his full height. He slapped the boy's back, causing him to spill his beer. "No thanks, man." Josh squeezed the boy's shoulder, tight, tighter, tighter. Until he could see pain on the boy's face. "I'll stay here." He shook the boy's shoulder and smiled, slapping it once more.

A picket fence countered the edge of the back yard. The fence bounded at least sixty teenagers. Some dressed in swimming gear, others soaked to their skin in their everyday clothes. Floaties of all colors covered the bleached-blue water. Some towels hung over pool chairs; others laid across the concrete. Galvanized tubs, filled with ice, water, soda, and beer, were tucked into every possible corner of the backyard. Two tables, covered with food, stood on the patio. Whoever this girl was, she knew how to throw a party. They never had snacks in his day.

A girl about five foot five, strutted toward Josh and welcomed him. Jackie, he guessed. Josh smiled. The girl looked exactly like he imagined a Jackie would look: slick blond hair with hazel eyes. Pretty, but not like Olivia.

His sister's smiling voice drifted into earshot. Josh lifted his eyes over Jackie. Veronica and her friend walked toward them, chatting endlessly. They stopped behind Jackie. Veronica looked up. An innocent shock covered her face. "I thought you had other plans?"

Josh shrugged.

Veronica focused on Jackie and the other girl. "This is my brother, Josh."

Jackie smiled at Josh, batting her eyelashes, "I'm glad you came," she said.

Josh looked over Jackie's head and combed his fingers threw his hair. He hoofed, leaned his weight one foot, and crossed his arms over his chest. He nodded.

Maybe this had been a bad idea.

Olivia checked her mom's text message to reassure herself she had the right address. She read the house number on the text message then the one by the front door. This was the one. She slid her phone in her jean pocket and closed the pickup door. She scanned the street, amazed at the number of vehicles parked on it.

Olivia halted. Behind her, to the right side, stood Josh's pickup. She blinked. Didn't he have plans today? It could be that someone else had the same vehicle.

She walked to the front door. Music blared inside the house. People laughed and shouted. She glanced through the window, passed the dining room, into the back yard. Teens surrounded the pool, boys jumped in. Some lounged in the living room, some looked bored; others snuggled with their partner. A girl looked out the window and spotted Olivia.

She jerked back, standing between the door and the window, holding still. The front door opened and Olivia cringed. She tightened the grip on her folded hands. "Can I help you?"

She released her breath and turned around. She stepped closer and dangled her arms beside her hips. "Yes, I'm here to pick up something for Lindy Unruh, my mom."

The girl looked confused.

"Your mom and my mom met at the grocery store the other day and your mom had offered to lend her your drink dispensers for a party she's throwing next weekend. I'm here to pick them up."

"My mom's not home right now, come back another time." The girl pretended to smile and stepped underneath the door frame.

Olivia leaped in front of the door frame. "Can you not get them for me? We live twenty miles away. My step-dad needed parts for a piece of machinery, that's the only reason I'm in town to—" Josh swayed through the living room, toward her.

"Olivia." His big, genuine smile warmed her heart. "What are you doing here?"

He wore a maroon T-shirt with tan cargo pants. His dark, thick hair brushed to one side. The sleeves on his T-shirt fit snug around his biceps. Surely, he'd never looked better. Her stomach fluttered and her arms tingled. Out of everyone here, he approached her. Happy to see her.

"I'm here to pick up something for my mom. I was in town anyways, getting parts for Dave." Dressed in her work clothes, covered in dirt and grime. She scooted her ankles closer together and hugged her ribs. Everyone here looked appropriately dressed for a party. "I just got off work. Well, I'm not technically *off* work. Getting parts for Dave is work, but running an errand for Mom wouldn't be."

Olivia shut her mouth. She squeezed her triceps and tightened her grip on her forearms. She was beginning to sound like Sam.

Josh's eyes smiled. His everything smiled. Olivia glanced down.

"You two know each other?" the girl standing between them asked.

Josh kept his eyes on Olivia. "Yeah, we're dating."

The flutters worsened. This must be how Nicholas Sparks' characters feel. She had never read one of his novels. Surely, she was living in one. She wanted nothing more than to be held in his arms. She wanted to show appreciation for the love she felt.

Josh reached out his hand. Olivia loosened her grip on her arms and placed a hand in his. He shook his chin sideways. "C'mon." He squeezed her hand. She stepped over the threshold. "I'll show you around," he said.

She could get the drink dispensers later.

Olivia surveyed the room as she followed Josh. The girl that had opened the door stood in the kitchen, holding a solo cup, talking to a group of girls. Every girl eyed Olivia. She trailed her eyes down to Josh's shoes until she stepped out the open sliding door, onto the deck. This looked nothing like the junior high party she'd gone to years ago.

Girls talked to the guys. By their flirtatious body movements Olivia could tell their actions were loaded with confidence. The guys threw footballs in the pool, jumping in after them. They cheered the girls on as they jumped off the diving board. Some did tricks, others simply fell in. They teased and dared, the up-beat feel-good music obviously increasing the party mood. Where were the neighbors? How had the host not received complaints? Or gotten called in. There was evidence of underage drinking lying all over the freshly cut grass.

Josh stopped in front of a galvanized tub filled with melting ice and cold cans. "What do you want?" he asked.

Olivia studied the beverage station. Soda, water and beer. "Water please."

"Are you sure you don't want a beer?"

Olivia glanced at the beer cans; she leaned in close to Josh's ear and quietly said, "I've never had one."

Josh smiled. He raised his shoulders and draped his left arm around her waist, then pulled her close, until their bodies formed a V shape. He rubbed his palm on her ribs. "Then let today be the first time." He looked down at her. "How about it?"

Could she still drive home after one beer? If she waited a while after drinking it, before she drove home, she should be fine, right? She didn't know. In school she had overheard stories about weekend parties. The after effects sounded gross and uncomfortable.

Josh removed his arm around her and reached down into the tub. "Two beers coming up. One for me, one for you."

"Thanks." She shyly accepted the beer and opened the can. Olivia brought the beverage to her lips. Maybe she could pour it out behind a bush when no one was looking. Not that it tasted bad. After the day she'd had, an ice-cold beer tasted refreshing. More than the sweet tea she would've had at home.

"I guess we can make it official? I can call you my girlfriend?"

Girlfriend. The word tasted warm and sweet, like fresh banana muffins out of the oven on a crisp rainy day. She would have someone to go out with—anytime, anywhere. She would have someone to call. Someone to take to school events—not that she'd ever gone to any. She would be his and he would be hers. Someone who would love her.

Olivia nodded.

How would it feel to be appreciated without constantly working for it? Olivia brought her beer to her chest and nestled against Josh's chest. He kept his arm extended for a while, then gently pushed against her spine. He held her close and lowered his cheek to the top of her head.

All she needed was a blanket wrapped around her and she'd feel the comfort of their two-story suburban home in

Topeka. With her dad slouching crisscross on the floor beside her, building a model train track. Olivia bit the inside flesh of her lower lip. The hole in her heart became evident like a sink-hole at night. She pushed herself against Josh and he held her tighter. She bit her lip painfully hard and scraped her forehead downward against Josh's chest.

She missed Dad. So much.

Olivia stepped back, slid her free arm down Josh's forearm and curled her fingers around his knuckles. She smiled at him.

"If I didn't know any better, I'd say something was wrong." Josh searched her face. His lips smiled, but his eyes looked worried.

"Not at all." Some people would consider that a lie. But Josh didn't need to know her inward life. It wouldn't do him any good. And when it came to Josh, nothing was wrong.

Olivia sipped her beer. She swallowed and gestured her beer toward the girls walking their way. "Looks like we're getting company."

Olivia felt Josh's eyes shift off her, his body turning forward, watching the girls approach. He slurped up a hefty gulp of beer and said, "That's my sister."

"Which one?"

"The one in the red T-shirt."

She eyed the girl over another sip of beer. The girl wore a summer red V-neck T-shirt, with medium-tinted blue denim shorts. Her silver anklet displayed the baby-soft skin on her bare feet. Olivia's feet felt trapped in her work boots. Like clown shoes, standing out for everyone to see. If only she could slide her boot-cut jeans over her toes. No wonder all the girls stared.

A boy about her age trotted up to Josh's sister and stopped her from heading their direction. The girls in his sister's group gave her "the look." The "Girl, you're about to get lucky" look. Olivia had seen plenty of other girls in school receive that look. She'd never been told the true meaning, but she knew enough of her own kind to know. The girls said their "see-yas" and their "have-funs," then they walked to another group.

Obviously, Josh had also noticed. He stretched to his full height and shifted his weight from foot to foot. Like a female tiger, waiting to pounce on her prey.

"Is he not a good guy?" Olivia looked up at her boyfriend.

"I don't know," Josh paused, "I don't know him."

CHAPTER TWELVE

If Olivia had used all her senses, she would have left. But clearly, she'd burned a few cookies in the oven. Otherwise, she wouldn't be standing in Dave's kitchen explaining to her mom why she hadn't gotten the beverage set. The woman didn't care where her daughter had been the last three hours. She simply wanted to know if she'd still be able to use the beverage set for her party next weekend.

Mom had a summer party planned for all of Dave's family. She wanted the set so she could display a buffet just like she'd seen on Pinterest. Mom figured everyone loved a good party. It'd be the perfect way to warm her way into Dave's family. She wanted to be one of them.

Mom shrugged and tilted her head. She'd buy one. She couldn't always depend on lending one anyways. On Saturday, after she'd completed all her chores, she would head to town and buy the necessities. She didn't think they had enough chairs either; she'd have to buy some of those as well.

Dave's eyes listened eagerly. Olivia was fully aware of his keen hearing. The idea that Dave might have a sense of smell like a track hound, made her uncomfortable. She watched him without entirely looking at him, like one did a bull. Mom wouldn't stop planning her to-do list long enough to smell the alcohol on her breath, but Dave observed every bit of this scene.

At last Mom flipped open her planner and began to reassure her schedule for the next week. She stopped talking and mumbled to herself, while flipping pages.

The woman never once looked up to ask Olivia if she'd eaten dinner. Not once. The last hour she'd spent with Josh her stomach had rumbled. He offered her dinner. She declined because she didn't have any money with her. To assume he'd pay was unfair. Yet now she wished she would have.

She could have driven home to get her wallet, driven to town again, eaten a one-hour-dinner, taken a leisurely stroll around town and Mom still wouldn't have asked, "What took so long."

"I'm going to bed." Olivia turned slowly. After the one beer she'd drank, she'd felt tipsier than she should. The two hours spent mini golfing had taken the edge off a bit, but she didn't want to risk showing any signs.

"Eh-em." Dave cleared his throat. Olivia stopped underneath the frame that separated the living and dining room. She envisioned Dave straightening in his chair. Demanding full authority over his household. "Olivia."

She turned on one foot and stepped toward the round dining table. "Yes."

Dave glanced at Mom, who stood staring at him. "As the leader of this family, I would really appreciate it if you could let us know where you are next time and let us know that you'll be home later than you thought." Dave stretched up off the bar stool. "You can take the pickup anytime, just let us know."

Olivia fixed her gaze on the dark stained oak cabinets. Anger simmered in her system. It bubbled above her heart, like a sauce bubbling over a heat source. *The leader of the house.* No one had *led* her, since her father passed. If anything, she'd been the leader. One couldn't call a mom who never invested time in her whereabouts, a leader.

Yet, she couldn't bring herself to burst out her anger. It stopped simmering; the flame underneath puffed out.

"Okay." Olivia looked at Dave, showing her acknowledgement. "Goodnight."

Mom didn't care. She never had. Her step-father cared more than her birth mom did. Olivia did everything for her. Every day after school she had worked at the restaurant. She had worked at the restaurant on weekends; she had stayed up till twelve finishing her homework; she'd done her house chores in the mornings before school. She'd done everything for Mom.

Why didn't she care?

What kind of a daughter did she need to be to earn her mother's love? To earn her forgiveness.

Olivia pressed her palms against her cheek bones. She

squeezed her eyes shut, and inhaled deeply. The air pierced her lungs. She gasped through the pain. Her mom would never forgive her. She couldn't be forgiven. She couldn't expect her mom to love her, to care about her. No one else knew, but Mom knew. She knew the truth.

But to not love your own flesh and blood. To never care. Never wonder if they're okay, never want the best for them. Had she messed up that bad? Bad enough to erase every humanely motherly feeling.

Olivia bumped her toe against the top of the stairs, stumbling to the middle of the hallway. *Yes. You selfish child. Remember what you did.* No, no. She wanted to scream. To stomp her throbbing foot against the floor. It couldn't be true.

To never truly be loved again. Whole-heartedly, fully and truly loved. By no one.

Her heart crushed, shattered. She pressed her forearm against her chest. The limb felt unattached to shoulder. She rubbed the skin, the palm. How could she never be loved? Did anyone truly love her now? She breathed heavily, welcoming the air, allowing it to float to her heart. The fresh air in her body, made her feel less alone.

Exhaustion overtook her. Her eyelids became weights she could no longer hold up. She dragged her feet into her room, breathing shallow, short breaths. She needed to rest. She wanted to rest. To lie down on a soft mattress, under warm, fluffy covers.

Thinking back, the less painful decision would have been to continue with the schedule and retrieve Keith's package from Colorado. He knew this when he decided to attend Jackie's pool party. But if he had done that, he wouldn't have made Olivia his girlfriend. He smiled. "Oh!" The blow to his intestines cringed his lips into a wrinkly O shape.

If a knuckle beating was his punishment for missing one trip, what would Keith do when he found out he planned to quit? He could handle a little bone-to-bone friendliness—not that he wanted to join in, fighting had never been his strong suit—but who knew what else these men stored in their sheds? Josh figured, the less he protested, the sooner they would stop. All they wanted was to see him suffer a bit.

The man's knuckles popped as they hit Josh's head. He dangled his head on his neck. His head throbbed. He knew he could endure more, but they didn't need to know that.

He'd never acted in any school plays, but he watched enough action movies to know how to act defeated. If he could trick his history teacher into believing the history book was wrong, then he could trick these guys into believing his defeat. If they wanted to kill him, they would have already.

"That'll be enough." Keith sat in a wooden seventies style chair, rolling his cigar between his lips. He used the arm rest to straightened his back. He shook his head over his shoulder, motioning for Ron to leave. Ron disappeared into the only room within the shop.

Josh wiggled his wrist, using the rope to itch a sore spot.

He lifted his head, groaning. He shifted his feet on the ground, wanting Keith to think he could hardly hold himself up. The pole that stretched along his back had clunked against his spine several times. That hurt. He'd give them that.

"A month ago, when I agreed to this, you seemed friendlier." Josh smiled with his eyes.

Keith removed the cigar from his mouth and huffed. He held the roll-up between his index finger and his middle finger, balancing his elbow on the narrow arm rest. "I am friendly." Keith slowly smiled. Like a rotten animal that grew more disgusting over time. "Sometimes people just need"—he puffed another smoke—"a"—he waved the cigar around with the flick of his wrist—"reminder."

"Reminder of what?"

"Not to mess with a plan."

A boy too small for his boots clopped toward Keith and Josh. His face. Something about it looked familiar. The boy couldn't be more than eighteen years old. He walked without watching where he stepped. As if he expected all the crawling insects and rodents to race out of his path. No doubt they hid nervously behind any crack they could find.

"If Keith tells you to run an errand, you do it." The boy glanced at Keith then back at Josh. "You don't protest and you don't ask questions."

Ron stood behind the boy, in front of Keith. Obviously, Ron was the guy they called to do the dirty work.

"I had other obligations."

The boy nodded; walked back and forth in front of Josh, like a determined woman in a conference meeting. "Yes, I'm sure you did." The boy jerked his head up, smiling at Josh. "Attending a party with your girlfriend is something you wouldn't want to miss." He stopped in front of him, hands behind his back. He looked at Keith, Ron. "We all like to have a good time, don't we boys?"

Ron smiled inappropriately. Disgust shadowed Josh's face. He could only imagine the good time these men liked to have.

Josh looked at the boy again.

The party. That's where he'd seen him. He was the guy who'd left with his sister. He'd been flirting with her all evening. Anger sparked friction in his joints. His sister would never be involved in this boy's "good time."

"You ratted me out." Josh's head sat firmly, lifted high, glaring at the guys in front of him. His bruised spine stretched out to its full length, the muscles around it tensed and flexed.

"Ah." The boy shrugged. "They would have found out anyways."

Josh pressed his fingers onto his palm, flexing his forearm. He lifted his chin slightly. "Why are you here?"

Keith removed the cigar from his lips and flicked the ash off the end. Scattered clumps of gray had accumulated on the stained concrete floor. "The boy's good at trash talk." Keith extended his arm, letting it balance on the arm rest.

The boy stayed in his position. Josh saw the expression change on his face. Keith didn't. The irritation mixed with disappointment on the boy's face lightened Josh's mood. Obviously, the boy was hoping to climb the "business" ladder.

"And," Keith leisurely stood up from his chair, leaned backward to pop his spine, then stepped up beside the boy, "he has a business plan I'm interested in."

"How does that include me?"

The boy folded his arms across his chest, setting his feet too far apart. The kid's face was enough to drive anger through every fiber of Josh's being. His voice was reason enough not to like him.

Keith stroked the dirt on the concrete with his shoe-covered toes, shifted his feet and looked at Josh. "Meet your partner." Keith looked at the boy.

No! Josh's fearful eyes scanned the three guys. *No!*

Olivia stood in front of the kitchen window, holding a plate for Sam to put the avocado in. White foldable tables, covered with red and white checkered tablecloths, were lined up in one ten-foot row. White foldable chairs stood around them, placed at a comfortable distance. On the little concrete patio, in the corner where the day's first shadows appeared, Mom put two tables with white tablecloths neatly displaying every option on the menu. By the drink dispensers, she set a sunflower and daisy bouquet that she'd bought at Shallow River's flower shop. The flowers in her garden wouldn't bloom for another month.

At six o'clock Mary, her husband, and Sam arrived. Great-Grandma, Grandma, Wyatt, and Nate had yet to arrive. That was fine. Mom said six was plenty early. Of course, she didn't say that in front of Mary. But Olivia heard her and Dave talking upstairs, when Mary and her husband's vehicle parked in front of the house. Mary and Sam would have to help with the final touches, Mom said. And that's why Mary had insisted they come early, she wanted to help.

Sam sliced open the first avocado. She giggled, moving her body like an air tube-man. "Don't you just love cutting an avocado that's ripened to perfection?" Sam tilted the avocado toward Olivia. "Look. It doesn't get better than that." Sam smiled, showing all her teeth, squeezing her shoulders. "This'll be good."

Olivia stared at Sam. What kind of person would perk up about an avocado? The same person who rollerblades up and down the sidewalks on Friday nights, just for fun. Sam placed the green slices neatly on the white plate. If Sam ever did find a husband, he would be a man with unfailing love; one who sees beauty in everything around him.

"Is Josh coming?" Sam took the plate and held it in front of Olivia.

"No. I thought maybe it was too soon."

Sam nodded and stepped around Olivia. When she walked back from the patio, into the kitchen, she asked, "I heard Nate's coming. Any idea when he's going to be here?"

Olivia shrugged. It felt wrong to wait for Nate instead

of Josh. The thought of talking to Nate excited her. The guy was fun to work with. They'd never seen each other outside of work. She wanted to know who he was when he wasn't covered in grease and dirt.

Maybe she should have invited Josh. But she didn't want to scare him off by taking things to serious right away.

Sam's shoulders sagged; her eyebrows dropped; her hands clung to the edge of the bar table as she stared out the dining room window. As if a familiar thought settled itself within her. Olivia stepped closer. She felt like she needed to reach out and squeeze her shoulders.

No. Olivia planted her feet onto the wood flooring.

Sam slid her folded hands across the counter and rested her elbows on the white Formica. "Sometimes I feel lonely. Talking for miles without end doesn't replace the desire to share a conversation with someone."

Sam feeling lonely? Here stood a girl who marched through doors and demanded attention.

"Do you suppose that's why guys don't talk to me?" Sam straightened her back, reached for the plastic picnicware and began placing silverware into the entertaining basket. "Oh, they talk to me. A few words, just to be polite. Guys can be very nice you know." Sam shot Olivia a glance. Olivia nodded. "But I don't remember a guy ever showing interest in me."

Sam removed the sturdy red plates from the plastic bag. "I've heard guys like to pursue. Not be pursued. It's part of their need to be the leader of things. Kind of like those males on Animal Planet. Did you know polar bears will walk for miles and miles just to find a lady?"

Sam grabbed the plates and red solo cups, nodding toward the silverware. "Can you bring that?" Sam headed toward the patio screen door. "We should've gotten steak knives; no one can cut through a steak with plastic."

"Less dishes," Olivia said.

"Yes. Plastic knives will work. Besides, Dave cooks a tender steak. Juicy and well-seasoned. I can taste it already."

The rumbling of an engine rolled down the driveway, stopping in front of the house.

"Do you think that's—" Sam's face turned red. She lowered her attention to the beverage table, pretending to busy herself arranging the solo cups.

Olivia hid a smile behind her lips. It most likely was Nate. It sounded like his pickup. Any minute Nate would walk out the patio doors. Nerves tickled her colon. She glanced at the outfit she'd chosen for the day: a faded pair of dark blue boot-cut jeans and a gray and white graphic tee with a woven cream and black striped sweater. The spring air made the sweater seem appropriate.

Sam wore a mid-length sage colored midi skirt, a white T-shirt, with a brown belt to tie it together. It highlighted her shoulder length blond hair perfectly, making her delightful appearance even more welcoming.

Olivia could never compete with that. Even if she'd worn a dress.

She rolled her eyes away, scanning the area. Early evening light shone on the dark green wheat leaves behind the neatly trimmed buffalo grass. Sixty feet to the right of Olivia stood a shadowing Locust tree, claiming its place beside the white and red chicken coop. The chickens pecked and waddled around in their run. Some stuck their head through the square fencing, picking at the buffalo grass.

Between the coop and the dining tables nested Mom's prospering garden. Olivia hadn't thought Mom could grow a single plant, but there it was. A thirty-by-twenty-foot garden, growing vegetables and flowers.

Chatter filled the farm yard. Cash sat beside the grill, tongue hanging out, as if he knew steaks would soon cover the propane fire.

Olivia could nearly sense Dad's presence beside her. A part of her wanted to turn her head, to believe she would see his clean-shaven, friendly face. Fear of realizing the truth—again—kept her head from turning.

Olivia lowered her eyes. Her knees wobbled. Her arms dangled like spaghetti noodles. She should never enjoy herself in this way. Like she did on her dates with Josh. She remembered the vow she'd made when the paster at Dad's funeral said, "everyone deserves joy." She had thought all the other God-fearing-hypocrite-Christians could have her joy. She didn't need it.

You need it.

"Why the sad face?" Nate stood beside her, hands in his pockets.

His blond, curly hair framed his scratchy, bearded face. His light-blue eyes cheered her heart immediately. She'd never been happier to see him. He wore a blue and white snap-on checkered shirt tucked in behind his boot-cut blue jeans. He'd rolled up his sleeves, showing his tan, muscular arms. Olivia wanted nothing more than to lean against his chest and have him wrap his arms around her.

But that couldn't happen. She had a boyfriend.

She had a boyfriend. She should never have thought that way about another guy. Shame covered her heart. She could only imagine the hurt Josh would feel if he knew her thoughts. Olivia lowered her gaze, feeling worse now than before.

"You okay?" Nate asked. He looked genuinely concerned.

"Yes." Olivia smiled at the concrete. She needed something to do.

"Then why won't you look at me?"

Olivia looked around, scanning past Nate. She needed to convince him, but how?

"I have to go to the restroom." She turned and strode into the house.

The restroom? Really? Now he would think she had the "runs."

Ugh!

She walked through the dining room, into the laundry room. She turned toward the restroom. She might as well go.

CHAPTER THIRTEEN

Who had she become? First, she had the *"runs,"* and now she spilled ice tea all over her jeans. Olivia stood up and walked to the buffet table to grab more napkins. She glanced at everyone lounging in the chairs, toothpicks balancing between their teeth, exchanging casual conversations. The sun had set behind the corrals; the last light slowly fading. The *"kids,"* Nate, Olivia, Sam and Wyatt, sat a comfortable distance from the others, underneath the patio light glow.

With the sunlight gone, maybe no one would spot the moisture on her thighs. She sat down in the freshly wiped chair, reaching for her phone vibrating on the table. Everyone glanced at the lit screen. The phone moved closer to the stacked trash plates. It read *"Josh,"* with a picture she'd taken the other night. Olivia grabbed the phone, heat rising up her cheeks.

She pushed the chair back; striding toward the chicken coop, she answered the phone. "Hey."

"I've missed you." Her muscles relaxed. Her breathing

calmed, bringing a smile to her lips. She sensed his smile over the phone. "What are you doing tonight?"

She should have told him. She should have invited him. She closed her eyes, remembering her thoughts toward Nate.

"I thought maybe we could hang out. Still have a few hours."

"I'd like that." As if time with Josh would justify her thoughts. "What did you have in mind?"

"I could come over."

She breathed, studying the bottom of the clothes line pole. Mom wouldn't mind.

Everyone chatted around the tables, undisturbed, unrushed. She lowered her gaze toward her boots, poking the grass beneath them. Everyone would ask, why didn't you invite him for supper? Nate and Josh, in one space, with her. Olivia shook her head.

"I could meet you somewhere."

"Meet me at the valley. It's on your way to town, a few miles east of the highway," he paused. "If I leave now, I could be there by eight thirty."

She couldn't. She'd have to leave her guest. She sighed. "Dave's family is here."

"Oh."

"How 'bout after they leave?"

She glanced in the family's direction. Everyone laughed, leaning back in their chairs, listening to Mary's husband tell another story.

"If they haven't left by nine, I'll tell them I have some-where I need to be." Olivia's black hair hung over her cheeks, blocking her face.

"You could just tell them you're meeting your boyfriend. Unless you're trying to hide me." He pretended to tease, try-ing to hide the serious tone underneath.

"No. Not at all." Olivia carefully considered the words on her tongue. "We can chill. Privately. This way."

"Privately, huh?"

Yes. Her stomach tingled.

"I'll see you there Olivia."

The call stayed open. She could hear his breath. "See you there," she said.

Did he want to say something? One second, two sec-onds … nothing. She removed the screen from her cheek and hung up. She slid the phone inside her pocket. She'd take the blue pickup.

Crickets chirped in the crisp air. Voices echoed from behind her. Every animal slept. The wheat stood straight, not a breeze waving through. She hugged her sweater around her waist, looking up at the early night sky. A lonesome star shone boldly, a perfect five-pointed star. On the horizon, orange highlighted the narrow clouds above the unseen sun. The longer she looked, the more stars popped up, the more the orange faded from the clouds.

"It's beautiful."

Olivia turned her head to see Nate standing a foot behind

her, to her side, with his hand in his pockets. He stepped closer, a few feet beside her. She smiled, then looked at the sky, above the chicken coop.

"The sky," she searched for words, "it's different every day. Never the same, but always," she paused, sighing, "beautiful."

"Just like you."

Olivia lowered her head. He shouldn't say those things. He knew she had a boyfriend. She lifted her chin, focusing on the chicken coop.

"I'm always the same."

He tore his focus away from the sky to look at her. "That's not what I meant."

She nodded, lifting her eyes to the sky. "If I could paint, I'd paint that." Pure, spotless, radiant beauty.

"God's painting," Nate said. "New every day." He slid his hands in his pockets, puffing his chest in and out. "Every day's a blank canvas."

He lowered his eyes; noticed her studying him. She didn't care. "What's your story?" she asked.

His thin beard countered his jaw. His kind eyes, questioning her. Like they often did. "What's yours?"

He stepped closer, reaching his hand up. Was he about to brush the hair behind her ear, or hold her hand? Whatever he thought about doing, he didn't do. He slid his hand back in his pocket. "I have a feeling there's a lot more to your story than there is to mine." He looked deep into her eyes. She couldn't look away.

"Someday, I hope you'll tell me."

Olivia parted her lips. Inches away from unloading every miserable moment, every heartbreaking, unhuman thing she had ever thought or did. About the rejection. The constant reminder to be there for a woman who didn't care whether she lived or died. To tell another living soul. To tell and still be loved. To hear someone say, "It's okay. I still love you." She wanted to cover the distance between them, more than she'd ever wanted anything in her whole life.

Nate broke eye contact. He stared over her shoulder, "Olivia," he faced her, "be careful around Josh. I know him. He's not who he seems."

"He's a good guy."

"Promise me you'll be careful." His eyes pleaded more than his words. "I don't want anything to happen to you."

Olivia straightened her neck; stretched out her spine, setting her shoulders firmly. "I'll be fine."

Nate nodded. Olivia wrapped her arms around herself.

"I'm gonna go," he said. "Tell your mom I said thanks for inviting me. I had a good time."

Olivia nodded. Nate stepped past her, around the clothesline pole. Her eyes following his footsteps, she said, "have a good night."

Not good. This was not what he'd planned. When had he ever heard of someone entering the "*drug*" business and things didn't go south? Or west, in his case. Every week he headed west for his weekly run to Colorado. Except for last week. When he'd been lured to a *meeting*. A meeting that left him bruised. He held in a whimper every time Olivia grazed her hand along his back.

He couldn't tell her to stop. Her fingers running down his spine, wrapping around his ribs; her body leaning against his. Even now his heart raced, remembering. He had allowed his mind to wonder, but he would never do anything about it. The feeling he experienced every time she held him was enough.

At nine-forty Olivia had jogged around the corner, behind the round-top. She held in the gasps, but her silent, heavy breathing showed she didn't run often. It didn't matter, she was the prettiest thing he'd seen all week. The starlight glistened on her wavy hair, making it appear even darker. Her skin glowed. So much, that he had brought her closer and grazed a finger down her cheek.

When Cash galloped around the corner, barking vigorously, Olivia jumped, sharply abrupted their embrace and persuaded Cash to shut his yapping jaw. That dog ended their evening when it was just getting started. Josh hadn't planned to leave that early. He didn't mind meeting Olivia at the farm, instead of at the valley. But he would've wanted to leave at one or two o'clock.

Olivia insisted on walking inside before Dave or her mom became suspicious. But he would drive the forty miles again just to see her and hold her.

Especially tonight. He'd rather be anywhere else than where he was. Saturday night should be spent with his girlfriend. Even a board game with his sister would be better than this. At least his sister wasn't with Steve. Who'd name their child *Steve?* Steve, the kid born with deceit, sat in the passenger seat of Josh's pickup. Josh glanced at the boy. Veronica and Steve. Their names didn't even go together.

Josh lifted the roll-up to his lips. He held the smoke behind his lips for several seconds, then exhaled. He shouldn't be indulging while driving, but if he was doing all this for the drug, he might as well use it. Cars zipped past them, some honked and others looked out their window, squinting their eyes to see who would drive fifty-five in a sixty-five.

What was the hurry? He wasn't going to see Olivia tonight.

Josh peeked at Steve. Steve sat up straight, eyes focused on the road. Elbow propped on the door-window frame, smoking like an elderly official, contemplating in his study.

Josh wrinkled his nose, looking away.

Every time he asked himself why he agreed to this, he remembered the beating he had received on Tuesday. It had cost him two days off work, three days away from Olivia, and several lies to his sister, persuading her not to come over. He couldn't risk either one seeing him in that condition. Veronica couldn't handle it. A fifteen-year-old girl should never be exposed to such sights or stories. Especially not ones that involved her only brother.

Josh took another puff and glanced at the boy. Josh

adjusted his grip on the steering wheel and asked, "How long have you and my sister been going out?"

Steve smiled.

What had he done? Why would he smile? Josh glanced at him again. Still, he held that mischief, boyish grin.

Slowly Steve brought the joint to his lips, huffed, and propped his elbow on the door frame. "Not long," he said.

Josh's right hand tingled. He used every sense in his being not to pull over and punch the kid. Right, on his slick, sly, too-high-on-his-horse, good-for-nothing grin.

Instead, he said, "She's too young to date."

"Relax, big brother." *Don't call me that,* Josh thought. "I haven't seen her since the party," Steve said.

Why not? Was his sister not good enough for him? "Have you called her? Talked to her?"

Steve shot Josh a frustrated look. "Dude, chill out." He shook his head, then stared out the windshield again. "Turn left here." Steve gestured to the dirt road, exiting the highway.

Josh merged onto the shoulder and turned left. The dirt road gravel nicked the bottom of his pickup. Josh slowed his speed.

No sense in asking Steve more questions. He'd have to talk to his sister instead. Maybe tomorrow he could take his bike out of his parent's garage and they could ride around town. Later, he could meet up with Olivia.

Josh pressed the smoke into the ash tray and placed both hands on the steering wheel.

It'd be a better Sunday than the ones in the past.

Would his life be a routine of trips to Colorado? Was this all he'd amount up to? Failure. He'd been raised to know better. He came from people who did better. Men who finished college. Men who ran million-dollar dairy operations; men who strode into a bank every morning, working eagerly at their desk. Men who received hundreds of thousands of dollars every year, crunching other people's finances. Doctors, attorneys—respectable citizens. Those were the kind of people his parents surrounded him with all his life.

He'd make sure his sister would become one of those people. A woman whose husband could proudly call her his. A woman who marched around the community with authority and a kind spirit.

Like his mom. After that, Veronica was on her own. But if she ever neglected her children, he'd come knocking. He didn't have an older sibling to help him when Mom and Dad were too busy. Veronica's children might not either.

"Turn right." Steve gestured his high head toward a *village* on the right side of the dirt road.

Josh crept onto the property. Eight dogs scattered on the lawn. Around the shop, the greenhouse, the trailer house, and the shed. A silver chain was locked onto their collar. Their nails clawed into the soil. They backed up, jumped forward, yanking on the chain. Several more leaped around the rusty vehicles, snapping loud, angry barks at Josh's pickup.

Josh gripped the gearstick. He lingered at every gear,

holding in the brakes. *Notch…notch… notch.* A German Shepherd jumped forward, locked his jaw and growled. *Notch.* Josh released the brakes. He leaned back in his seat. Instead of crawling underneath the dashboard, he looked at Steve.

"He got a few more," Steve said. "Angrier than I remember." Steve leaned back in his seat and nestled in. "We'll wait."

A long nose and big eyes appeared at Steve's window. The face nodded toward the shed. Josh nodded.

"She wants us to go, Steve."

The kid nodded. "I know," he said, looking at the woman standing outside his window.

Josh would rather be at the other seller. They didn't have sister-dating boys, ankle-biting dogs, and weight-lifting-sized women. But like Keith and Steve said, this one would bring four times the hassle, four-times the effects and four times the money.

The galvanized pail, half full of eggs, rocked in Lindy's hand. She stepped over a puddle, walking from the coop to the house. Last night's shower brought little more than tenth of an inch. The lawn sprinkler she'd forgotten about had created the puddles. Heavy breathing neared her shoulder, she lowered her head to watch Cash trot toward her from the fuel tanks.

She bent down to scratch behind the dog's ears. His tongue hung out. His innocent brown eyes watched Lindy, clearly enjoying the love. A lukewarm breeze brushed her hair down her shoulders. Lindy patted the dog's head and stood up straight. She really needed a haircut. She hadn't found a salon she trusted with her hair.

Among the six salons in Shallow River, she should have found at least one she liked. But she didn't want to volunteer her hair for the experiment. But she couldn't let it grow any longer. She dreaded brushing her hair at night for fear of noticing the split ends. Her hair color could use a touch up as well.

She could see the dirty dishes on the kitchen counter, through the screen door. The sight of bread rolls cooling beside the oven made the cleanup worth it. She'd stuff the dishes in the dish washer, wipe the counter, then season the chicken legs. At four thirty she should have plenty of time to cook a hearty meal and prepare a breakfast casserole for tomorrow morning.

Lindy placed a hand on the screen door frame, working to slide the hiking boots off her feet.

The tractor engine churned next to the barn. Inside the cab, Nate operated the fork lift, moving twenty-foot iron post. Dave hollered at Olivia. Lindy breathed in, smiling to herself. She loved the activity. A part of Topeka she sometimes missed. But Topeka didn't have the earthy-crop smell she'd grown to love.

"Lift up," Dave yelled.

Nate lifted the iron post, attempting to drive through

the gate without hitting the corral panels. Dave had sold the posts to a neighbor, who wanted to build a horse fence for their kids. On the northwest side of the barn, out of eyeshot, Dave stored all the valuable things that could one day be used. Even Dave knew some things were too good to throw away. That didn't mean it needed to look messy. He asked Olivia to trim around them every other week.

Olivia stood beside the gate, watching Nate's every move. Dave stood to the side, hand held high, instructing Nate where to drive.

The fork lift tilted down.

Lindy pushed her palm against the doorframe, standing still, watching. One post rolled forward a few inches.

"Woa!" Dave yelled.

CHAPTER FOURTEEN

U p." Dave pointed his thumb to the sky. "Up." He bobbed his fist upward.

The posts rolled forward. The forklift yanked up. It slammed down a few inches. The first post rolled off the tips of the fork. The others following, like a group held together with magnets. Never too far apart, yet never clinging together. One hit the ground, then the other, one after another. They clunked and banged against each other. The sounds echoing off the barn tin, like a trumpet playing over the farm.

Dave! Lindy screamed inwardly.

Her feet raced to the barn, hardly touching the ground. *Did something happen to him? What happened?* A hundred thoughts swirled in her mind. She repeated his name. As if screaming it silently brought her closer to him. Surely, he'd be okay. *He had to be okay.*

Lindy leaped around the post lying by Olivia's feet. She looked up. He was here. Standing. Not under heavy, rusted, long-tubed post. Lindy examined the medium-sized, scruffy farmer. He was here. Unmarked. Unfazed. Studying her, like he would an anteater at the zoo.

Lindy lowered her eyes and stepped closer to Dave. *Thank the Lord he was here. With her.* She wrapped her arms around him and breathed. Her heart rate slowed, her muscles easing. She rested her cheek on his chest. He wrapped his right arm around her. His scarred, callused hand pressing against her ribs. A perfect fit. Made to hold her.

"Are you okay?" Nate asked someone.

Lindy turned, careful not to lose Dave's embrace. Nate observed the scene he'd caused.

"Yes." Olivia nodded. Her eyes glistened. Her lips a straight line.

A pink and red scab covered her left arm. Blood ran down her left leg, staining her jeans. It disappeared above her ankle, most likely puddling in her boot. Several posts rested on her feet.

"I'll help you to the house." Nate studied the posts on Olivia's feet. "Let me move these." Nate lifted the edge of a post, moving one end at a time.

"I'll help." Dave forced his body away from Lindy and picked up the opposite end of the post.

Olivia's eyes rolled toward Lindy. Lindy looked at the dirt, folding her hands in front of her. She glanced up. Olivia focused on Dave and Nate. As if she would take one step, she would fall over Nate's back and topple onto the iron posts.

Dave straightened his spine, breathing hard. Concern

shadowing his face. "Will you be able to walk?" he asked Olivia.

She nodded.

"We can get the four-wheeler, drive you to the front porch," Dave said.

"Do you want to take your boots off?" Nate nodded toward the boots.

"No." She shook her head.

Olivia turned, an inch at a time. They watched her move like a sloth crossing the street.

Lindy glanced at the men. Olivia would never accept their help. After her father passed, independence crept into her bones.

The men looked at Lindy. Silently questioning her, as though they expected something. Dave's forehead lines deepened. Disappointment? Confusion? Sympathy? Lindy couldn't tell. Nate lowered his gaze. Lindy looked away, step-ping around the posts.

A sticker hooked into her heal. She'd taken off her shoes. She tiptoed over toward the corral panels, weed stems pok-ing her feet. She balanced herself on a panel, pulling out the sticker. She stepped around the end post, onto the gravel, wincing every time she stepped forward.

Behind her, the men talked. The posts clinking against each other. Olivia stepped onto the sidewalk. Cash trot-ted over the lawn, toward Olivia. The dog walked beside her, sniffing her legs. Olivia kept her head lifted, her arms hanging down her shoulders, limping. She couldn't tell which leg Olivia favored.

When Olivia wanted to learn how to ride a skateboard, she'd taken it too far and decided to skate downhill. She fell, skidded, and rolled down the street, stopping when she hit the curb. That's how Olivia looked now. Except as an eleven-year-old, she ran home to Erick, who applied a salve and wrapped up the scabs while Olivia let a few tears slip out.

Olivia climbed up the steps, holding on to the railing. Lindy offered Olivia her shoulder, but she shook her head.

"I'm fine," she said.

She made it up the steps and across the porch. In front of the door, she clenched her jaw, and attempted to slide off a boot. She squinted, inhaled, and tried again.

"Sit down and I'll help." If she sat on the bench swing, Lindy could slide the boots off Olivia's feet.

Olivia held herself up by the doorframe. She slid her foot up, through the boot shaft, pursing her lips together. The blood-stained sock, leaked onto the concrete. Permanently marking the day that she could have lost another husband. Lindy wanted to run into the laundry room, get a bucket of sudsy water and scrub. Scrub the memory out of the concrete.

She couldn't go on without Dave. She couldn't go through that again. She finally had a family. The first true family she had since her parents' death.

The screen door banged against the frame. Lindy's head jerked up. Olivia limped into the living room, disappearing behind the wall. A trail of blood following her. Lindy bolted inside.

"Olivia, wait." She ran into the laundry room and grabbed a rag from the cabinet. Olivia watched Lindy like a stranger who couldn't speak. "Walk into the mudroom and wash off the blood. Then you can put bandages on the scars."

Olivia dragged her feet through the dining room.

The area around Olivia seemed blocked off. Like an invisible barrier that traveled with her. The foundation she stood on, seemed forbidden. Who had this girl become? When had she changed from Erick's little girl, to … this?

Lindy lowered her gaze. She hunched over the red drops and wiped the floor. She knew.

Her own words echoed in her mind. *"Get out!" "Get out!"*

Lindy's upper body tightened. As if someone whacked a bat against her back. How could she have yelled at a fourteen-year-old child? And with such anger.

She could still see Olivia standing in the doorway. Like an infant. Her hands hanging down, her eyes swollen from tears, her dark hair tangled, clinging to her cheeks. She never saw Erick's little girl again. Maybe she passed away with her father. Left there at the burial site.

Shouldn't she, her *mother,* have revived Olivia?

A tear hit the wood floor. In the mudroom faucet water dribbled into the sink. Olivia's pant sleeve was rolled up; a cloth wrapped around the scar to stop the bleeding. The faucet stopped dribbling. Olivia's feet stepped backward.

Lindy quickly scooted along and finished wiping the rest of the drops.

She stood up, the rag dangling from her fingers. Her eyes following Olivia as she wobbled past her, toward the stairs. The scab on her arm had turned a shade of purple and red, the colors darkening by the minute. Most likely her feet looked the same.

"Can I get you anything? Cream for your arm? Ibuprofen for the pain?" Lindy asked.

"I'm fine." Olivia made her way through the main floor and up the stairs.

Lindy turned her focus to the pile of dishes on the counter. The dinner rolls needed to be put away before they dried out. She still needed to prepare the chicken legs, steam the vegetables, and make mashed potatoes.

She sighed, stepping into the mudroom to throw the dirty rag in the washer.

Intense, cramping, pain tightened her lower right side. The rag flung against her hips; her palms pressing against her abdomen. She hunched down, staring at the floor, groaning. Her eyelids fell shut. Nausea overtook her. She squeezed her palms against her body. Another stab pounded against a throbbing organ.

She blinked, rocking up and down, ready to fall. Ready to lay on the floor, hug her knees and rock on her hip.

Outside men talked; the tractor had shut off; something bustled.

Ow! Lindy cramped her intestines. Another sharp pain hit and clung. She began to straighten her back. The pain worsened, her face muscles tightening. *Nope.* Nope, that wouldn't help. The pain jabbed the inside of her, like a hundred needles piercing, poking. She pressed her arms against her ribs.

Ow! She silently cried as she reached for a chair by the dining table.

She sat down, hugging her stomach, rocking her upper body. Why was she having these pains?

Her conscience whispered to her, slowing her rocking. A punishment?

An image of *her* played in her mind. Her slick black hair, her graceful face, smiling at Lindy in the well-furnished, perfectly-styled living room. A living room where she had once sat, beside *him,* never fully accepted, but welcomed. A part of *them.*

Lindy remembered everything. She remembered the love, the purity. The salty tears on her lips, the gut pounding truth, her heart shattering, like a windshield hit with hail. The years after, the warm, cozy home, with plenty of everything. The phone ringing on the couch, the hesitant, shaky voice that told her, "Your husband died." The life draining from Olivia's face when she heard. Every angry, blame-pointing thought she had toward the child, she remembered everything.

She still felt the chill on campus. The empty sidewalks, the dead grass, the bare branches. She remembered the brown leather jacket Erick had worn. His blue eyes, shining with moisture. The steady breeze lifting his thick, wavy hair.

"What about her?" she had asked Erick. *"How will our life work?"*

She had sensed the longing in his eyes. She had wanted to believe him.

"God will provide a way. Our God is a God who forgives and forgets." She saw the determination in his eyes. He believed every word he found in his new Bible.

A tear slipped from Lindy's eye. *Oh God.* Her rocking quickened. *Why have you asked this of me? I can't do it. I can't forget.*

Everything else was new.

Everything except the injured girl upstairs. Every time she looked at Olivia, she saw *her.*

How could she forget?

Olivia slouched behind her desk, looking out the window. Her arm stung. It rested on the wooden desktop. The cloth above her knee, damp with blood. She'd have to change the bandage soon. The leg stretched out, toes resting against the desk drawers. She should change. She dreaded brushing jeans over the cracked skin.

She studied the farm. Her chin lowered; her hair pulled back. In front of the corrals, Nate and Dave loaded the post onto the neighbor's bumper-pull trailer. The neighbor and his son followed their system. The calf and cow napped next to each other in separate pens. Horses scratched their necks on the end posts. The chickens pecked near the barn door. A rooster pranced from one hen to the other, pecked the ground, then strutted to another hen.

The sun glistened against Nate's pickup in front of the round-top. Olivia blinked, her lips a straight line. She should talk to Nate, later, before he left. She'd hate for him to blame himself. She'd be fine. She intended to rake the alfalfa field tomorrow.

Olivia closed her eyes.

It made sense that Mom would worry about Dave's safety before hers. He was her husband after all.

She had leaped past Olivia. Hadn't Mom seen the post falling on her?

Olivia dropped her head back. A headache rushed through, her eyes spun, neon lights swirling behind her eyelids. It didn't mean that Mom didn't care.

Nate had jumped off the tractor steps and rushed to her aid. Mom had embraced Dave, as if she would let go, he'd break down and slip out of her arms.

As a short five-year-old, with smooth, even-clipped bangs covering her forehead, she had run after a butterfly, off the park lawn, onto the street. Dad had yanked her arm and pulled her to the side. Seconds later a vehicle zipped by, honking. She'd cried, the pain in her shoulder ruining the evening. Dad had carried her back to the lawn, sitting her down beside Mom.

"Never cross the street without your mom or me. Do you understand?" he had said.

Olivia nodded. Her hair bobbing back and forth. Dad brushed her cheeks with his thumb and held her close, until she forgot about the pain.

Olivia breathed heavily.

Every day she missed her father. Every day.

She lifted her head, opening her eyes. Her mother would never love her like her father had. If she stood in front of a driving car, would Mom yank her arm? Olivia doubted it.

Every morning she woke up with a goal to be the daughter Mom needed. She reminded herself she was the reason Mom's world crashed. It was she who had caused the unwanted update in their life. And Mom knew it too. Every cold stare when she sipped her coffee, every lingering glance told Olivia Mom's secret thoughts.

Did Mom still have those thoughts? She shouldn't.

For nearly three years Olivia had done everything she possibly could to restore her mom's happiness. To *take care of her,* like she'd promised her dad.

When would Mom love her? Her *daughter?* When would they have a mother-daughter relationship?

Like Sam and Mary.

Olivia sat up straight. Her mother would never love her like Mary loved Sam. She would never value their conversations.

Olivia stood up, pain shooting through her hip and down her leg. After waiting for it to pass, she wobbled to her closet. She couldn't do it any longer. She *would not* do it any longer! Olivia stretched her rib cage, wiggling her fingers, reaching the duffle bag on the shelf. She pulled it down and watched it hit the floor.

She could go anywhere, anywhere but here. She would live with Josh if she had to. Mom wouldn't care. Olivia sat the duffle bag on the bed, and fluffed it out. She would find a job somewhere in town. She could work at the thrift store. She'd never run into Mom there.

CHAPTER FIFTEEN

Olivia yanked clothes off their hangers and pulled undergarments out from the chest drawers. She stuffed them into the bag. For nearly seventeen years Mom could have put forth effort. Not once did she bring cupcakes to school on her birthday. She never took her to the park—just the two of them—she never taught her how to drive. Never. In seventeen years.

Olivia pounded the clothes down.

Why not? What had she done so wrong? Mom's first husband died because of her, but before that. What kind of a child had she been that her own mother would resent her?

Olivia crumpled dresses together, adding another layer. Could she leave her mom? Could she leave her only parent?

Mom had Dave.

Olivia loaded the duffle bag to the top and zipped it shut. She pressed her palms on it, leaning, thinking, what to take and what to leave.

She'd have to leave it all. She couldn't take it and she wouldn't come back for it. Olivia limped to the window to sort through her wallet. She would need the essentials. She pulled out a few wrinkled dollar bills. Her fingers flipped through the sections. Not much. Her debit card, her license, and a few gift cards.

She zipped it shut. She would withdraw money from her bank account in case Josh wanted rent up front, although that would be unlike him. Should she ask him first before she showed up expecting to move in?

An engine started. She looked out the window. The neighbor's pickup. The neighbor, Nate, and Dave stood around the front end of the vehicle with its hood popped up. Cash sat a safe distance from their feet. The neighbor's son sat in the pickup, obviously starting the engine for the men. Did they have a good relationship? By the way the neighbor looked at his son, Olivia guessed so.

She had that once. She had the most amazing father anyone could ask for. She promised him she would look out for his wife—always. At the funeral, at the grave, before they moved. She couldn't break that promise.

She couldn't breathe, knowing she had let him down, twice.

Would he know? Did he really *know*?

Olivia scraped her callused hands over her face. If he knew, what would he say? Would he blame her for tearing their family apart, again?

If he never heard her at the funeral, was she even breaking a promise?

Olivia stepped toward the bed and sat on the edge. She rested her hands in her lap, her head heavy. Emotions bubbled up inside her body like lava, simmering, rising higher. Olivia fell on her side and cradled her knees. A groaning, aching sob escaped her lips. She hugged her ankles. The flood of tears soaking into the quilt.

I should have never called him that night. I should have sat patiently with Mom. Olivia tucked her chin against her chest. Why hadn't she been smarter?

Gripping her ankles, silent tears rolled down her face. Lips parted, breathing in the dry air. *Why?* she whispered.

Lindy scrubbed propane stove racks in the deep, farmhouse sink. She moved the rack back and forth underneath the running faucet, rinsing the suds off the edges. The lukewarm twilight air seeped through the kitchen window screen, decreasing the drying time. A lit candle flickered on the freshly cleaned bar table, highlighting the recipe books underneath the calendar.

The mudroom door notched shut. Boots clapped against the floor; Lindy envisioned Dave setting them neatly against the wall. The floor creaked with every step. Coins rattled against the counter top as Dave emptied out his pockets.

"One day we should get new flooring and cabinets," Lindy said, placing the racks over the burners.

Dave slid a chair away from the bar table. He sat down,

and leaned against the calendar wall. "What's wrong with these?"

"They're out-dated. The whole place was built before either one of us was born." Lindy hung the kitchen cloth over the edge of the sink. "The whole house should be refinished."

"Remodeling costs a lot of money."

Lindy walked to the bar stools and sat down across from Dave. She propped her elbow on the counter and rested her head in her hand. "The upstairs carpet has stains older than us."

Dave shrugged. "Chris and Lauren designed this house."

"And we'd keep it the same way. Just renew everything." Lindy smiled. "I'm sure your former employers wouldn't mind. They had to have known that changes would be made when they sold the farm to you."

Dave smiled. "Maybe one day."

Lindy sighed, sitting up straight, smiling at Dave. He cleared his throat, his face sobering. Lindy tensed. She lifted her chin, stretching out her arm across the counter. She knew that look. Had Dave noticed something when she didn't fuss about Olivia's injury? What would she say if he asked her?

"Why do you treat Olivia the way you do?"

Lindy stared at him. Should she tell him the truth? He was her husband. Rightfully she should.

She sighed; shrugging, shaking her head. If she told him, what would stop him from telling his family? Could she stand to lose another family?

She could beat around the bush, say, *"Mothering doesn't*

come natural to me." She couldn't do it. Her head dangling on her neck, like a rag doll, slowly shaking. She couldn't lie to her husband.

"Lindy?" Dave searched her face.

She lifted her head. The man who held her heart, who she loved with all her life, sat in front of her, waiting for an answer that would forever change the way he looked at her. Her stomach churned, the words floating to her tongue.

Her lips wouldn't open.

She could get up, ignore his question, and tell him to never bring it up again.

Yet, her legs wouldn't move. Her bottom stuck to the chair, like superglue that fastened with every second it dried. The weight in her chest, anchoring her down.

She shouldn't have to explain this. It shouldn't be on her. Her life should be fresh. Her past erased. Instead, she brought *it* with her. Cared for it and raised it.

"What is it?" Dave asked.

Whiskers countered his jaw line. A few wrinkles outlined his faded blue eyes. His mid-length hair, still thick with a hint of gray, brushed to the side. This man loved her. He married her. He was honored to call her his wife. How could she break his heart, by admitting to her past, admitting she kept it from him? From *everyone.*

Tell him! A voice echoed behind her thoughts. *If you don't tell him now, it'll only get harder.*

Lindy's lips parted. She sucked in a load of seasoned air.

"It's okay." Dave scooted off his chair. He stepped over to her side. "We can talk about it another time." He kissed her cheek, rubbing her shoulder. "I'm going to bed. Join me in a bit?" Dave asked.

Lindy nodded.

He removed his hand from her shoulder and kissed her cheek again. He stepped away, creaking across the living room, toward their bedroom. A part of her wanted to reach out, pull him back and tell him everything.

She lowered her head.

Maybe this was for the best. Eventually she'd have to tell him. It wasn't fair to keep secrets from him. She should have told him years ago. What had she thought? That her past would roll up into the rug and be donated to the nearest thrift store in Topeka? She had brought it with her. It would be a part of her life until she died.

She would lift her head from the bacon every morning and see her come down the stairs. She would look out the window and see her drive farm equipment onto the yard. She would watch boys fall in love with her, turning their heads simply to look twice at her natural beauty. Like everyone used to looked at *her*.

Olivia stared at the abandoned tank-tops in her drawer. How comfortable they'd feel in the summer heat. Air flowing underneath her arms instead of sweat sticking sleeves onto her arm pits. She'd wear shorts every day, if work allowed it. She didn't want to scrape her legs every time she carried a gearbox along an irrigation sprinkler. The tank-tops in her drawer would distract her coworker, especially if she wore them for irrigation repairs. They would definitely distract her date.

She shook her head and reached for a graphic T-shirt instead. The AC blowing through the vent, lifted the summer dress she'd thrown on the floor. She'd worn a dress on the last couple dates. Plus, shorts and T-shirts were made for county fairs.

She stood in front of the full-length mirror, lifting her hair in a ponytail. She turned sideways, tilting her head side to side. Up or down? Down. She released the ponytail, letting her hair drape over her shoulders. She'd pair her outfit with the boots Dave gave her and call it good. She scanned her room for a hair tie just in case she'd want one.

Her stomach gurgled. Dinner smelled delicious. Mom and Dave's voices drifted up from the back patio, through the decades-old insulation.

The days for open windows had passed. Only after sunset did they let the night air cool the house. She preferred to start each day with fresh air blowing through the window screen, brushing the wool rug underneath her bed.

Olivia reached for the hair tie on her chest and slid it onto her wrist. She grabbed the dress off the floor, the AC blowing onto her knees. Underneath the hem of the dresses hanging in her closet, her duffle bag sat, packed, ready to go.

She could take it tonight, ask Josh, not come home. Move in with a man she'd known for two months.

Olivia hung up the dress and brushed her hair to one side.

She could forget about everything. Move on.

She closed her eyes.

She could move on, but she'd never be loved. He didn't know her. Didn't know her past. He would ask, "What happened to your dad?" "What happened between you and your mom?" If he thought he loved her now, he wouldn't love her after he found out the truth.

She squeezed her eyelids, clenched her jaw, and breathed in.

Tonight, she wouldn't think of her life.

Her eyes opened and the room seemed lighter than before. She would stroll from one entertainment to the other, holding Josh's hand, inhaling the smell of funnel cakes and popcorn, sipping her Coke. She didn't deserve it, but she'd take it.

Her sock-covered feet trotted down the steps until they landed on the wood flooring in the living room. The carpet upstairs looked stingy compared to the wood planks. If she'd designed this house, she would have put wood planks everywhere, with woven rugs underneath the beds, instead of carpet.

"I'm not gonna be home for dinner. Josh is picking me up soon," she said, walking into the kitchen.

Mom nodded. "I'll keep your portion in the fridge."

Mom diced potatoes. Her thin skin revealed the veins on

her hands. Wrinkled, aged fingers clawed the potato in place; the knife chopping closer and closer to her nails. "We're going to the fair. They're serving brisket."

Mom looked over her shoulder. She nodded so lightly Olivia nearly missed it.

Olivia glanced at the clock, hanging between the living room entrance and the pantry door.

"You can help me while you wait." Mom scraped the diced potatoes off the cutting board into a bowl.

"Josh will be here soon."

Olivia walked into the mudroom and retrieved her boots from the closet. The woman didn't want her. Why would she waste her energy?

CHAPTER SIXTEEN

If it wasn't for the rapid pounding in her chest, Olivia would have thought her heart quit beating. The tickle in her stomach assured her she was very much alive. How could a simple graze against Josh's shoulder steal her breath away?

Josh hovered the popcorn bucket in front of her, strolling through the fair. She carefully picked out a few kernels. In the light of the food stands, game booths and spinning carnival rides, Josh looked more handsome than she remembered. The army-green tee clinging to his masculine shoulders, gradually loosening from his chest down, didn't help her admiration. To think that those arms might wrap around her later.

They sub-consciously made their way to the game booths, standing at a distance, eyeing the options. Olivia sipped Coke up a straw out of a disposable paper cup and reached for more popcorn. Children of all ages pumped water down PVC pipes, threw baseballs at bottles, or shot ducks on a treadmill. Whatever the booths had to offer, they played.

"Which one?" Josh looked at her.

Her lips formed a smile, she lingered, pleasantly study-ing the features of his face—again. She tore her focus away and scanned the booths.

She needed to control herself.

Shooting ducks looked tempting. She hadn't aimed a toy gun or a real gun at anything since her dad's passing. She kept her knowledge, but that didn't mean she kept her ability to shoot.

"The duck ranges?" Josh asked. "I see you staring at it?"

Olivia nodded, smiling. The line was empty. She grabbed Josh's hand and hurriedly lead him to the booth. She set her drink down at the make-shift wooden table and gathered her hair, draping it over her left shoulder.

"Who goes first?" she asked.

He smiled humorously. An *I-love-that-I'm-here-with-you* smile. For a second, Olivia forgot where she was.

He stepped back. "You can go first."

Olivia turned her attention to the boy standing behind the table. Was that how it felt to be cherished?

Olivia handed the boy the tickets and picked up the pel-let gun. A scene flashed through her memory.

The shooting ranges. Ten miles out of Topeka. On a grassy meadow, with trees all around. She could still feel the warm air against her cheeks. "That's it," her dad had said, as she positioned her first gun. A .22 rifle, small, yet mighty.

Olivia closed her eyes. *Keep it in. Not now.*

"Olivia." Josh's gentle voice opened her eyes. In front of her, chain-ducks ran along the board.

Olivia cranked the gun and pressed the trigger. Each time the pellet banged against a wooden bird. *Crank, shoot, crank shoot, crank shoot*, again and again until her time ended.

"Wow! Way to go, Olivia." Josh stepped up behind her, placing his hand on her back. He counted the fallen ducks. "I'd say that's unbeatable."

Olivia smiled, mumbling her thanks.

The boy handed her the traditional stuffed animal; after Josh gave him the tickets, he handed Josh a pellet gun. She shouldn't brag about her aim, but Josh did hit one less than she did. Maybe he'd done it on purpose. Either way, she wasn't going to mention it.

Josh turned around and stepped toward her. He looked up, his smile fading. Olivia turned her head, searching the crowds. Among the hundreds of town folk swarming the flat green buffalo grass, she couldn't spot anyone she knew Josh disliked. Josh spat out words, nasty enough to make her want to wash out her ears.

She followed his gaze.

Veronica and the boy from the party stepped away from the dinner-selling shed. They held two red and white paper bowls, and one overly large soda. Surely those words weren't aimed toward his sister.

Olivia looked up at Josh. He hadn't liked his sister's date the day they first saw Veronica with him. Did Josh know something she didn't?

"She shouldn't be with him," Josh demanded. His jaw

clenched shut. His shoulders stood a bit higher; his head fastened securely to his neck. His body in perfect control, flexed and steady.

Olivia sensed the presence of someone in front of her and lowered her eyes. Veronica and her date said their "Hellos," then took turns sipping their soda. Olivia smiled politely, waiting for someone to make small talk. Veronica's date spoke; all eyes went to him.

"I thought you'd be busy tonight," he paused, "since you often are."

"Not tonight." The two guys stared at each other, their eyes at equal height.

"Have you two talked after the party?" Veronica asked.

They nodded.

Veronica's date lowered his head, stepping closer to Josh's sister. He put his arm around her and pulled her close. The couple smiling at each other made Olivia want to look down, or pretend to examine something in the distance. The boy looked up, and scanned their faces.

"We work together," he said.

The veins in Josh's arms popped out. Maybe he only looked mad. If she wrapped her elbow around his arm and nestled next to him, would he remember where he was? She wanted to try. She didn't know how. How could she embrace a high-line pole? Olivia kept her arms to herself.

Veronica looked from one man to the other. "Really? I

didn't know you worked at the irrigation shop." Veronica focused on her date.

Her date stroked her back, snuggling her closer yet. Fifteen-year-old Veronica loved every bit of it. Too much, from what Olivia could tell. How long had they dated?

"I don't."

Olivia looked at the guys. Veronica's date glared at Josh. His relaxed body wrapped in her embrace, while his eyes threatened. Veronica couldn't see it, but Olivia did. Why did Veronica like him? He wasn't attractive. Easy on the eyes, but not attractive. Compared to Josh, the boy looked fresh out of puberty. She guessed him to be her age, seventeen, eighteen at the most.

"Olivia and I are leaving. You're coming with us, Veronica." Josh stepped forward, nudging a hand between the couple. He placed it on Veronica's shoulder, and urged her away from her date.

"I'm here with Steve." Veronica and her date simultaneously stepped back.

"You shouldn't be with him." Josh's gaze hovered over his sister. Sadness, almost pain clouded his cheek. Why did this mean so much to him?

"Please, Veronica? Trust me." He dipped his head slightly. Sincere, truthfully wanting the best for his sister. Olivia would go with him. If that would satisfy him. But it wasn't her he wanted.

"No." Veronica shook her head.

Their age number might only put them two years apart, but Olivia felt decades older.

"Sis," Josh turned from a caring brother to a concerned father, "you don't know what you're getting yourself into."

Josh's expression caught Olivia's focus. He knew something she didn't.

"What am I getting myself into? A relationship?"

Josh stared at his sister, obviously displeased.

Steve stepped away from Veronica, releasing his embrace. His affection grew cold. Like blocks of dry ice, fogging away. Veronica studied her date, too confused to notice.

"Let's go." Josh placed a hand on his sister's shoulder, urging her to turn around. But she stepped away, staring at Steve.

"I don't understand." She shook her head.

Neither did Olivia.

Josh looked angrier than before. His fingers pressed against Veronica's shoulder. He shoved her forward. Veronica trotted a few steps to keep her balance. "Josh!" she yelled.

Olivia looked around. She ducked her head and followed her boyfriend, glancing back. Steve stood in his spot, his dinner bowl in one hand; a large soda in the other hand. He looked at her and Olivia yanked her head forward. She halted, nearly running into a man.

"Nate."

The name came out more surprised than she wanted to appear.

Olivia scanned past him. Josh and his sister dodged the

crowds, heading for the exit. By now they looked more like friends walking together, not an officer arresting a fugitive.

"Who are you looking for?" Nate asked.

Olivia jerked her head in Nate's direction. Beside him stood a tall, auburn-haired girl. His date? She stood a few inches shorter than Nate. Olivia glanced at her feet; no heels.

"Josh." Olivia looked at Nate.

"Is everything all right?"

"I … don't know."

For a moment they studied each other. Guilt fogged her conscience. How would this exchange look from his date's point of view?

"I've got to go." Olivia looked at both. "See you guys."

She stepped around them and strode off in the direction she last saw her boyfriend. After several feet, she looked back. The two stood close to each other, friendly, sharing a conversation, waiting in the Ferris wheel line. Olivia looked ahead, striding forward, dodging people, strollers and dogs.

Everyone knew why a couple rode the Ferris wheel. Her insides churned. She shouldn't care who Nate dated. Or who he kissed. She wanted to bite her lips. To keep nausea at bay—maybe a bit of jealousy? She shook her head. Her date was waiting in his pickup.

Had she been pretty? Olivia couldn't remember. She'd worn a homemade dress. The kind she'd seen Mennonites wear around town. Nate's parents would like that.

They would never approve of her.

Suddenly, her legs felt bare, like revealed items for everyone to stare at. She hurried through the exit and trotted over the asphalt, onto the grassy parking lot.

Olivia didn't want to be here, but she felt she had to. Not only because Josh was her ride home, but in case he needed her.

Veronica resembled a child who'd recently been sent to her room. She swung open the front door to their parents' house, grabbed a water bottle from the fridge and sat down by the large island. The island separated the kitchen and the dining room.

Marble countertops rested on the cabinets. A modern, sleek feel flowed throughout the house. Accent walls and beautiful but maybe unnecessary features scattered throughout the open floor plan. Olivia bit her jaw, knowing if she released, she'd gawk in awe of the half-million-dollar house.

Olivia hoped Josh's parents weren't home. She wasn't dressed to meet his parents. Olivia scratched her leg with her sock-covered foot. What should she wear when she met his parents? They lived in farm country. Their son worked at a repair shop. They wouldn't expect anything fancy, would they?

Veronica slumped over the island, barely sitting on the stool. "I don't understand, Josh." She looked up, irritated. "If you dislike him so much, why didn't you tell me when you first met him?"

"Trust me," he said, leaning against the fridge.

Veronica shook her head, stood up and marched out onto the back patio.

Josh leaned forward, sighing.

Before he took a step, Olivia waved him down. She followed Veronica's trail; her eyes fixed on the glass patio doors. The small young woman sat in one of the chairs around the outdoor table. Her head lowered over her knees, sliding her fingers along the edges of her phone.

Olivia stepped onto the wooden planks and slid the door shut. The stars and moon lit the table, keeping the mosquitos at bay. Kids played in their back yards; cattle mooed in the distance. After two months, the mixture of sounds still sounded strange.

Veronica sniffled.

Olivia, folded her hands in her lap; twiddled her thumbs. How would she succeed in comforting a confused teenage girl when she herself longed for comfort? When she understood about as much as Veronica did?

"My parents are never around," Veronica paused, "that's why Josh makes it his responsibility to humiliate me." She spun her phone between her fingers.

"I don't think he was trying to."

Veronica shook her head. "He doesn't know what he's doing half the time."

Olivia studied Veronica. "Is he not a good brother?"

Veronica straightened her back, looking directly at Olivia.

"He's the best. If he would have had an older sibling to help him, he probably wouldn't have dropped out of college."

Olivia's eyes scanned over Veronica's shoulder, to the inside of the lit home. Josh sat in the living room, head down. She never wondered why a twenty-year-old man still lived in his home town. She figured he had never enrolled. Nate never had. Her eyes rolled toward Veronica. What else did she not know?

Veronica sighed. "I don't know what's worse, my brother embarrassing me, or Steve stepping away." She looked to the left, scanning the neighborhood, until her gaze landed on her lap. "I guess he didn't like me the way I thought he did."

A shadow of emotions clouded Veronica's expression. Pain? Regret? Olivia wanted to ask more questions about Josh. But the girl had bigger concerns. Olivia looked at her sock-covered feet, brushing her toes against the patio. What could she say to her?

"I should've known better." Olivia lifted her head as Veronica leaned hers back.

She turned her focus on the table. "Some boys only stick around when it's fun." She looked at Olivia. "Is this what high school dating is?"

Olivia didn't know.

She looked past Veronica and stared at Josh. If she knew anything about guys, she wouldn't question her boyfriend's motives. She hadn't, until now.

At ten o'clock Josh pulled onto the farm yard. Earlier than Olivia had hoped. He parked beside the round-top, with the windshield facing the blacktop. Visible from the house, yet not close enough to feel spied on. The radio played the latest country song as the engine wound down. Josh nestled against the seat next to her. The digital clock displayed one hour of freedom. Free to sit in the middle of Josh's pickup and spend every second of the next sixty minutes with him.

She waited for Josh to wrap his arm around her and pull her close. He stared at the gauges; arms draped over his legs. Olivia opened her mouth. He looked at her expectedly. She pressed her lips together and shrugged. Why wasn't he making the first move?

"I'm sorry about tonight." He picked at the steering wheel with his finger nails. "I wish it would have turned out differently."

Olivia looked at the floorboards. So did she. She breathed in, turning her body toward him, propping her elbow on the seat.

"If you knew him, you wouldn't question me."

"I wasn't questioning you."

Josh jerked his head toward her. "I saw it in your eyes."

"And I saw intense anger in yours." Olivia stretched out her chest, straightening her neck. "Curse words I never wanted to hear."

"I'm sorry." The words spat out, much like the words he'd directed at Steve.

Olivia's throat tightened. She should open the door and leave. Disbelief kept her seated. She wanted to stay. Wanted him to take back his words.

She looked into his eyes, holding his gaze; all her senses drained. She swallowed, lowering her head, unable to take it. This. It wasn't like her. She needed to leave. He'd given her every reason to walk out, to forget they'd ever dated.

"I'm sorry." Softly, the words evaporated into the cab. He took her hand, "I'm sorry," stroking his thumb over her knuckles.

She wanted him to stop. But it was *his* touch. Josh's, the person who invited her into his pickup—into his life. She blinked, tightening her jaw, breathing in. It was Josh who sat beside her.

Olivia gripped his hand, holding his thumb in place. She slid her fingers over his palm, intwining her fingers between his. "I'm sorry too."

"You have nothing to be sorry about."

She lifted her chin, her eyes searching his.

"It's not your fault," he shook his head, leaning closer, wrapping his arm around her waist. "It's not your fault." He shook his head, leaning in, until his lips landed on hers.

Olivia closed her eyes. Every burden-filled thought, every rejected moment, fled her mind. She leaned into his warm, comforting embrace.

CHAPTER SEVENTEEN

W ho is she?" Sam asked, balancing a bag of grain on her shoulder, watching Olivia empty a bag into a barrel. "Do I know her? Oh," Sam's lips formed an *O* shape, her eyes following Olivia's every move. "I bet it's Anna. I've known her for years and she's always had eyes for Nate." Sam nodded. "I bet that's who it is."

Olivia lifted her arms out of the barrel and stretched them toward Sam. Sam glared at the half-filled barrel of chicken feed. Olivia lifted the paper bag off Sam's shoulders. She ripped the top open, steadying it between her stomach and the barrel, holding it up with her leg.

"Are you sure you saw him with someone?" Sam asked.

Olivia pointed the open end into the barrel. Kernels slid against the rough paper, forming a brown-grayish mountain. She crumbled the bag, dust releasing into the air.

"Yes."

Sam lowered her eyelids, nodding.

"I'm sorry."

Nate could have decided he didn't like her. It could have

been a one-night thing. But it was better not to build Sam's hopes. Sam would never have a chance with Nate. He never gave her a second look. He never sought her out for a simple conversation. He acknowledged her presence and kindly answered her questions, replying to her when expected. He didn't talk to Sam the way he did to her.

"My mom won't be. She nagged me about giving up for almost a year now. I don't know if she didn't like him or if she simply worried that I'd fall in love and get married." Sam shrugged. "I suppose it's for the best. It'll take a while before I get over Nate and this way, I'll for sure be around to help Mom when the baby's born. Of course, Dad will help the most."

Olivia stepped around Sam.

"What if I'm not busy enough?" Sam followed Olivia. "Then all I'll do is think about Nate. How will I ever get over him if I'm always thinking about him?" They stepped over the concrete door frame, onto the grass, where the open pickup bed stood loaded with feed sacks.

Sam focused on the dropped tailgate, waiting for Olivia to dump a sack on her outstretched arms.

"I thought for sure he liked you. Nate has never looked at a girl the way he looks at you." Sam shrugged. "After watching you run after Josh last night, I bet he's glad he found someone else. No point in loving someone who doesn't love you back."

Sam made a face. "Listen to me. I should take my own advice." She shook her head, then nodded. "I'll get over Nate, now that I know I don't stand a chance."

Olivia's body temperature heated. She glanced at Sam, then at Nate. He stood beside the bed, elbow propped up on the edge, facing the mint green grass. How much had he heard? The corner of his lips lifted, his smile wrinkling his cheeks. He'd heard everything.

Olivia wanted to crunch down and hide. She felt like the monkey in the middle, on display for everyone to see.

He forced his smile away, clearing his throat. "Let me help."

Sam looked up, baffled.

Nate stepped between them, smiling at Olivia. He slid a bag toward him and smiled at Sam. Couldn't Sam have kept her mouth shut, for once?

He lifted a bag onto his shoulder and walked toward the barrels.

Sam nibbled her lower lip. She buried her face in her palms; shaking her head. She looked up and breathed in, her face red like a tomato. "I have to go." She shook her head. "To get water, or something." She turned and walked toward the house.

Nate's footsteps stopped behind Olivia. She felt his tall tower overlooking her head.

"Is she okay?" Nate asked.

"She will be."

Olivia turned her attention toward the pickup bed and tugged a bag of feed onto the tailgate. Nate followed her to the feed barrels. He set a bag on the ground, leaning it against the barrel, and studied Olivia.

"She's not wrong."

Olivia tore the bag open. "About what?"

"I did like you."

The grain poured out the paper bag, burying the ends in the feed. *Did.* The word pierced through. Olivia shook the bag, removing every kernel.

"But Sam's right. 'No point in loving someone who doesn't love you back.'"

Olivia froze. She gripped the barrel rim, dropping the empty bag. He could have loved her. Could he have known, and still loved her? She turned her head, facing Nate.

"Anna," she swallowed the word, "she loves you back?"

Nate shrugged. "She doesn't have a boyfriend."

Her gaze lowered to the packed dirt floor. She almost broke up with Josh. Almost. Thought about it; couldn't do it. Instead, she'd kissed him. Like never before. She could have chosen Nate. Could've walked out on Josh.

She lifted her chin. "Good for you. You're moving on."

A shock passed through his eyes. He studied her, searching her expression. He had shaved his beard, trimmed his hair. She liked his beard; his long hair.

"Unless you don't want me to."

Olivia stared at him. He would choose her. If she told him to leave Anna, he would. She lowered her eyes, gazing over his shoulder into the stall.

"Olivia," Nate stepped closer, placing his hand on her shoulder, "you don't have to be with him."

She rolled her eyes toward his, squaring her shoulders. "I want to." She stepped sideways, forcing his hand to drop from her shoulder.

He puffed out his chest, straightening his spine. "Then be careful."

Why? *What did he know that she didn't?*

"Promise me?"

She'd made enough promises in her life. She shouldn't promise him anything.

"Promise me, before it's too late, you'll leave him?"

"I can't promise that." Olivia backed up, raising to her full height. "I'm sorry Nate."

Red, white and blue decked every front porch railing on Maine Street. The flag flapped in front of the courthouse higher than the three-story red-brick building, proudly waving in the Kansas wind.

The dark-green, waist-high corn demanded everyone's attention. It claimed every available section, squeezing in between the remaining golden wheat fields, standing next to every concrete edge in town. A person couldn't walk into the grocery store without hearing the corn grow.

The bell above the door jingled, interrupting the whooping and gurgling of the semi-trucks driving by. After nearly three months of living in solitude, even the bustle of wheat harvest in a seven thousand population town was too loud.

Lindy placed her wallet in her basket and walked down the narrow aisles. Her flip-flops clapped against the once-white vinyl; the chill of the open fridge reminding her of her bare legs. She walked down the dry goods aisle, stopping at the baking section. Lindy scanned down her list, overhearing raspy voices whispering her name. She laid cocoa and baking powder in her basket, then tip-toed closer to the end of the row, hoping to hear the gossip on the other side.

She glanced behind her, making sure no one was around, then leaned forward, holding the basket against her legs. A foot away from the rack of nearly expired bread.

"I heard her first husband passed away three years ago."

An elderly lady's voice. Lindy tilted her ear toward the conversation.

"No, it'll be three years in September is what she said."

Mrs. Bell! The name felt like an anchor, dropping to the bottom of her lungs.

"And already remarried. My, she didn't waste any time."

Lindy's jaw dropped open.

"The women in that family..." Lindy could picture Mrs. Bell shaking her head. A familiar picture. "You know Olivia started dating Josh only a month after they moved here."

The other woman tsked. "Those girls move in quick, don't they?"

Both ladies giggled.

Lindy's breath caught in her throat, unable to escape through her open mouth. She closed her eyes.

They didn't know about the days she went into the office to say, "dinner's ready" and then saw the empty chair sitting motionless in front of the computer. To relive the gut stabbing realization that her husband was gone. Never to sit in that chair again. They didn't know how it felt to walk back into the kitchen—the cold, light footsteps.

Mrs. Bell's laughter faded into a sigh. She said, "If I were Lindy, I would steer my daughter away from Josh. Force her to stay home, if I had too. The things I've heard of him." She tsked.

"Ooohh," the other woman chimed in, "I know. Do you think Lindy knows?"

Lindy's eyes flashed open. *Know what?*

She leaned forward; skidding her toes to keep her balance, the flipflops stopped against the sticky vinyl. Her upper body gained momentum, wobbling over her own basket. Her face above the bread rack.

"Woah…" Lindy hopped forward, hitting her basket against the bread basket. The rack tilted, tipping the basket out. The basket rolled by Lindy's feet, to the middle of the dry goods aisle.

She surveyed the scene.

"Lindy."

Her head jerked up. Mrs. Bell and the other elderly lady walked toward her.

"We were just talking about you," Mrs. Bell said, stretching her hands out, grasping Lindy's right hand, shaking it while she smiled.

Lindy let the woman shake her wobbly arm. She scanned over both lady's faces. "Yes, I heard," she said to Mrs. Bell.

The two ladies widened their eyes and made a face at each other. Guiltless, mocking their accuser. Their wrinkly smiles saying, "We didn't mean any harm," while their eyes sparkled with mischief.

Lindy pressed the automatic closing button on the trunk and carried the remaining groceries toward the house. Cash's nose bumped against the bags. He received a harsh "No!" from his mistress. The dog lowered his tale and backed off. He stood on the lush buffalo grass, his eyes begging for an explanation. Lindy tore her eyes away. She marched into the house and let the screen door slam shut behind her.

She pushed the groceries onto the counter. The AC turned on; Lindy strode to latch the front door. She turned around, her eyes catching a glimpse of Olivia through the dining room window. She lingered, long enough to see her walking from the round-top to the barn, Nate following. He ran up in front of her, stopping Olivia in her tracks. Olivia looked up at him. He curled his fingers around her wrists and stepped toward her. Olivia did not protest.

"*No!*" Lindy nearly yelled out loud. "*No,*" she repeated in her head. "*She wouldn't. She couldn't. Not Olivia. Back away,*" she begged silently.

Lindy tore her eyes away. She leaped toward the counter

and began unpacking produce from the paper bags. She couldn't let this happen. She shook her head, walking from the fridge to the counter, to the pantry, to the cabinets and back to the counter.

She crumpled the paper bags, wringing them in her hands. Fear freezing her body.

"I ran into her at Patrick's. Nothing was supposed to happen," Erick said. "It doesn't change anything," Erick pleaded, reaching for her.

She yanked away. "It changes everything," the words spat out.

"I didn't feel anything." His eyes filled with tears.

She had held in a sand-papered laugh. "You don't sleep with your high school sweetheart and feel nothing!" she had yelled..

The mudroom door swung open. The memory vanished. Lindy stared at the oak dining table.

"Lindy," Dave stood underneath the dining room entry frame, "are you okay?"

CHAPTER EIGHTEEN

The whole place stank. The dog beds smelled of urine. The cushions and linens smelled of sour milk, resembling spoiled pancake dough, with dots of cotton mold on the edges. The carpets smelled of unflushed toilets, left for weeks on end. The kitchen smelled of rotten cantaloupes and sweaty underwear.

On the table lay dozens of half-eaten burritos, sandwiches and cut-open soda cans. Mouse droppings dotted the torn seventies-style chairs. Pointy noses and tiny black eyes squeaked out of the door-less cabinet. Cornflakes dribbled off the cabinet shelves, the bags getting vandalized by gray, fury rodents.

True or not, Josh felt lice crawl up his legs, nestling in his leg hair. Powdery dust drifted up his nostrils; landing in his hair.

The door behind him shut, locking out any natural light. For the first time, and without a doubt the last time, he appreciated Steve standing beside him.

Used, cut up straws were organized in bowls and displayed on the coffee table. Lighters were scattered over every horizontal surface. Obviously, Keith's dealers enjoyed their product.

Steve leaned sideways, closer to Josh's ears. "Why are we doing this?"

Josh eyed the dog sitting against the lumpy coach. The dog's slick fur revealed his broad rib cage. His curled lips showed his yellow teeth. "You're doing it 'cause of the money, I'm doing it 'cause you dragged me here."

"You dragged yourself into this," Steve whispered.

Not a lie, he thought.

The wide boned lady with skin like sandpaper and hair like a horse's tail stepped out of the back room. She carried boxes stacked up to her whiskery chin; ignoring the lizard racing across the hard kitchen floor and up the refrigerator. She set the boxes on the dog-hair-covered Lazyboy. She sniffed, balling her tongue against her cheeks, sliding it down her lower lip.

"Stuffed newspaper in 'em so they wouldn't make a sound." She showed her teeth. "Get pulled over, tell the cops you're moving." She swished saliva from cheek to cheek. "They'll believe you."

Would they believe the truth? If he opened the boxes; showed them the drugs, would that get him out of this mess? He was tempted to try.

Josh popped open a beer bottle and flicked the cap into the trash can. He brought the small round end to his lips, cherishing every sip. He lowered his hand, letting the alcohol linger underneath his tongue for a while, then swallowed. He repeated the process several times, until it brought the little bit of comfort it had to offer.

He planned to sit on the couch, kick his feet up and enjoy every sip to the fullest. After today, he might need several bottles. Josh turned around and grabbed two more out of the fridge. He grabbed the bottle opener off the counter. The cold bottles, firmly grasped between his fingers, clinked against each other. Wherever Wyatt was, he could stay there all night.

His sock covered feet indented the soft carpet as he walked into the living room. His calves touched the edge of the couch; he breathed deeply and sank into not-nearly-fluffy-enough cushions. Better than the ones in the trashed trailer house the lady lived in. Josh shuddered with his head resting on the back of the couch. He straightened his neck and brought the bottle rim to his lips. He dropped his head back. How could anyone live in such an inhumane place?

Josh turned his head to the side, staring at the TV stand where the broken VCR player hid his stash. He could light a roll-up and inhale the toxic herb. The desire to do so was what got him in this mess in the first place. He rolled his eyes up to the ceiling.

If the man behind the counter hadn't sold him the twenty-four pack, he'd probably do it. The woman never sold him anything, no matter how he tried to charm her. Josh sat up and took another gulp, then rested the bottle on his knee. When would this part of his life end?

The ceiling fan went round, round, swaying, shaking the light string. A black spider crawled on the popcorn ceiling. When had he gone from a rich boy with a promising future and a long time to get there, to a middle-class man earning minimum wage, hauling illegal drugs with his teenage sister's boyfriend—ex-boyfriend?

Someone knocked on the front door.

Josh turned his head, looking out the dark window. The yellow porch light lit the front yard, showing a new model SUV parked beside the curb. *Oh.* Josh relaxed his squinted eyes, swinging his head straight, looking up. His sister.

He lifted his chin. "Come in," he yelled.

The door hinges squeaked open; light feet stepped over the threshold; the door latched shut.

"You know you're not supposed to drive. I think I told you that last time already."

Sniffling. Why was she sniffling?

Josh propped his elbow on top of the couch and looked behind him. Veronica stood barefoot on the patch of vinyl flooring in front of the door. Her cropped jeans revealed the scratches on her ankles. Her arms dangled beside her hips. Her damp hair hung over her chest, covering half her face.

"What happened?"

Veronica bit her lip.

"I'll get you a towel." Josh stood up, setting his beer on

the TV stand. He retrieved a blanket from the colorful pile in the hallway closet.

When he came back, Veronica stood in the same spot. He handed her the blanket and led her to the couch. Where had she been? Why hadn't she gone home to Mom and Dad? It was Saturday … their parents were probably at a party somewhere. Steve … she wouldn't be with him after he told her not to.

"I'll get you something to drink." Josh walked into the kitchen. He spoke over the bar table, "Hot cocoa? Wait," he looked at the cabinets, "we don't have any. How 'bout coffee?" He glanced at his sister.

"No, I'm fine," she muffled.

Josh studied her. Sympathy and confusion overtook him. She'd obviously gotten into some trouble. He wished he could lie and tell her the scar on her arm was a mark of a warrior, like he had when she'd fallen off her bike.

How could he fix this?

He looked at the floor, walking to the couch, sitting down beside her. He propped his elbows on his knees, rubbed his hands together, and looked ahead at the coffee table, "What happened?" he asked.

Veronica sniffed. Josh rolled his eyes toward her. She searched the room. "Where's Olivia?" she asked.

"Raking alfalfa."

Veronica nodded and lowered her gaze.

"Are you going to tell me what happened?"

"Steve left some of his stuff at Jackie's house the night of the party, told her I'd give it back to him. Still hadn't, so I figured why not stop by and give it to him. I forgot that his parents would be at the booster club meeting."

Veronica drew on the tan colored carpet with her toes, tucking her hair behind her ear. A red-blueish bruise dotted her jaw line.

Josh straightened his back to get a better look. "He didn't hit you, did he?" Josh pushed his palm against his knee, biting his jaw.

She shook her head. "He invited me—a few of his friends were there. Or that's who I thought they were. Turned out they were his co-workers."

Keith.

"Was one medium build with dark hair, seemed like a harmless goofball at times? The other looked like a body builder?" asked Josh.

Veronica nodded.

No. Josh looked away, scratching his neck. How long would it take until they involved his sister? She was fifteen, how could she possibly be of any use to them? He huffed, dangling his head from his neck. His forearm propped on his leg, keeping him balanced. He shut his eyes. Gruesome stories filled the news stations. What was to stop such a story from happening here?

Josh opened his eyes and pushed himself off the couch. Anything. Anything could happen.

He lifted his hand in Veronica's direction. "How'd you get that bruise?"

He searched her expression. For anything, any sign. But all he saw was innocent confusion. Sadness. Regret. Embarrassment, maybe.

"They scared me. I wasn't used to their jokes and…" she shook her head, "You don't have to be over eighteen to know what they were doing."

The ceiling fan and the refrigerator, hummed. Vehicles drove pass the house, glaring light through the window. Josh, stared at his sister, waiting for her to speak.

"When I wanted to leave, Steve tried convincing me to stay. He scared me, gripping my arm so I'd come closer to him." She wrung her hands, looking up at Josh. "I ran out of the house, tripped down the stairs just as the sprinklers went on." She pointed at her right jaw line. "That's how this happened. I didn't want to go home, all by myself, so I came here."

Josh shook his head, lifting his eyes to the corner of the yellow stained walls. He breathed deeply. Veronica didn't have to know anything. As far as she knew, Steve was just a boy she met at the party whom her brother didn't like. And that Steve and his much older friends did drugs.

Josh placed his hands on his hips. This could play in his favor. Now his sister would stay away from him.

Josh dropped his head. What if they didn't stay away from her?

"I'm so stupid." Veronica spoke the word like tasting expired cream cheese.

He looked at her.

"You're not stupid."

He sat down at the end of the couch. "But I told you to stay away from him; you didn't."

Veronica looked into the kitchen. "I will now," she said, twiddling her thumbs in her lap. "Any one with such a disgusting habit isn't worth knowing." She looked at the coffee table. "Why do people do it?"

Josh looked away from his sister. "I don't know," he said, staring into space.

Olivia lifted her head off Josh's shoulder, sliding her hand over his rib cage, looking up at him. "Why didn't you take me here sooner?" The ridges on the tailgate nudged her hip, cramping her vein.

"I tried." Josh looked at her. His fingers curled around her waist, his arm stretched down her back, holding her close. "You changed the plans."

She remembered. Weeks ago, she'd planned to meet him at the valley. Why had she changed her mind?

She glanced at the edge of the tailgate. Nate. She had allowed him to play with her mind. To tug on her heart.

Not anymore.

She lifted her eyes, smiling. "I like it here. With you."

She looked into his eyes. Every sound evaporated from her mind. The way he looked at her. His eyes, filled with affection. Nate made her feel things, but not like this.

"Are you sure? Nowhere else you'd rather be?"

He teased, but she saw it. Concern, spreading over his eyes. What had he heard?

"There's no place I'd rather be."

He dipped his chin. Or did she imagine it? Her stomach tingled, stronger than flutters. Stronger than anything she'd ever felt. She should lower her eyes. Look away before she said or did something she'd regret. Did he feel it too?

"Olivia." *Yes, yes tell me. Tell me what you're thinking.*

He removed her hand from his ribs, intwining his fingers between hers. He gripped her palm, squeezing her knuckles so hard it hurt. "I'm glad I got kicked out of college."

She broke eye contact. What? "Your sister said you dropped out."

Josh froze. His grip loosened around her hand. He sniffed, lifting his arm up, setting it between them. He looked at the pond in front of them, hands folded on his lap.

"I told everyone that." He glanced down. "I was too embarrassed to tell them the truth."

Olivia shifted her hips, relieving the cramping vein. She straightened her posture.

Flies hopped around on the pond. Clouds reflected against the still water, mirroring the colors of the sky. She rested both hands on her lap.

"I'm glad you told me." She said, her feet dangling, her flipflops hanging from her toes.

"There's a lot you don't know about me."

She faced him. He didn't know the half of her.

"I want to tell you. One day." He leveled his chin, and brushed her hair behind her ear. "One day, years from now."

His hand rested on her shoulder, he curled his fingers against her neck, sending shivers down her body.

"Do you think we'll have a one day?" she asked.

Josh slid his hand across her back, up her shoulder. He lifted his arm; wrapped her hand in both of his. "I hope. Because, I love you, Olivia." He squeezed her hand. "I don't want a life without you."

Her breath caught in her throat. She closed her eyes. He didn't love her. Not all of her. He thought he did. How could he? No one could ever love all of her.

Josh touched her chin. The world stopped spinning.

"Hey," he wiped a tear off her cheek, "what's wrong? Usually, girls don't cry when someone tells them they love them."

Olivia opened her eyes. Tears fogging her vision. She grabbed his hand, moving it away from her chin. "I love you, Josh."

He smiled, nodding slowly, his smile growing.

"I do." A warm breeze flowed over them, landing in the trees. "I really do love you. Not anyone else. Only you," she whispered.

Josh's smiled lifted into his eyes. He kissed her. His lips

inches away from hers, he whispered, "You don't know how happy that makes me."

She smiled, lowering her head onto his shoulder. He wrapped his arms around her and held her close. A bird sang in the trees, the evening light shining onto the leaves. She closed her eyes, stroking Josh's back.

It hurt to admit she loved someone who might never love her. Openly allowing herself the possibility of another rejection. To spend years hoping for another person's love, knowing they could end up resenting her, like her mom did. Could she spend years fearfully waiting for that "one day?"

CHAPTER NINETEEN

She should look away. What if he noticed her watching him? She'd seen him often, felt the muscles on his back, felt his firm biceps; she'd ran her fingers through his thick, dark hair, yet she couldn't look away. Rather, she didn't want to.

His shoulders flexed as he paddled the kayak in front of her. His hair brushed his sunburned neck. He turned his chin over his shoulder, and smiled at her. His smile. The same slick smile he smiled the first time they met, yet different. Bigger? Better?

"There's a clearing up ahead that I want to show you." He looked ahead, paddling.

Left, right, left right, flex, flex.

Her kayak halted. She jerked forward, and bounced against her seat. Her paddle scraped against her kayak, whacking the branches around her. The tip of the kayak nested underneath a fallen branch.

"Josh?" She lifted her chin. Where had he gone? She pushed her palms against the edge of the kayak, trying to look over the branches.

Dirty, open water stretched along the tree line. Underneath the branches flies hopped on the water. Turtles crawled off the bank, out of the grass, into the lake.

Olivia leaned back, trying to glance around the corner of the tree line. In the distance blue shimmered on the water. She looked down. Maybe she could get out on her own.

She scanned the branches. A snake dangled on the branch above her kayak. Its eyes, glaring at her. Its smooth skin, slipping downward. If she pushed against the branches it could slip into her kayak.

Just grab it, she told herself. *It's a water snake.* Its slim body, covered in dark brown stripes, lifted itself, crawling to the edge of the branch. Its jaw open, it wiggled its needle tongue, mocking her. Its head slithered off the branch, pointing at her.

She stepped onto her seat. Her paddle slid backward, hitting her ankles. She grabbed the paddle, poking one end into the water, trying to reach the bottom. The paddle tapped against a hard surface. She angled it, pushing the kayak backward. The paddle slipped, knocking the branches. The kayak teeter-tottered, branches scraping against the kayaks.

She stretched out her arms, reaching for a branch.

She wrapped her palm around a warm stick. It curled up around her hand. Olivia looked to her right. She opened her mouth, breathing deeply. Slowly loosening her grip, releasing the snake covered branch. She shook her hand, forcing the snake off.

"Olivia?" Josh yelled.

The snake fell onto the edge of her kayak. She released the other branch, bent down, and reached for the paddle.

"Olivia!" His voice sounded closer. Olivia yanked her head around, checking for Josh. Her vision blurred, flashing down, as her knees gave out. The kayak dumped her through the branches, into the water. Algae wrapped around her arms; brush tickled her legs. Her head sank, until the bottom slime swallowed her feet. She kicked, flapping her arms, pushing herself up.

Her chin popped out of the lake, between the branches. The sunshine glared in the blue sky; vibrant tree leaves hung above her. A turtle wobbled off a log, into the water. Something tickled her legs. She spat, thinking of everything swimming around her.

"Olivia." She turned around, kicking her ankles, keeping afloat. Josh hovered behind her. Wet hair stroked back, bare shoulders poking out of the water. "I turned around, looking for you. When I saw you fall, I jumped in after you."

He swam closer, lifting his arm out of the water. He brushed her chin, and scanned her forehead. "You're hurt."

She shrugged. "They're only scratches."

Josh shook his head. "Let's get you out of here. This place is full of snakes."

Olivia nodded, biting her lip, thinking about the one on her kayak.

Underneath the poplar trees, beside Josh's pickup, he laid

a blanket. The kayaks rested on the shore, away from the branches.

Josh stood behind the open passenger side door. He latched the glove department, and stepped back, swinging the door shut. He carried a black and red pouch. The branches cracked as he walked through the grass.

"My sister took this from my parent's medicine cabinet when she found out I was taking you to the lake." He sat down on his knees. "I was hoping I wouldn't need it." He unzipped the pouch, removing wipes and bandages.

"It's fine. Honestly, it's not that bad."

Josh scooted closer, wrinkling the red-checkered blanket. He'd slipped on his T-shirt, after they secured the kayaks on the shore. "They'll get infected." He reached out, dabbing the wipe against the scar on her forehead.

It stung like the sting of ten ants. He paused, glancing down at her. She rolled her eyes up, questioning him. They questioned each other, he smiled and continued wiping the scratch. Olivia held still, lowering her gaze.

"You don't show pain, do you?"

"Try not to."

"Why?" He set the wipe down and grabbed another one. He began wiping the scar on her cheek.

"A habit, I guess."

"Habits come from somewhere." He set the wipe down, looking at her.

She looked at him. "Some habits come naturally."

He lowered, passing his face inches from hers. She wanted to kiss him.

He leaned back, sitting on his heels. *Do it.* He turned his head, reaching into the first aid kit. He peeled the paper off a band aide and placed it over the scar on her forehead. He gently rubbed his thumb over it, sticking it onto her skin. He repeated the process with the scratch on her cheek.

"What about your legs or arms?" he asked.

They spotted a scratch above her knee, releasing clumps of blood.

He handed her the wipes, cream and bandages. He looked at her, "Maybe you should do that one."

She scanned his expression. What did he think would happen if he cleaned the scar? The two of them on a picnic blanket, not another eye around for miles. A perfect scene. Would she regret it?

Another guy might have tried.

Olivia lowered her gaze, and focused on her right leg. *"Love is patient, love is kind."* Wiping her leg, she remembered the words her dad told her.

"You never did tell me how that happened." Josh nodded toward the scar on her left leg.

She could tell him how it happened. Nate lost control of the fork, dropping a dozen iron posts on her. But he wouldn't know what hurt the most that day. He wouldn't know about the duffle bag that still lay half packed in her closet.

"An iron post fell on me. I'd rather not talk about it."

Olivia lifted her knee off the ground, and began wrapping the gauze bandage around her leg.

Josh nodded. He took the bandage roll, and put everything back into the first aid kit. Olivia touched the band aides on her face. Her face wouldn't look the same. She'd keep scars for at least a month. Everyone would notice.

"You look beautiful." Josh marveled at her.

She could feel heat rising in her cheeks.

"I mean it. I noticed it the first time I saw you." Josh stood up, extending his hands toward her. She placed her palms in his and stood up. He squeezed her hands, pulling her closer. "Bandages can't hide it."

Olivia smiled. He kissed her cheek, then her lips. He pulled back, smiling. His smile shining through his eyes.

Someone loved her.

Josh jumped off the driver's seat. Coffee seeped out of the lids, onto his hands. He shoved the pickup door shut with his elbow. The kayaks shaded the sidewalk in front of Nate's double-wide.

"Shouldn't you be in church?" Nate leaned his head against the siding, the lawn chair tipped back.

Josh stepped into the sun, his spitfire boots clearing the dew on the over grown grass. "I should ask you the same thing."

Josh extended the paper cup toward Nate. His untrimmed face looked up, questioning him.

"It's coffee. Take it."

Nate leveled his chair, reaching for the cup. "Thanks."

Josh dipped his head, backing up toward the concrete steps. He sat down. One foot dangling, holding a coffee cup on his leg.

"If it's donuts you wanted, I don't have any."

Josh chuckled.

The midmorning sun shone on the chest high corn field across the road. The leaves glistened, covered in dew. Josh sipped his coffee. He missed it here.

He'd take it all back. He'd drive the ten minutes to work every day; pay the extra fuel. He'd do anything, anything to go back.

How far back would he go?

He sipped his coffee.

"At least you came sober this time."

Josh looked at Nate. Nate forgave, but he didn't forget. He never would. Josh glanced at the grass, tipping his coffee downward.

"You still need to mow."

Nate looked up, holding his coffee off the edge of the arm rest. "Why are you here?"

Josh shrugged. He scooted backward; leaned against the door. He breathed in the moist air, listening to the stillness. A bird's call sounded from the highline wire nearby. A vehicle passed by on the blacktop, behind the shop.

"How's Olivia?" Nate's voice broke the silence.

"Fine. Why do you ask?"

"I told you not to go out with her."

Nate didn't know about the weekly runs to Colorado. He didn't know about Keith, or about Steve. He didn't know the danger he'd put his sister in. What would Nate say now? If he knew, would he tell her? Would he tell her to stay away from him?

"Don't hurt her."

Josh straightened his neck, swirling his coffee in his cup. He looked at the kayaks on his pickup bed, replaying yesterday's scenes. Bandages on her face, her hair a mess, her skin flushed, yet she looked beautiful. If anyone else would have fallen in the water because of a water snake, he would have laughed. Even at his sister.

He looked at Nate. "I won't."

Olivia giggled. She squeezed Josh's fingers, forcing the tickling to stop. She held his hands against her waist, watching him laugh. He wiggled free, tickling her ribcage. She laughed, throwing her forehead on his shoulder, nestling her face against his neck.

She giggled, lifting her head. "If I didn't love you…"

"Then what?" He wrapped his arms around her, pulling her closer, rocking her slightly.

"I would've walked inside by now." She looked at him, scooting up his lap.

A light flashed. They looked at the dining room window. Dave's shadow walked past the window, into the living room. The living room light switched on.

"I think he's hinting for me to leave." Josh turned his chin, looking up at her.

Olivia glanced at the clock on the radio. Green numbers, 11:03, glared through the plastic. She sighed, tipping her head sideways, moving her hair out of her face. "I am late."

The living room light flashed. Olivia leaned her chest against Josh's. If she closed her eyes maybe he'd go away.

"I better go." Josh placed his palms on her upper arms, pushing her back.

Olivia nodded, reaching for the door handle. She opened the door, placing her boots on the doorstep. She ran her fingers through her hair, looking up at the stars, inhaling the warm summer breeze.

"'God's painting,'" she mumbled.

"I've heard Nate say that."

Olivia nodded. "Nothing beats it." The sky shimmered. Silver lights, lighting a black globe.

"Maybe a Kansas sunset." Josh brushed her back, curling his fingers around her waist. The warmth sent shivers up her spine. "You."

Olivia looked down, meeting Josh's eyes. In the cab light she could see the love in his eyes. She looked at the sky.

"I don't know about that," she said.

A coyote howled. Josh stroked her back.

"You used to live with Nate." She looked at him. "Why did you move out?"

He looked shocked. His lips straightened. His hand paused, resting on her spine.

The screen door creaked open. The wood frame bounced against the door trim. Dave glanced at them, then watched his steps down the stairs. A blue T-shirt and cargo shorts, something she'd never seen him wear before. His bare feet patted down the sidewalk.

Josh pressed his hand against her lower back. He balanced his leg on the ball of his foot, lifting his leg off the seat. Olivia balanced on his leg, holding on to the steering wheel. Dave approached, clearing his throat.

Olivia stepped onto the footrail, slowly climbing down.

"I was just leaving." Josh straightened his back, placing his fingers over the ignition.

"That's too bad." Dave studied Josh.

Olivia scraped the gravel with her boot, her hands resting in her jean pockets.

"Why don't you and I sit on the porch for a bit?" Dave glared at Josh. "It's too fine of a night to sleep anyways. What do you say?"

"I don't want to keep you up. We both have work tomorrow."

Dave turned, looking past Olivia. "Should've thought about that sooner." He stepped onto the grass, underneath the tree canopy, strolling toward the porch.

Josh slid the keys out of the ignition. He jumped off the

seat, landing in front of Olivia. She smiled at him. He leaned down and kissed her cheek. His lips curved upward, slightly.

"Good luck," Olivia whispered.

They stepped away from the door frame. Josh pushed the door shut.

"Olivia, you might as well go to bed. You'll need the sleep if you're getting up at four tomorrow." Dave pushed his knees in, then out, swinging the porch swing back and forth.

Crickets chirped in the grass.

Olivia sighed, letting her hands fall out of her pockets. She stepped toward Josh, and grabbed his hand. "Call me?"

He nodded, squeezing her knuckles. She smiled, released his hand, and faced the sidewalk.

Olivia stood in front of her bedroom window, brushing her hair. The yard light shimmered on the silver round-top, fading over the corrals. The taillights on Josh's pickup shone against the gravel. The thirty-foot-high tree in front of her window blocked the view of the rest of the pickup.

She tapped her phone laying on the desk in front of her. The screen lit up, showing eleven thirty-eight. How long could they talk? There was only so much a twenty-year-old and a thirty-nine-year-old could talk about. Olivia leaned forward. Should she? Olivia placed her fingertips against the window frame.

Olivia slid the window open. Crickets chirped; the moist air rattled the blinds at the top of the window. She reached up to hold them in place. Muffled voices drifted up the white stucco. The screen door swung shut; the exterior door latched. Josh walked down the sidewalk, reaching into his pocket. Gravel crushed underneath his feet as he disappeared behind the tree leaves.

Underneath her chin, her phone lit up, bringing extra light to the dimly lit room. She dropped the brush, rapidly clicking the volume button on the side of the phone. *Pick up.* She brought the phone to her ear, sighing.

"I heard you, listening in on us," Josh teased.

"I wouldn't," she teased, stepping into the bed. She pulled the quilt toward her, nestling her bare legs underneath the bedding.

"I had fun tonight."

Oliva propped one pillow against the headboard, cuddled the other pillow against her belly, and leaned back. "So did I."

"I hadn't heard you laugh before—not like tonight," he paused, "I like it."

Olivia's face sobered. "I hadn't shown that side of me in a long time." She twiddled the pillow case between her fingers. "I forgot I had it."

"Why? You should let more people hear your laugh."

Why? The last several years zipped through her mind. Olivia stared at the pillow. *Why?* She lifted her chin, focusing on the door. "No one makes me laugh like you do."

"I'll take it."

Olivia listened to the signal light clicking. The music playing in the background. She pulled the quilt further up, snuggling into the mattress.

"What did you guys talk about?"

"You. Me. Us."

"What did you tell him?"

"That I'm not going anywhere."

Olivia smiled, remembering Josh, handsome Josh. His hand in hers, his arms around her, his laugh; the look in his eyes. She squeezed the pillow, pushing it against her stomach. *Her Josh.*

"I like that," she mumbled.

CHAPTER TWENTY

She should have put her hair in a bun. Veronica winced, detangling her braids. Open hair, clinging to her neck would've been better than this. The towel wrapped around her waist came undone. It dangled over her hips, dragging on the concrete sidewalk. Veronica grabbed one end, holding on to her braid with the other hand.

Mrs. McCormick stood on her front porch, watering flowers. Her head tilted, glaring at Veronica. "Summer heat getting to you girl?"

The lawn sprinkler across the street squirted water onto the neighbor's house. The evening sun peeked through the neighborhood trees, casting shade over Mrs. McCormick.

"How are you, Mrs. McCormick?"

She nodded, lowering her gaze to the red and blue supertunia plants. She circled the watering can around the edge of the container, moving into the middle. "I saw your brother pull into the shed a few minutes ago. With two kayaks." Mrs. McCormick looked up. "Is he still dating the girl your mom told us about?"

She could feel the entire neighborhood listening. "As far as I know."

Mrs. McCormick nodded, watering the second container.

Veronica wrapped the towel around her hips and tucked one edge behind it. She lifted both hands to undo the last braid. Her eyes focused on the concrete in front of her pink toes, her flipflops clapping against her parent's driveway. Mrs. McCormick knew everyone in the neighborhood better than they knew themselves. A sweet lady, playing her cards right.

Kayaks banged against the concrete inside the shed. Veronica stepped onto the threshold, swinging the unlatched door open. Josh stood on the pickup bed, tossing paddles and life-jackets onto the glossy floor. She stepped into the shed, latching the door behind her.

"Make sure you're ready to confront Dad if you're going to scratch his twelve-thousand-dollar floor."

Veronica undid the towel and dropped it inside the outdoor clothing hamper. Goose-bumps immediately covered her exposed legs. She placed her pool flipflops on the shoe rack, and slid into her Tory Burch sandals.

Josh scanned the floor. "It's fine," he said, jumping off the tailgate.

"You've changed since you started working at a mechanic shop."

"You notice that after almost two years?"

Veronica shrugged. Josh balanced a kayak above his head, walking toward the racks against the wall. "How'd it go Saturday? Was it as romantic as it sounded?" Veronica leaned against the taillight.

"Does falling into the lake sound romantic?" Josh leveled the kayak parallel to the wall and secured it with a rubber strap.

"Depends," Veronica giggled.

Josh looked over his shoulder. He narrowed his eyebrows, focusing on her. "My love life isn't your business."

"Your love life, huh?" Veronica folded her arms across her chest.

Josh smiled, shaking his head.

"Someone's in lo-o-v-v-e." Veronica danced to her song, turning toward the passenger door. "I'll get the first-aid kit. Parents are talking about going to the lake this weekend. You know Mom won't leave without it."

What would it be like to have a boyfriend? Besides Steve. Someone who liked her the way Josh liked Olivia. Someone who took her on real dates; blushed when he talked about her.

Veronica scanned the cab. Nothing. She pulled the handle on the glove department until it clicked open, allowing the door to slowly lower. A black pouch with a red zipper and a red plus symbol glared at her. She retrieved the pouch and closed the department. A package bounced onto the all-weather mat.

Veronica stretched out her neck, looking out the rear window. Josh stood in the corner, hanging up paddles. He still needed to return the lifejackets. Veronica lowered her shoulders, picked up the package and set her elbows on the seat.

It was wrapped in a brown sandwich bag with clear packing tape around it.

She brought it to her nose. She had seen these at Steve's house. Veronica sniffed it. It smelled like the men she'd met at Steve's house. Why would her brother have it? Why hadn't he said something when she told him about her experience? At the time he seemed angry, worried.

Worried that she would find his stash?

The package was soft, crinkling when she squeezed it. Why would he do it? He lied to her. He let her believe he was better than them.

If she was hiding drugs, she would lie about it too. Why would he have them unless he was using them?

"We work together." Steve's words echoed through her mind. At the fair, Steve said he worked with Josh. What kind of work? Drug related work?

"Okay, I'm gonna head out." Josh's voice came closer.

"Um," she brushed her fingers against the tape, "why not stay for dinner?" She squished the bag; it deflated some. She tucked it into her shorts and pulled her swimsuit cover over it.

"I got some place," Josh paused, becoming puzzled. He stepped closer to her. "What did you do?"

"Me? I got the first aid kit. See?" She searched the cab for the kit, snatched it off the seat and held it in front of her.

"What else did you do?"

"Nothing, why?"

Josh stared at her, questioning her.

"You think I'm lying," she paused, "what else would I have done?"

"You are lying. Everyone knows when you lie, your eyebrow twitches."

She needed to itch the skin underneath the package. She needed to hold her eyebrow in place. She needed to tell Josh the truth. To have him tell her the truth.

"You're lying to me," she said.

Josh's expression changed. He lifted his chin; his eyes opened further. He *was* lying to her.

"What makes you say that?"

"You know you are. Why?"

Josh's phone rang. It vibrated on the passenger seat. Veronica glanced at it. *Steve.*

"You're talking to him after you told me not to."

Josh tore his focus off her and stepped toward the seat. "I'm an adult."

"He said you two worked together. You instantly knew who his "co-workers" were. Why?" Josh picked up the phone, he scanned Veronica as he answered.

Veronica quieted her tone. "What are you not telling me?"

Josh looked at her. She could hear Steve over the phone. *"You're late,"* he said.

"Late for what?" Veronica asked.

"I'm sorry," Josh mouthed, then stepped around her; walked around the hood, and toward the driver door.

"I'm just leaving," he said into his phone, climbing into his pickup.

Veronica watched him turn the ignition. He opened the garage door with the push of a button and placed the pickup in gear. She stepped back and closed the passenger door. She placed a hand over the package in her shorts. She breathed out. Her brother. Who was he?

CHAPTER TWENTY-ONE

Rain showered the house. It flowed down the roof, dribbling into the puddles in front of the porch. Moist air sifted through the dining room window. The breeze waved the tablecloth, patting it against the dining chairs.

Olivia wrapped a towel around the basket filled with warm dinner rolls and set it on the middle of the table. She wiggled her fingers into the bowl and tore off a nibble. She popped the buttery morsel into her mouth and tucked the towel underneath the basket, savoring the taste.

The crackling in the cast iron stopped. Mom removed the last pieces of chicken from the oil and turned off the burner. She placed them in a towel layered bowl, and wrapped the edges of the towel over the chicken. Unwanted chicken skin and chicken fat laid on the Formica countertop, beside the white clay sink. Olivia scooped it into her palm, ready to toss it in the trash can.

"No," Mom stood beside her, holding the bowl of chicken, "it'll stink up the place. Throw it outside."

Olivia glanced at the skin in her hands. "I'll do it later." She dumped it on the edge of the sink and rinsed her hands.

Her bare feet padded toward the fridge. She curled her toes underneath her feet, protecting them from the cold air. She retrieved the glass pitcher of iced tea, stepped back, and shut the door. Three glasses stood on the bar table. Olivia pulled back a chair, filled a glass of ice tea and listened to the rain clattering against the windows.

Mom rounded the bar table and opened the cutlery drawer. She fiddled around. Olivia's eyes turned to her mom's hands. She needed three forks and three knives: picking out silverware shouldn't be difficult.

"How's Josh?" Mom asked, gripping the knife handles.

Olivia set her glass down. "Good, why?"

Mom didn't care about her dating life. What had Dave told her?

"I was just wondering," she shrugged her shoulders, pushing the drawer closed. "I don't see much of him."

"Because you purposely stay away from us, from me."

Mom looked up at the flickering kitchen light. Thunder rumbled behind the house; they looked out the window. The clouds became thicker, darkening the dining room.

Mom lowered her focus to Olivia. "Is he good to you? Does he treat you well?"

Better than you ever did.

"Because I've heard some things, and I," Mom laid the silverware on the counter, "I don't want this relationship to go wrong."

Olivia rubbed her thumb against the glass she held,

condensation moistening her palm. "What things? Why would it go wrong? What did Dave tell you about him?"

Mom shook her head, lowering her chin. "Nothing." She inhaled, then looked up. "A few weeks ago, I heard a couple of ladies talking about him."

Gossip. Ladies loved gossip.

"It just seems like the town knows more about him than we do."

The screen door creaked open. Boots stomped on the concrete porch. "It's raining," Dave said.

Why had she asked? Mom relaxed her thin shoulders, straightened her back and shook her upper body. She painted a smile on her face and brushed her blond hair over her shoulder. She bunched the silverware in one hand and walked to the dining table.

Olivia turned on the barstool.

"You hear that Lindy, that's the sound of sweet, sweet rain." Dave set his boots in front of the stucco and stepped into the house. His folded-up jeans reached to the middle of his calves. His wet hair collided with his scruffy beard.

He kissed Lindy's cheek and walked into the mudroom. "We needed it. Thank the Lord, he sent it at the right time." Water poured out of the faucet. "The hay's still on the ground, but if we hadn't gotten a rain soon, the corn wouldn't have made it." The faucet shut off. "The hay will grow again. This rain will help for the next cutting."

Dave stopped underneath the doorway to the dining room,

flipping the dining room light switch. "It smells good in here." Dave pulled out the chair from his usual spot. "Ladies, you don't know what this does for a farmer's soul," he said, sitting down.

Olivia itched her elbow, stepping closer to the register. She scanned the chalk board menu, setting her phone on the wooden counter. Ninety degrees outside and the guys ordered coffee. The cashier tapped the screen in front of her and looked up.

"Three iced vanilla lattes, please. No whip cream."

She held Dave's farm card between her fingers, resting her wrist on the edge of the counter. Watercolor paintings of the town hung on the walls. Black piping, topped with wooden shelves lined one wall. The shelves held books and games. On the coffee and side tables laid traveling magazines and copies of the local newspaper.

People sat scattered amongst the tables and couches. Women laughed, chatting, gossiping. Some rocked their babies in car seats, others talked about their eighteen-year-olds joining the army. Young men sat in front of the window, typing, folders lying beside their laptops.

"Twelve-o-six," the cashier said.

Olivia turned her focus to the card reader below her.

Approved. She removed the card, thanked the cashier, and stepped toward the end of the counter, past the cinnamon rolls and chocolate chip cookies. Veronica lounged on an armchair in the corner of the room, staring into a travel magazine.

How did girlfriends act around their boyfriend's sister? Like friends, right? Olivia slid her phone and the card into her jean pocket and stepped into the armchair-square. Veronica lowered the magazine and looked up.

"Hey." Olivia smiled. "How—"

Veronica lifted the magazine in front of her face, flipping pages faster than she could read them.

"Are you planning on traveling to Wisconsin?"

Veronica shrugged.

Olivia scanned the room, glancing over the customers. She slid her hands in her pockets and sat down on the edge of the armchair. The ladies behind the counter pumped syrups into to-go cups, blended ice, and twirled whip cream on top of the drinks. Hopefully her order would be next.

"I can't talk to you," Veronica said.

She focused on Veronica. "Why not?"

"I'm not mad at you, it's just better I don't."

Olivia nodded, lowering her eyes to the coffee table in front of her. She glanced at the counter. No drinks.

"You're an awesome girlfriend—to Josh."

Olivia looked at Veronica. The girl clenched her hand around the tightly rolled magazine, jabbing her knuckles onto her coral skirt, denting her flesh.

"But you don't have to date him, if you don't want to." Veronica's shoulders stiffened, pulling in her spine.

"He's a nice guy." Attractive, loves her, why wouldn't she date him?

Veronica nodded, her curly hair bouncing above her shoulders. Anyone could tell the girl came from a rich family. Her cream-colored tee tied at the waist above her skirt, showing an inch of skin. Two necklaces countering her collar bones, hair and makeup done perfectly. And it was only a Thursday.

She aimed her large eyes at the foot of the coffee table, straightening her lips, arching her eyebrows. Slowly releasing the magazine, relaxing her hand.

Olivia looked over her shoulder, glancing past the people standing beside her. She pressed her palms down in her pockets.

Olivia leaned over the arm rest, lowering her voice. "If there's something bothering you—"

"—I can't tell you." Veronica stood up.

"I meant, talk to your parents about it, your brother, your friends."

"I can't tell anyone," Veronica said, setting the rounded magazine on the side table.

Veronica wrapped her fingers around the strap of the leather bag that hung off her shoulders. She stared at the rounded magazine, moving her hand up and down the strap.

"Do you…" Olivia paused. Veronica needed something. She looked more troubled than when Steve dumped her. Veronica straightened the magazine, attempting to undo the fold. "Maybe you can buy a copy," Olivia paused, "somewhere."

Veronica lifted her gaze. She looked at Olivia. Her face looked like she was begging for something, yet she said nothing. She dipped her head. "It was nice to see you," she said, then stepped out of the seating area.

Olivia slid her hands out of her pockets, rubbing her legs. Dirt crumbled loose, into the crack of the cushions. She stopped, folding her hands between her legs.

She should call Josh.

Tonight.

After five.

She'd catch him on his way home from work.

"Olivia," a lady behind the counter called.

She thanked the lady, lifted the drinks, and blindly walked through the crowd. Should she talk to Josh about his sister?

She lifted her eyes to the man holding the door open in the afternoon sun. "Thank you."

Everyone except for his high school buddies stood in the crowd, holding a red solo cup, dressed in their Sunday best. The girls that used to nervously giggle when he'd speak to them strutted past him with confidence. They held their head high, careful not to let their hair fall out of place. He tried to imagine Olivia in a pencil dress.

The image didn't suit her.

He liked her in jeans, a T-shirt and a messy braid. The way she looked when he first saw her. Confident in manure-covered sneakers. Sebrina and Jessica never looked that beautiful. If they had, he hadn't noticed.

Josh leaned on the deck railing, sipping his iced tea. Jessica sat several tables away from Sebrina, both crossed their legs above their knee, displaying their subtle tanned skin. One of them scanned her phone, while the other one scanned the crowd.

Josh lowered his chin, shifting his feet. He should've brought Olivia. His ex-girlfriends, had grown into their woman-shaped bodies, yet they could never measure up to Olivia's beauty.

He grabbed his phone out of his pocket. No message. He slipped it back in his pocket, sagging his shoulders; he propped an elbow on the railing.

Nearly two years had passed since his celebratory college party. The dads that slapped his shoulder, wished him well; the moms that asked about his plans, his goals; not one of them noticed him now. He was last year's football gear—forgotten, filthy, left in the back of the closet behind the new shoulder pads and purple uniform.

Josh brought the solo cup to his mouth, halfway wishing it contained more than tea. He should've brought Olivia, mostly for company, but also because it'd do him good to show everyone he'd found a girl he loved. It'd do his family good to show people he'd made one good decision.

His sister spoke to everyone she passed, laughing and smiling. Dad called her. He waved her toward him, Mr. and Mrs.

Morgan, and Mr. and Mrs. Stevenson. He wrapped his arm around her shoulders, raving about her academics.

Josh gazed over the golf field, at the pasture. Barbed fencing lined the mint green, ankle high buffalo grass. Cattle dotted the pasture, like flies on a sticky trap. He sipped his tea, ice clattering in his cup.

"I heard they're still searching," Mrs. Stevenson said.

Josh rolled his eyes sideways, glancing at Mrs. Stevenson.

"Well, John said they just recently discovered it. Said they found ten packages scattered out on road K," Mr. Morgan said.

"It's sad to think about crime in Shallow River. Not too long ago one could leave their door unlocked at night, now you can't go to the post office without thinking the worst." Mrs. Morgan shook her head, scanning the group.

"Do you ever notice anything in school, Veronica?" she asked.

"About drugs? No, I wouldn't know anything." She shook her head, her voice trailing off. "I never notice anything—in school, I mean."

Mrs. Morgan nodded, eyeing Veronica.

Josh glared at Veronica, scratching his thumb on the solo cup. A tall figure blocked his view.

"I saw you walking around town the other day, noticed you weren't alone. How'd you get a pretty girl like that to go out with you?"

Josh looked up and straightened his body. "Hey Clint." Josh smiled, "just smile at 'em, it works every time." He slapped Clint's shoulder and glanced around him. "Hey man, I got to go. Don't have too much fun." He tapped his shoulder again and backed away from Clint. "We'll see ya, later."

He turned around and scanned the crowd for his sister. She'd left their dad and wasn't with her friends.

The eyes of the guests felt like ants he needed to shake off. No one noticed him, so why did it feel like he was the giant in the room?

He opened the patio door, and walked into the living room. The house remained untouched, except for the dusty footprints trailing to the bedrooms. Heels clicked in the hallway.

"Veronica?"

Josh walked down the hallway. The door to his sister's room stood open. She had updated it since he left. The room looked like a guest bedroom, instead of a teenage girl's room. A chair sat in the corner next to a window. A magazine was lying on the chair next to the throw blanket. A dresser with minimal décor stood opposite of the window. A lamp stood on each night stand. On one night stand there was a coaster, a phone charger, and a water bottle. On the other one stood a picture frame.

Josh walked into the room to look at the picture in the frame. The four of them, when Josh was twelve and Veronica was eight. Before they realized the absence of their parents. Before they realized there was *something* that their family never had. Or at least before he realized it.

The drawer to the nightstand peeked open. Josh glanced

inside. Instead of books or pens, a brown package kept the drawer from closing. It looked like the ones he'd seen. *It couldn't be, but what if it was?* He laid his fingers on the drawer handle. He opened it an inch. It looked like what he had stashed away underneath the dash of his pickup.

He squeezed it out of the drawer. Exactly like what he had.

The toilet flushed. Water started running out the bathroom faucet. That must have been where Veronica went. He should put the package back; walk out of her room. What *was* he doing inside his sister's room? He should be outside, with the guests.

"Josh?" Veronica stood underneath the doorway.

He felt guilty, caught in the middle of a crime.

He looked at the package in his hand. But this was *her* room, *her* package. She was the one who'd been caught. If it was what he thought it was.

"What is this?" Josh held the package in front of him.

"Something I found."

"Where?"

She stared at him. As if he should know the answer to his question. *His* pickup? When was the last time he checked underneath his dash?

"Did you …" he trailed off. He couldn't ask her. What if it wasn't from his stash?

"Yes." Veronica stepped into the room and shut the door behind her. "It's from your pickup," she said through her teeth. "What are you doing with drugs?"

"Ssh."

"Don't *ssh* me." Veronica set her jaw firmly. Her back slightly arched. "Answer me."

"What are *you* doing with it?" Josh threw it onto the sage duvet cover. "Tell me you haven't used it."

It looked unopened. But she could have taped it shut again.

"I don't even know how to use it."

"Then why do you have it?"

"Josh," she changed her tone, "why do *you* have it?" He didn't hear or see her disappointment as much as he felt it.

He was her older brother. The one who was supposed to set an example. He wanted a better life for Veronica. He wanted to make sure she wouldn't turn out like him. He had failed. Miserably. What could he tell her? The truth? She would never look at him the same again. Or would she? Did his sister appreciate him as much as he always thought? Could he tell her everything and still be wanted, still be respected?

"What kind of *work* do you and Steve do?"

Josh's memory flashed back to the night of the fair. *Steve.* He would like to hurt Steve and his big mouth. Physically, emotionally, he didn't care. He'd like to pound him against a pole, the same way Roy had done to him. He'd like to turn his family against him. He'd like to see him alone and hurting. The kid deserved it.

What about you? Don't you deserve it?

Veronica picked the package off the bed and hid it in the nightstand drawer next to her. She folded her arms across her chest, as if to protect herself. Her hair draped over her ears, covering half her cheeks. She didn't tuck it behind her ears. She let her hair cover her. She looked at him, the determination she'd shown a second ago was fading. Was she realizing the truth? Was she giving up on him?

"Are you gonna answer me? If not, then you can go. There's a party waiting for you."

The party wasn't for him. He didn't even want to be here.

"I can't tell you." *I wish I could.*

"Does Olivia know?"

He shook his head.

"She likes you."

It was more than that.

"Maybe you should tell her. She's a sweet girl," Veronica paused, "if you think you can trust her more than you can trust me."

"Veronica…"

"You're in trouble. I can tell. You need to do something about it."

He was in trouble. But he couldn't do anything about it. Or could he? Would his sister know what to do? His fifteen-year-old sister?

"You should go. People will start to wonder."

Josh walked around the bed and stopped at the nightstand behind her. She faced him, holding her hand out.

"No. It stays here. You didn't answer me."

"What if Mom or Dad find it?"

"I'll tell them it's yours."

Would she do that? Would she rat him out like that? Without a second thought.

Maybe she should. Maybe his parents could help him find a way out.

He looked at the door and turned toward it. They would shun him. They would find a way to keep everything quiet. They couldn't risk ruining their reputation. But would they help him? He doubted it.

CHAPTER TWENTY-TWO

Granny placed New Year cookies in the center of the table. If frogs had warts, they'd look like Granny's New Year cookies. Neatly bunched on a napkin, inside a red fast-food container, faded raisins peaked through the fried dough. A layer of grease coated the cookies, soaking into the napkin.

"Try one." Grandma nodded toward the cookies, eyeing Olivia.

Olivia nodded. She should. According to Sam, New Year cookies were a treat. Every December Granny stood over a hot frying pan for hours on end. Mary, Sam and Grandma cooked the rest of the dinner, but Granny made the New Year cookies. A tradition that Granny would do until the good Lord called her home.

Granny's eyes sparkled. Like a child showing his parents his artwork.

Olivia lifted her hand, itched her elbow and hovered her arm above the white table-cloth. Her fingers inches away from the cookies.

Granny's laugh broke the silence. "Goodness child, you

can spit it out if it's that bad. You von't be the first person that didn't like them."

Olivia grabbed one, the grease wetting her finger tips. She brought it to her lips.

"Honey," Mary said.

Olivia eyed her, holding the cookie in the air.

"You need honey." She stood up and retrieved a jar of raw honey from a kitchen cupboard. She set a plate underneath the cookie Olivia held and swirled a dap of honey on the plate. She closed the honey jar. "There, now try it."

Olivia dipped the cookie into the honey and clenched her teeth through the fried dough. Sweet and salty blended together.

"So?" Sam asked.

"Give her some time," Grandma said.

"On New Year's we serve coffee, cookies, and honey all day," Sam said.

"All day, huh?" Olivia wiped honey off the corner of her mouth.

"Do you like them?" Granny asked. Her eyes kind and patient. The black head covering pulled an inch from her forehead, lining her wrinkled cheeks. A crumb dangled on the knot that fastened the covering to her head.

"You're a good cook, Granny. I'm sure you make the best New Year cookies." Olivia smiled, taking another bite.

Granny smiled ear to ear. She relaxed her shoulders, bit off a strawberry roll, and hovered her chin over her plate.

"But why make them in August?" Olivia asked.

Granny set the strawberry roll on her plate and bunched the chewed roll in her cheek. "I vanted to. Now you'll know vat to expect on New Year's."

Olivia smiled. "I'm sure it will be a lot of fun."

"You're very kind." Grandma squeezed Olivia's hand. "Must be something you get from your mom."

Mom choked on her coffee. She thumped the mug on the table, coughing into her palm.

"Excuse me." Mom cleared her throat. Everyone stared at her.

Olivia shifted her shoulders, scooting further into the chair. She set the cookie down and sipped her coffee. Mom hid her disagreement well. But Olivia knew what her mom thought of her.

Olivia set the mug down, and ate the last of her cocoa cookie. She rested her wrist on the edge of the table and stared at the corner of the ceiling.

"Are you all right?" Grandma asked.

Olivia rolled her eyes toward her mom, gripping the mug with both hands. Mom wouldn't be able to hide her disgust for her daughter much longer.

"Yes, I'm fine." Mom wiped her lips.

"Well," Grandma straightened her back, scanning the food, "perhaps it is time we clean up."

Sam stood up. "Olivia and I will do it." She picked up the plate of rolls and cocoa cookies, and looked at Olivia. "If you're done?"

Olivia snapped out of her glare. "Yes." She scooted her chair back and picked up the basket of New Year cookies.

Olivia stepped around the half wall, that separated the kitchen from the dining room. She set the basket on the island, beside the strawberry rolls and cocoa cookies. Sam began piling the cling-wrapped cocoa cookies into a Tupperware container.

She scanned the cabinets. Where did Granny store the storage containers? Olivia looked at Sam. "Where—"

"How's Josh?" Sam closed the container. She swung around and retrieved another Tupperware container from an upper cabinet.

"He's fine."

Sam set the container in front of Olivia, then scooped the rolls back into the casserole dish. Strawberry glaze covered the tips of her fingers. Olivia would have licked it off her own fingers. Her mouth watered at the thought. No one could compete with Granny's baking.

"Does he treat you with respect?"

Olivia grabbed the container, and slid it toward her. "Of course he does." Olivia piled the New Year cookies into the container. "Why wouldn't he?"

Sam shrugged. "From the stuff I've heard about—I'm just concerned."

Well don't be. She bit her tongue, keeping the words in.

Sam clasped a lid onto the casserole dish, and placed it in the freezer.

"What do you know about him, that I don't?" Olivia set the fast-food basket in the sink. "Everyone seems to know something I don't."

Sam sat down on a bar-stool; leaned her body forward and rested her elbows on the counter. "He has a bad reputation. I'm surprised you haven't heard about it." Sam opened her palms, pointing her fingers at the salt and pepper shakers. "He got kicked out of college—"

"—I knew that." But how did Sam know that?

"Every girl in high school liked him and he enjoyed every bit of it. The girls he did date never stuck around for too long. He'd spend every weekend drinking, smoking, trespassing, doing who knows what." Sam sighed. "Nate dislikes him. After a lifetime of friendship, the two suddenly never speak. What does that tell you?"

Olivia closed the container and rested her palms on the countertop. "I know all of this. Maybe Nate has an unrelatable reason to dislike Josh. Whatever is going on between them is their business."

Olivia carried the New Year cookies to the freezer. "People change. Dave knows it, but you and Nate refuse to believe that it's possible for Josh." Olivia opened the freezer door.

"Not there."

Olivia paused.

"Set them on the countertop. They'll eat them for dinner."

Olivia set them beside the toaster oven.

"Dave doesn't listen to gossip."

Olivia faced Sam. "Neither should you."

Sam looked at Olivia. Her face dropped. She focused on the salt and pepper shakers, folding her hands. She stood up, pushed the stool against the island and walked around to the sink.

"Just don't say I didn't warn you."

She opened the faucet, wetting the dishcloth. "You should break up with him."

The breeze flapped her skirt against her ankles, lifting strands of hair out her loose braid. She pulled it from between her lips and tucked it behind her ear. Street-lights shone onto windshields; American flags waved beneath every light.

Olivia glanced at Josh.

She looked at the picnic table cemented into the sidewalk, in front of the ice cream shop.

"I can drive myself next time." She looked at him.

"No." He brought his hands to his pockets. She wanted to grab his hand, to feel his fingers wrap around her knuckles. He slid both hands into his pockets, looking ahead. "I don't mind the drive."

Josh's overgrown hair dipped into his eye. She wanted to wrap her fingers around his elbow, face him and brush his hair back. The way he used to wear it. She wanted to look him in the eye and ask what had gone wrong.

Olivia paused in front of the picnic table. "How about an ice cream?" She smiled. "My treat."

His lips curved up, but the smile didn't reach his eyes. "I'll buy you one."

"That's not why I asked." Olivia smiled, stepping closer to Josh.

Josh's focus drifted away, his smile fading. Olivia looked down. She folded her hands and twiddled her fingers. She pulled them apart, sighed and lifted her shoulders, scanning the street.

Movie posters hung inside plastic boxes beside the front entrance. A large family walked into the theater. The mom carried a tote around her shoulder, urging the youngest to step inside.

"Are you okay?" Josh asked.

Olivia hadn't noticed her expression changing. She faced Josh, shaking away any memory of her childhood. She looked into his eyes. "I'm fine." *Are you?* she wanted to ask.

Josh lowered his eyes. He believed her.

Olivia rolled her eyes past his shoulder. She was fine.

"Olivia, I—" She straightened her posture and looked at him. He stepped closer, sliding his hand down her forearm, until he reached her palm. He squeezed her hand, stroking her knuckles with his thumb. "I love you, you know that, right?"

She remembered Sam's words, *"Every girl in high school liked him and he enjoyed every bit of it."* But he loved her.

As he stroked her hand, Olivia's body tingled. Smiling, she said, "I know."

He looked into her eyes. In the past she had always seen

his love, but today she saw concern—worry. Her stomach knotted. What did he want to tell her? He lifted his eyes over her, looking into the distance. Olivia looked over her shoulder.

The boy they saw at the fair with Veronica stepped out of a pickup.

Josh stepped back, urging her forward. "Let's go."

She looked up at him, multiple questions running through her mind. She followed Josh's gaze and watched the boy walk the other direction. The tension left; Josh lowered to his regular height.

He released his hold on her, and ran his fingers through his hair. "I'm sorry about my behavior tonight." He studied her, his expression filled with sympathy. "Is it all right if we call it a night?"

Her heart sank. She would be home over an hour earlier than her curfew. Time she could have spent with Josh.

"*Just don't say I didn't warn you.*" She looked at Josh. Warn her about what? What did Sam know that she didn't know? Olivia opened her mouth, the questions balancing on her tongue.

"Wh—"

The worrisome looked returned, more intense than before.

Olivia closed her mouth. She had never witnessed a grown man's eyes fill with fear. She had never expected it out of Josh.

Suddenly, she wanted to comfort him more than she wanted answers.

Olivia squatted in the cucumber patch, balancing on the balls of her feet. Vines stretched out underneath her heels, beside her hips, in front of her face. She held the basket in one hand, searching for cucumbers with the other.

The breeze carried Nate's voice across the gravel patch.

Olivia yanked a small cucumber off the vine, shaving the peel off the stem. *Ugh.* A yellow bloom blossomed at the tip of the cucumber. *Too young.*

Nate laughed into his phone, loading tools onto the bed of his farm pickup.

Cucumber leaves crackled. The dog walked through the vines, poking his nose between the leaves, sniffing the ground. Olivia itched her arm. Red lines covered her underarm, like a tree trunk damaged by cat claws.

A bucket drummed against the house. Mom scraped out the last bit of leftovers into the dog's bowl. The dog's ears poked up, his body completely still, eyes turned back. Mom whistled. He leaped out of the patch and trotted toward his bowl.

Footprints crushed gravel. Nate walked to the shop, switching his phone from one ear to the other. Most likely speaking to Anna.

Olivia sat the basket down and stretched to her full height. The front door squeaked open.

She stepped through the vines and onto the buffalo grass. A hen flapped her wings, scattering out of Olivia's way. It clucked, running toward the hen house.

The porch swing chain creaked, rubbing against the metal hooks. Olivia redid her ponytail as she walked across the gravel toward the shop. Nate walked out of the round-top, sliding his phone into his pocket. He stopped in front of his farm pickup, watching her.

Hydraulic oil covered his T-shirt. Grease streaks stained his jeans. His hair, clumped together with dirt, flared to the side underneath his John Deere hat. The same way he often looked. Had Anna seen him like this?

"Long day?" Olivia asked.

"Pickup's running, you're good to drive it wherever you want."

"Thanks."

He nodded, studying her.

The dog's bowl scraped against the concrete pad.

Olivia looked into Nate's eyes. Would he tell her the truth? What if he did? What if he told her something she would have never expected?

Nate broke eye contact. "See you tomorrow," he said, stepping past her.

"Wait." Olivia lowered her voice. She turned around. "I need to talk to you about something."

Nate removed his fingers from the door handle and faced her. "What do you need to talk about?"

Olivia glanced at the slab. Dave sat on the porch swing, watching them. How much could he hear? Should she wait until another time? After the way Josh acted last night—she needed to know. Olivia stretched to her full height. Oil covered Nate's left cheek. Somehow his eyes looked bluer today.

"What do you know about Josh that I don't?"

Nate lifted his eyelids, shock piercing through. "What do you want to know?"

"What's he hiding from me?"

His eyes widened. Like he'd feared this question. He blinked. "I think you should ask him."

"I'm asking you."

His arms dangled beside his hips. Pity covering his face. Olivia parted her lips.

Should she ask again?

She breathed in. *Yes.*

"Tell me what you know that I don't."

She curled her fingers, scraping her palm. Nate stared over her shoulder. What did he know that required so much thought? She pushed her fingernails into her skin.

He looked at her, serious and focused. "A month ago, in the barn, I was out of line." Nate slid his hands into his pockets. "Josh cares about you. He would never hurt you on purpose."

Olivia exhaled, releasing her fists. "What's he hiding from me?"

Nate searched her expression. A sympathetic look on his face. She filled her lungs with air, straightening her spine.

"You know something I don't," she said

Nate gazed at her. He lifted his hands; Olivia stepped

back, expecting him to touch her. Instead, he slid his hands into his pockets.

"No," he said, in a rough whisper, "I don't."

She searched his eyes. Why would he sympathize with her if he didn't know anything? His lips curved down; his cheeks fell.

"Don't lie to me," she said.

"I would never want to."

Nate removed his hands from his pockets, and placed one hand on the door handle. "Next time, talk to Josh about it. He's your boyfriend, so don't come to me."

She stared at him.

"If you're gonna date him," he glanced down, "then don't come to me about your problems."

Nate opened the door and turned toward it. His eyes staying on her. "It'll be for the best."

Olivia looked at the front porch. Dave no longer sat on the swing. Nate's words stung, but he was right. She looked at him. She should have never asked.

He climbed into his pickup. The cracked windshield darkened his face. The barrier somehow sealed his words. He nodded a goodbye. The engine started; the pickup rolled off the concrete. Olivia looked at the wheat stubble behind the house.

She remembered Josh's words, "*I want to tell you, one day, years from now.*"

...years from now. When would she tell Josh her secret?

Nate didn't know her secret, what made her think he knew Josh's secrets. Whatever Josh was hiding from her, would never compare to what she was hiding from him.

Some secrets were better left untold.

CHAPTER TWENTY-THREE

Josh scooted out from underneath the pickup, his belt scraping against the concrete. He wiped the oil off his hands and slid the rag into his back pocket. A neighborhood boy bicycled past the house, staring at Josh. Josh itched his lip with his sleeve and bent down to pick up his supplies. An engine shut off. He looked at the street.

Nate. What would he want?

Josh released the oil filter and stood up straight, watching him walk across the grass. Nate stopped at the pickup's taillight and rested his arm on the bed. He glanced at the concrete.

"Olivia came to me today," he tilted his head, "asked questions about you."

Josh lowered his eyes, glaring at the rear tire. "You told her." How had she not called him? How had she not broken up with him?

"I lied for you."

Josh looked up.

A part of him wished Olivia knew. Every morning when

he texted her, he felt the urge to tell her everything. Saturday it had taken all his self-control not to take her into his arms and beg her to stay, no matter what. If she left, he would live on. One way or the other. But the longer he waited to tell her, the more it would hurt.

"Olivia knows you're hiding something from her." Nate dropped his arm, straightening his body. "There's rumor of a drug operation in town."

Josh's eyelids jerked up.

"You can hide it from her, but you can't hide it from me." Nate stepped closer. "How deep in are you?"

"You didn't have to lie for me."

"I didn't. Olivia's different. If you tell her, it'll break her."

"She's strong."

Nate shook his head. "Not that strong."

How well did he know Olivia? They worked together, but how personal was their relationship?

"Get out of this mess, before anyone ever knows you were in it."

"I can't."

Josh bent down to pick up the oil filter and oil pan. "You don't know Keith." He walked into the garage and set the oil pan in a corner.

"Why not?" Nate nearly shouted.

Josh faced Nate, standing underneath the garage door.

"You should've seen what they did to me when I missed a meeting."

Nate stared at him, his expression calming down. "You've never been afraid of a fight." Nate walked to the hood of the pickup. "What's the real reason? Is it the money? The money's good, huh?"

"Man, shut up. You don't know the half of it."

Nate didn't know about the nights he'd sat in his pickup, cursing himself, thinking about how he got where he was.

"Then tell me."

Nate knew him better than anyone else. He'd been there through it all. From sneaking lizards into the girls' bathroom to sneaking drugs into his house. Nate never asked why. He never gave him a chance to explain. Why should he tell him now?

Kevin's pickup pulled onto the slab. He parked behind Josh's pickup. The door shut. Kevin walked beside the trucks, stopping beside Nate. He reached out his hand, clapping Nate's shoulder.

"Man, it's been too long," Kevin said. He stepped back, widening his stance. "What brings you here? Haven't seen you in so long, thought you might have packed up and moved to Florida for all I knew."

Nate chuckled. "Nah, I've been working."

Kevin finished his laugh, sighing. "Very good." He nodded. "But seriously, what brings you here?" Kevin stepped back. "Come in," he shook his head toward the mudroom door, "have a beer. Blake will be home soon. We'll have him cook up some dinner for us."

Nate opened his mouth to speak.

"He was just leaving."

Kevin stepped forward. "Come on, stay awhile. Josh is always gone. Hanging out with his girlfriend." Kevin said "girlfriend" like he was chewing sandpaper. "We'll play poker. What do ya say?"

"I'm good." Nate slapped Kevin's shoulder. "Maybe next time."

Nate looked at Josh, then turned around and walked toward his farm pickup.

How well did he know Olivia?

Josh popped the top off the bottle and tossed it inside the trashcan. It clinked against the empty soda cans. He set his bottle on the counter beside the plate of microwaved mac and cheese. He forked the noodles one by one and scraped them into his mouth.

Josh spat, dropping the noodles back into the plate. They tasted like microwavable plastic. He used a napkin to wipe the cheese out of his mouth and washed the rest down with beer. He should've gone to the bar with Kevin and Blake. Except everyone knew his ID was fake.

He opened the bottom cabinet, needing something to calm his growling stomach. He saw an open bag of Doritos. Josh snatched a few chips off the shelf and grabbed the bag. The bag caught against a nail in the wood. It tore apart, shedding Doritos on the floor and across the shelf.

Josh twisted the plastic, crumpling it over and over. He slid the bottle off the counter, holding it at the neck, he brought the rim to his mouth. He threw the bag in the trashcan and plopped down on the floor. He stretched out his legs, crossing them at the ankles. He selected the non-broken chips off the floor and ate his dinner.

His phone vibrated.

He set his beer down and grabbed it out of his back pocket. Keith. Another notification. Steve. What day was it? He glanced at the calendar on the wall. Tuesday. Steve could deliver them by himself. He leaned his head against the cabinet door and ate a Dorito, listening to the crunch in his mouth.

"If you tell her, it'll break her."

His phone vibrated.

"You're a hypocrite." Veronica's voice echoed through his mind. He lifted the bottle to his mouth. His phone vibrated. He glanced at the black screen, then at the bottle hovering underneath his chin. *"If you think you can trust her more than me."*

Who was he to influence a fifteen-year-old-girl?

Josh hurled the bottle across the room, smashing it against the refrigerator door. Beer foam seeped down the white plastic, puddling next to the broken glass. His parents loved Veronica. They cared about her more than him. They always had. She'd be fine without him in her life. What a fool to think that he could guide her toward a better life than he had.

Josh popped another chip in his mouth.

Girls' laughter came from the front yard. The front door knob clicked. Blake's voice came from the front porch. Josh peeked over the counter. The door swung open. Several girls followed Kevin into the house. A girl ducked her head, avoiding the door frame. She rode piggy-back on a guy Josh didn't know. The people kept coming.

His sister walked in the door, hugging herself. Josh jumped up. Where'd she come from? He twirled around, looking at the cracked chips and broken glass. He brushed his hair back and bent over to start cleaning.

"Josh," Blake yelled, "we got company."

"I can tell."

The noise stayed in the living room. Someone connected to their Bluetooth speaker and began playing music. Glass clunked onto the counter. He didn't have to see to know that several bottles of whiskey now stood on the bar table.

Josh scooped the glass together. Blood began flowing from his index finger. He shook his hand, then cupped the finger in his palm. He needed the broom, he stood up, where—the laundry room. Why keep a broom in the laundry room?

"Do we have cups?" Kevin asked. "Veronica, do you know?"

"In the cabinet above the bar table."

"Thanks." Kevin looked into the cabinet. "I'm mixing you the first drink."

Josh dropped his hands, leaping to the bar table. He

reached over the counter, yanking the solo cup out of Kevin's hand. "Dude, she's fifteen."

The room went silent. People glanced, but he wasn't sure who they were looking at. Him or Veronica?

"You're bleeding."

Blood seeped down the cup, dripping onto the counter. People began talking again; the music became louder.

Kevin scanned the kitchen floor. "What happened man?" he asked.

Josh dropped the cup on the counter. He walked around the bar table, chips crunching underneath his feet. His sister sat on the couch, holding her elbows. She bobbed her head to the music, flipping her hair over her shoulder. Like a twelve-year-old at her first boy-girl party. She spotted Josh and looked away.

He grabbed her elbow, lifting her off the couch. "I'm taking you home."

Veronica tore his fingers off her elbow and stepped in front of him. She dipped her head, her hair hanging over her cheeks.

"Let's go."

Veronica walked through the crowd. Girls stared at them, they scanned them over, then whispered to each other. Some giggled, a few winked at Josh, others watched Veronica with pity.

She walked into the hallway. Away from the music; away from listening ears and pitying eyes. She turned around, swinging her hair back.

"I'm serious, I'm taking you home."

"No."

"You can't stay here. These people are over half a decade older than you."

Veronica brushed her hair behind her ears, and hugged herself. "I'm not going home. Not with you," she mumbled, looking at the floor.

"Why not?"

"You're a bloody mess. I smell alcohol on your breath."

"By the end of tonight, every one of these people will be too drunk to drive you home."

"Amy drove me here," Veronica scratched her forearm. "She'll drive me home," she looked at Josh, "I trust her."

"I'm your brother. Trust me when I say, you don't want to be here."

She had never looked younger. Never more naïve. She needed to go home. To her room, behind a secured door. Away from lost optimist and gawking losers. To a quiet, comfortable place. To a house not contaminated with cigarette smoke and alcohol.

"I rather be with them than with someone who's lying to me."

"You have to trust me."

"How can I? If you don't trust me?" Her eyes bore into his.

Josh lifted his hand to his forehead, wanting to brush his hair. Blood flowed down his wrist. He lowered his arm, looking at his sister. He opened his mouth, but what could he say? The truth? The consequences that would come if she went down this path?

"Sis, I'm sorry." He shook his head, "You can't stay here. I won't allow it. I care about you too much."

"Then why don't you get it? You're my brother. I care about you. If you're in trouble I want to help."

"This is bigger than..." *than you*, he nearly said. If only she could, he would tell her. But how could a fifteen-year-old help him? He was supposed to help her; instead he was guiding her to a life of sin.

He placed his fingers on her elbow and faced the crowd. "You need to go home," he said.

Veronica stepped back, forcing Josh's hand to drop. "Amy will drive me home."

He propped his elbow on the middle console, holding the keys in the air. Card-board covered the inside of Keith's dining room window. Boxes were stacked on the front porch. An Amazon logo stamped on the sides, professional enough to fool anyone. He should've stayed at the house. He could've protected his sister. Dragged her out of the house—made sure she didn't drink too much.

He sat up straight, opening the door. Would it have made a difference? Would it have stopped her from drinking? Would it have stopped her from going to another party?

The door to the garage squeaked open. Keith didn't oil

hinges. The louder they squeaked, the better. Josh trotted up the carpeted staircase, onto the main level and into the house. Steve's voice drifted up the stairs. Tape unraveled from a roll, again and again.

Josh walked through the kitchen, and jogged down the concrete staircase, sliding his hand down the metal railing.

"Where've you been?" Keith looked up from the packages. "I called you, texted you like ten times."

"Doesn't matter." Josh shrugged, stopping at the end of the table.

"I need you to drive to Lamar." Keith started taping a bag.

"Tonight? That's a two-hour drive."

Keith tossed the bag on top of the others. He pulled the half-smoked cigar out from between his teeth, and looked at Josh. "Doesn't matter."

Josh slid his hands in his pockets, lifting his chin. "It's eight-thirty. I'm not driving in the middle of the night."

"I need it gone." He stuffed the cigar between his teeth, returning his focus to the table. He glanced at Josh. "You'll get it done."

"And if I don't?"

His stomach churned. He squared his shoulders.

Keith removed his cigar. He turned his body toward Josh.

"Remember our deal," Keith said.

"I remember."

Steve set his package on the table and looked at Josh.

"I changed my mind." His heart bounced against his chest. He rubbed his palms against his legs inside his pockets.

"No," Keith shook his head, "I—" Keith's focused drifted away. He stared at the concrete floor. "Listen." He held his cigar in front of him.

Someone knocked on the door.

"You expecting company?" Steve asked.

The ceiling creaked. They looked up, listening to footsteps.

"Anyone home?" A man's voice drifted down the stairs.

"You know him?" Steve asked.

Keith jerked his head toward Steve. "Sshh!"

"Hey," the man paused, "over here."

Josh knew that voice. The same voice that gave him his speeding ticket.

His knees weakened. He couldn't feel his feet in his shoes. He glanced at the staircase, then at Keith. The door above the stairs squeaked. Someone stepped on the first stair.

"Cops," Steve said.

Keith stuffed the cigar in his mouth. He nodded toward the fire exit behind the window. Josh stared at the drugs on the table. He could climb up the fire exit; drive away with a pickup they had already spotted. A license plate already written down. Or—or what? Or move, away from his family, away from Olivia.

The window slid open. The metal ladder clinked against the fire exit.

Away from everything. All his mistakes. Never return

to Shallow River. Who would his sister become? Footsteps creaked down the stairs. Josh looked at the ladder leading up the galvanized frame. Steve's feet disappeared at the top of the window frame.

"We have a warrant to search this house and everyone in it."

He could. He could run; fail his sister, himself, Olivia. A different state. A new life. Josh stared at the window.

"Turn around." He sensed the man standing behind him. "We have a few questions we'd like to ask you."

Josh looked over the drugs on the table. He let his gaze drift down to his toes.

"Turn around."

He lifted his chin, breathed deeply, and faced the cops.

CHAPTER TWENTY-FOUR

Lindy tilted her head back, breathing in the early morning air, the hot coffee warming her hands. She pulled the blanket over her shoulder and took a sip, the coffee steaming her nose. The mid-August sun peaked over the horizon, gleaming against the clouds. She teeter-tottered her feet, pushing the swing back and forth.

Spring birds no longer sung in the trees. Lindy closed her eyes. *Nothing.* Not a sound. She opened her eyes. The sun began to shine onto the end of the round-top. She brought the coffee to her mouth, breathing in the steam. She took another sip, savoring the flavor before it slid down her throat.

Inside the house, someone poured coffee into a cup. Lindy turned her head. Footsteps padded toward the screen door. Dave stepped onto the porch. Hair a mess, his eyes halfway open. Lindy slid to one end of the swing. She waved her head, urging Dave toward her. He smiled, sitting down next to her.

"I love it here."

Dave nodded. "Every morning I sat here, wishing I could share it with someone." He looked at her. "Here you are."

Here she was. With a lifetime of experiences behind her, feeling twenty years younger. Lindy lifted her coffee cup. "Here's to us."

Dave studied her. He lifted his cup, clicking it against hers. "Here's to us." He kissed her cheek and scooted closer, putting his arm around her shoulder.

The window next to the porch roof slid open.

Lindy sipped her coffee. Olivia would come downstairs soon. She needed to make breakfast for everyone. What would it be like to live without the obligation of a child? Like young newlyweds. Something she had never experienced.

Dave gulped his coffee. He balanced his cup on his leg. "Why do you treat Olivia the way you do?"

He'd noticed. After four months of marriage. Lindy gripped her cup, the warmth of the coffee rising up her body.

She leaned away from his embrace, and looked at him. "What do you mean?"

"It's different with you two." He looked at her. "You ignore her presence; the two of you never make plans together—unless it's work or somewhere both of you are expected to be."

"Maybe you're—" Something stabbed Lindy's belly button. She jerked forward. Increased pain scraped down her abdomen. Her mouth formed an O shape, shallow breaths escaped her lungs. The coffee cup shattered on the concrete porch, spilling coffee over her slippers.

'Lindy!" Dave put his hand on her back. "What's wrong?"

She pushed against her side, crunching her stomach, squeezing her eyes shut.

"Should I call an ambulance?"

She bit her teeth together, holding in a cry.

"I'm calling an ambulance." Dave jumped up. Lindy gripped his arm. She needed him here with her.

She breathed, the pain subsiding. A dull ache lingering on her right side.

Dave sat down, reaching for her hand. "What happened?"

Lindy rubbed her side with her free hand. "I'm not sure," she said.

What did other girls do when their boyfriend didn't answer his phone? Should she wait a day before she tried again? Olivia held her thumb above the call button. 5:37, he had been off work for over half an hour. Plenty of time to check his phone.

Olivia looked out of the windshield. Too young girls squalled in front of the feed store, fighting over Twizzlers. The bag ripped open, Twizzlers landed on the sidewalk, around their feet.

The store closed at six. She needed to get the feed if she wanted to be home before dinner. Could his phone have died or broken? He could've borrowed a phone. Maybe she should stop at his house. They hadn't spoken since Sunday. In the last five days he should've managed to talk to her, somehow.

Would she look desperate if she stopped by his house? She

clicked the lock button on her phone and shut off the engine. Probably. She would try again after dinner. If he didn't pick up, should she assume the worst?

The bell jingled above the glass door. She slid the keys into her pocket and walked toward the animal feed. Her boots clopped against the stained floor. She flung a bag of grain over her shoulder and squatted to pick up a bag of chicken feed.

She heaved the grain off her shoulder and onto the counter. "The one on the floor is chicken feed," she said to the clerk.

She stepped aside, waiting for the cashier to come around the counter. He searched the bag for a barcode. His mullet caught in the neckline of his shirt. A few whiskers popped out of his cheeks. She guessed him to be fourteen or fifteen years old. More her age than Josh or Nate.

"Could you add one more of each?"

The boy nodded.

Copies of the Shallow River newspaper were lying on the counter, beside the box of homemade caramel.

A picture of Josh. Olivia lifted a copy, reading the headline: *Josh Morgan Agrees to Criminal Charges.*

"It's too bad, isn't it?" the boy asked, ringing up the cost. "His family's the spectacle of perfection. They own nearly half of Shallow River. Rich boy's not so perfect after all."

Olivia's pulse bounced against her chest. *"Found in the basement of a local drug dealer…"* Olivia scanned the article. *"…currently at the county jail."* Her stomach dropped.

She looked at the picture again. Her boyfriend printed on the front page

"Can I go there?" Olivia looked at the boy.

"The jail?"

She stared at him.

"Maybe," he shrugged, "I—I don't know."

"Where is it?"

"Along Waterman Avenue."

Olivia held the paper between her fingers and lifted the feed off the counter, draping it over her shoulder. Questions swirled in her mind. He never told her. Probably never planned to.

"Put it on Dave Unruh's tab."

Olivia walked out the store, stood in front of the glass doors and breathed. She could throw up. Josh looked younger on the picture. Not like the Josh she'd grown to love. The Josh that said he loved her. She licked her lips, breathing in.

She flung the sack of feed onto the pickup bed and hopped into the cab. What would she say? She couldn't go home. Not after reading what she read. She needed to hear it from him.

Olivia filled her lungs, shifting the pickup into reverse.

Ten minutes later, she walked down the stairs of the local law enforcement office. She balled her fingers into her palm, trying to ease the tingling. Her stomach knotted. The painted brick walls smelled of dirt. Olivia looked at the top of the walls. The smell probably came from the crack in the window frames leveled at the ground.

She paused at the last step, hiding behind the wall. She smelled like motor oil and horse manure. Hair grazed her neck. By the end of the day, half of her hair usually stuck out of her braid. Why didn't she redo her hair before she came in?

A chair scraped against the concrete floor.

"Where are you going?"

Josh's voice. Olivia's breath caught in her throat. Her fingertips touched the cold, stained wall. She shouldn't feel nervous. The man that loved her, that cared about her, stood behind those bars.

"You have a visitor."

Olivia breathed deeply, lifted her head, and stepped around the stairway. Her breath caught in her stomach. Overgrown whiskers covered his face. Hair dangled over his ears.

The guard unlocked the door, he backed up, opening the cell. Josh looked at her. Olivia rubbed the goose bumps on her arms. She stepped in front of the bars. Had he slept at all in the last several days? His large pupils looked loaded with worry; dark blue lines countered his eye lashes.

"You can go in there or he can come out here," the guard said.

"How'd you find me?"

Olivia walked into the cell. The iron door swung, clunking against the frame. She breathed deeply, rubbing her fingers against her jeans. Her throat clogged. The newspaper, she'd left it in the pickup.

She swallowed, opening her throat. "I read it in the newspaper."

He let the words sink in, bobbing his chin. Like he'd expected it. He rubbed his jaw, inhaling deeply. What had he done?

He stepped forward, reaching for her hands. "I promise I never meant to hurt you, Olivia."

"You could have told me."

"I didn't think you'd go out with me if you knew."

He didn't know her secret. He didn't know that nothing he did could ever compare to her selfish act.

"I wouldn't have cared."

He searched her eyes, holding her hands. How could she judge anyone else's life, while hiding the greatest mistake anyone could ever make? Anyone who loved her, deserved all her love. For whatever it was worth.

She lowered her eyes to the floor. "Now what?"

She felt him staring at her. Something shifted. Had he looked away? Olivia looked out the corner of her eye. Josh stared at the wall, tears pooling in his eyes. He knew.

Olivia straightened, stealing his focus. Her stomach tightened. He planned on pleading guilty. He planned on leaving her.

"I was tired of running."

Her eyes widened. He couldn't leave.

"I needed to do something right."

"Something right?" she raised her voice. What about her? What about their relationship?

"All my life I've made mistakes." He gripped her palms. "It was time I did the right thing."

She squeezed his knuckles, shaking his hands. "No." *No, no, no,* she wanted to scream.

He stepped closer. "Olivia, don't make this harder than it already is." He stroked her knuckles. "I won't forget you."

"No," Olivia yelled. She stepped back, pushing his hands away. "No."

He reached for her hand. She slapped it away, eyes focused on him. "What about me? Did you not think about me at all?"

A tear escaped his eye. Uncombed hair poked his eye brows. She loved this man. He loved her. She saw it in his eyes; felt it in his touch. Why would he do this? Why would he separate himself from her?

"You're the only—" she choked. Why would she admit her sorrow to him? He wouldn't understand, he didn't know the full story. He never would.

She squeezed her eyes shut. *Stop staring at me.* She should leave before she cried.

She breathed deep and heavy, filling her body with air.

"I leave the day after tomorrow."

She opened her eyes, looking up at him. Her eyes burning. "When's your court date?"

"Tuesday."

"I won't see you again?"

His shoulders sagged, shriveled and vulnerable, appearing

five years older. The sadness evaporated from him, like steam. Not like the Josh she'd met four months ago.

He shook his head.

Olivia clenched her teeth and stepped forward. She lifted her arms, then dropped them, resisting the urge to embrace him. To feel his body next to hers. To feel his heartbeat in his chest. To feel his arms wrapped around her. To never let go.

He lifted his hand, tracing her temple. She held his hand, his rough fingers lingering on her cheek.

"I love you, Olivia," he said.

Did he? She closed her eyes. *Yes, he had.*

She nodded, afraid to speak.

He wrapped his hand around her fingers. He wanted to place her hand on his back and wrap his arms around her. He wanted to rest his head on hers and feel her body against his. He squeezed her fingers, so much that they probably hurt. She dropped her hand to her side; he didn't let go.

"I should go."

He stroked his thumb against the back of her hand. Their eyes met. He fought every urge to forgo common sense. He now knew what people meant when they said, their heart shattered. Every part of his being wanted to hold her; to ask her to wait for him.

"I..."

He wanted her to say it. He wanted to hear it one more

time. That she loved him. That she would wait for him. But he couldn't ask her to do that. He didn't know how long his sentence would be. He couldn't ask her to spend the rest of her youth waiting for a boyfriend in prison.

She needed to move on.

Josh lowered his eyes to her boots. He breathed, closing his eyes. She needed to forget about him. He needed to become the guy she once knew.

She cleared her throat. He looked up.

"I have to go." She released his hand.

She stared at him, leaving something unsaid. She leaned in and kissed his cheek. She lingered; placed her arms around his neck and stepped back, before he could hug her. She turned around and walked out of the cell.

He watched her. She wore boot-cut jeans instead of skinny jeans, but she still wore a T-shirt, still did her hair in a loose braid, and was still the prettiest girl he'd ever seen.

The deputy closed the cell door. It clinked into place. The sound echoed throughout the basement. He'd never felt more alone. He'd never been more aware of the stillness around him, the emptiness. He breathed, turning on his heels, backing up until his calves touched the cot. He sat down and looked up. At what, he didn't know.

Was God up there, or was He in his cell? Was he sitting beside him? Was God inside his heart? How could the King of the world live inside *his* heart?

"God," he said aloud, "if you're in here, don't leave me."

He felt a presence, something he had never felt. "Stay with me."

Lindy dipped her fingers into the bowl of buttered popcorn. It could have used more salt. She licked the residue off her teeth, washing it down with sweet tea. Less butter too. She stepped around the counter and sat down on a bar stool, fighting the urge to rub her feet.

A quick break before dinner. She scanned the counter for the latest newspaper. *Did they not have it yet? Dave must have the mail in his farm pickup.*

Voices drifted up the front porch steps. Lindy leaned back, peeking out the dining room window. Mary's Kia sat in front of the house. Lindy scanned the floor; her ankles, covered in grass clippings. She brushed the grass onto the floor and scurried to the mudroom. A few broom strokes piled the grass together. She swept it onto the dustpan, then dumped it into the trash can. Several knocks bounced against the door.

Lindy leaned the broom against the washing machine and strode toward the door. She calmed herself before she opened it.

"Come on in," she held the door open, "you're just in time for popcorn and sweet tea."

They left their flipflops on the porch. Both girls carried a slitted box with an image of a peach on the side.

"Thank you, but we stopped at Scooter's on our way back

from Colby." Mary heaved the box onto the dining table, careful not to bump her second trimester belly.

Sam set her box beside Mary's. She snuck her hand underneath the lid and lifted a peach out of the box. Lindy didn't remember ordering two boxes of peaches. Mary slid back a chair and sat down. She crossed her ankles, displaying her flip-flop-tanned feet.

"I told Granny that I'd offer to do it at our house, but John's still remodeling the kitchen. Why I let him convince me to remodel during pregnancy, I don't know." Mary rested a forearm on the table and leaned back in the chair. "Grandma talked about preserving the peaches this coming Monday, if that works for you?" Mary paused, watching Lindy. "You didn't know?" Mary raised her voice. "Oh, I thought Dave talked to you about it."

"No, he didn't."

Sam scrubbed the fuzz off her peach underneath the faucet. She shook the water off and closed the faucet. "How's Olivia doing?" she asked, opening the cutlery drawer.

"Why do you ask?"

Mary jerked her focus toward Sam, her face stern. Sam's skin turned cherry red. She pressed down on the peach, squeezing juice out as she peeled. Sam glanced at Lindy, then bit into the peach. Mary shifted, folding her hands in her lap.

Mary looked up. "Her boyfriend, Josh, was arrested Sunday."

"I'm worried about her." Sam wiped the peach juice off her

chin. "She defended Josh every time I mentioned something about him that she didn't like. I think she really liked him."

What would Mrs. Bell say now? *"How could a mother ever let her daughter go out with a guy like Josh."* Lindy could already hear it. She could hear the chatter in the house.

Lindy stepped toward the table and sat down behind the peaches. "Who told you?"

"It's in the newspaper." Sam rinsed off the knife and threw the peel into the trash.

Lindy opened her mouth. The waste belonged in the chicken scrap bucket.

"Where is Olivia? I'd like to talk to her. I'm sure she could use a friend right now."

Lindy closed her lips and shrugged. In the tractor, raking wheat straw. She wouldn't be done until later in the evening. But nothing would help Olivia. She would carry her feelings to the grave, unless someone pried them out of her.

"We should leave you to your thoughts." Mary stood up, using the table for support.

Lindy looked at Mary. What did Mary think of her? She would never have allowed Sam to date a boy almost four years older than her.

"We should go, Sam." Mary walked toward the door.

"Not on my part," Lindy said, looking at the peaches. Where would she store them?

Sam wiped the counter. "A few girls and I are going shopping tonight, for back to school. I'm home-schooled, but I'll use it as an excuse for new clothes." She laughed, stepping around the counter. "So, I should get home."

"And I have to cook dinner yet," Mary said.

Sam stood beside her mom. The two looked like sisters. They dressed similar; they did their hair the same.

"But if Olivia needs anything, let me know. Is she going to be off work early? She could join us, if she wants to. I'll text her. It'd be good for her to get her mind off things."

"I apologize for barging in with peaches. One would think we didn't have any manners."

Lindy lifted the corners of her lips, about to speak.

"If you prefer, we can do it at Granny's house. I'm sure we could work something out."

Lindy stood up. "No," she shook her head, "we can do it here." If they brought all the supplies. She should ask them to. Or she could buy her own. Would they think her unprepared if she didn't have anything for canning?

"Okay, so Monday it is?"

Lindy smiled. "Monday works." She'd go to town tomorrow and buy everything she needed. She'd have to Google a list of essentials.

CHAPTER TWENTY-FIVE

Lindy poured the sauce over the tortilla rolls. She licked the spatula and dropped it into the sink. The mudroom door opened; someone took off their boots. Lindy sprinkled cheese on top of the dish and slid the casserole onto the oven rack. She pulled out a stack of plates, setting them on the counter.

"Smells good in here," Dave said, walking into the dining room.

"I wasn't expecting you guys for another half-hour." Lindy opened the cutlery drawer, the forks clinking against each other.

"We had to quit for today. A part broke on the rake. The part store in Shallow River doesn't have a new one." Dave grabbed the newspaper off the counter and pulled a chair away from the table. "Nate's on his way to Leoti right now."

Dave sat down, shaking the newspaper open. "I called in, they said they'd have it sitting out for him."

Olivia walked into the kitchen. "I broke it." She opened a cabinet, placing three glasses on the counter, one by one. Straw shedding from her shirt, landing next to the cauliflower.

"Brush the dust—" Lindy stared at the endangered broccoli salad.

Olivia glanced down. She uttered a four-letter word. A word Lindy had never heard her say. Olivia brushed her hand down her belly, tapping dust into the air. She extended her elbow, bumping a drinking glass. The glass teeter-tottered until it fell into the sink, shattering. Another word escaped her lips.

"Those words are not allowed in this house," Dave said.

Olivia looked at Dave. She glanced at the newspaper in his hands. "Yes, sir."

An acknowledgement Erick taught her, something Olivia didn't say often. Lindy stepped toward the salad ingredients on the counter. She broke off a chunk of cauliflower and began breaking it into pieces.

"Sweep up the straw. It'll be okay."

Olivia studied the straw on the counter.

"Hey," Lindy stole her attention. She nodded toward the mudroom. "It'll be okay."

Olivia watched her; their eyes met. Lindy saw a deep sadness in her eyes, deeper than she'd ever seen it. How much pain could she take? What was going on inside that head of hers?

Lindy broke eye contact. She nodded toward the mudroom. "Go," she said.

Olivia stepped around her.

"Ouch!" Olivia pushed her hands against her hip.

"What happened?"

Olivia kicked the bottom cabinet. She hopped around, holding her left side.

"Sit down," Lindy said.

She stood up straight, in the middle of the kitchen. She filled her lungs, dropping her hands.

Dave laid the newspaper on the table. "It's been a long day. Why don't you rest." He stood up. "I'll sweep the straw."

Olivia walked out of the kitchen, into the living room, and up the stairs.

Lindy placed her palms on the edge of the counter. She looked at the broken glass splattered around the sink. She had broken several dishes in that clay sink, but Olivia hadn't. Olivia didn't mess up. She held herself together.

Lindy grabbed mayo out of the fridge. She set it beside the vinegar, and stared into the living room.

Dave detached the dustpan from the broom handle and started sweeping.

"Use the vacuum cleaner instead. The glass also needs to be cleaned up."

Dave clipped the dustpan onto the handle.

"Has she been like this all day?" Lindy measured out the dressing ingredients, pouring them into the wooden bowl.

Dave nodded. "I don't know what to do about it." He stared at the salad.

"Did you not see the front page?"

He shook his head. "I didn't have to. I was in the co-op

this morning, grabbing coffee." Dave leaned against the counter. "News spreads faster than the paper can print it."

Dave looked at her. "What are we going to do?"

Olivia never needed help. After her father passed, she became independent. She grew up instantly. She forced herself to. Rather, Lindy forced her to. The words she yelled at her the night of Erick's death—Lindy bit her teeth, closing her eyes.

"Lindy," Dave said.

Vinegar spilled over the tablespoon, onto the counter.

"Goodness." She set the vinegar down, staring at the puddle. Dave gave her a rag. "Thanks." She wiped it up and laid the rag beside the bowl.

How would she speak to a teenage girl? Where would she start? At the beginning, tell her everything. Would it help her, or make it worse?

"I thought he seemed like a good kid," Dave said.

Lindy mixed the salad.

"I guess he is, otherwise he wouldn't have admitted his wrong. Freedom or years in prison. A tough choice to make."

"Is that where he's going?" Lindy asked.

"Most likely. Drug trafficking is serious; it won't be handled lightly."

The boy Olivia thought she loved, gone. For how many years?

Lindy looked at Dave. "Do you think Olivia knows?"

Dave shrugged; his arms crossed over his chest. "That would explain her behavior. She probably feels betrayed."

Lindy remembered the feeling too well. She could still feel the bitter wind against her cheeks, the sting in her eyes from holding back tears. College campus never looked the same after that.

"Maybe I should have noticed something suspicious about him. I could have kept her from going out with him. I hate to see her hurting."

Lindy gave the salad a final stir and placed her hands on the edge of the counter. She helped raise Olivia. She witnessed all her heart-breaks, yet they never bothered her the way this bothered Dave. She closed the mayo lid. Nearly seventeen years of mothering, compared to four months of fathering. What was wrong with her?

Dave stood straight, scanning the counter. "Is dinner ready?"

"Five more minutes."

"I'll clean up Olivia's mess then." Dave stepped past her. "Wish I could clean up the other mess too."

Lindy wrinkled the dish cloth between her fingers. She knew where she went wrong. For sixteen years she'd known how to make it right. Lindy polished the counter. But she didn't. How could she? How could she forget a feeling like that? When Olivia reminded her of it every day.

It's not her fault.

She blamed Olivia for everything. The deepest pain she'd ever experienced, she blamed on a child. A child that did everything for her, until she gave up hope. Until she realized her mother would never love her the way her father had. Lindy wrung the cloth, squeezing vinegar onto the counter. Could she look at Olivia differently? Could she see her and not see the past?

The bailiff opened the mahogany gate. Josh rubbed the red cuff marks on his wrist. Mahogany furniture filled the room. A big room with no windows—too big. It made him feel small. Like a speck in someone's eye. Small, yet the center of attention. He scratched his chest, expecting it to fill his lungs. He inhaled the pine-sol scented air. But his lungs remained empty.

One person sat in the back. Josh would recognize her face anywhere. How did she get here? Their eyes met. He placed his hand on his chair, steadying himself. Would he see his sister again? What would he say to her if he did? Would he tell her the whole story? Would he explain the reason for his decisions? Or would he stay quiet, allowing her to believe the worst of him.

Josh faced forward.

The judge walked into the room, her gray hair swaying slightly above her shoulders. Tall and determined, like the woman behind the counter in the liquor store. Without the extra body fat.

The judge stepped onto the platform behind the bench. She laid a folder on the table and sat down.

She stared at Josh, dipping her long nose toward the seat.

"Sorry," he mumbled, screeching his chair toward the table.

Dry fingers slid across paper. The judge shuffled through them, glancing at him in between. She tapped them against the wood, straightened them and laid them down.

"You were charged with drug trafficking and possession of illegal drugs at the time of your arrest. Do you plead guilty or not guilty?"

In the hallway voices echoed. A bench squeaked behind him. He gripped his fingers, wringing his hands beneath the table.

"Do you plead guilty or not guilty?"

He glared at the judge. "Guilty."

Josh leaned his curved spine into the chair. Someone shifted on a bench behind him: Veronica. He rubbed his palm. He'd made enough bad decisions, he hoped this would never be one of them.

The judge glanced at the papers, and returned her focus to Josh. "This hearing is adjourned until further notice." She clopped the gavel against the table, picked up the folder and left the room.

He breathed in, puffing out his chest. He looked at his sister. She held on to her handbag, appearing several years older than her age. Josh lowered his chin, brushing the red marks around his wrist. How long would they make him wait? Another day, another week?

He stood up, waiting for the bailiff. The bailiff grabbed his elbow and escorted him out of the court room.

The cell smelled of urine and mold. The state could afford better. The prisoners deserved better—some of them. Josh exhaled, sitting down on the cot. The door shut; he winced. He wouldn't be here long. They'd transport him to prison, eventually.

He laid down, the springs squeaking. At least the mattress didn't have lumps. His stomach growled. If he closed his eyes, he could almost forget the urine smell. He could smell the fried chicken his mom used to bring home. Or the ribs they used to order at Sandy's. He could nearly feel the steam from the potatoes on his nose.

The sheriff's voice broke his reverie. He opened his eyes. Two years, five years, how long would he go without lunch at Sandy's? He turned on his side, using his elbow as a pillow. *Lord God, help me.* He closed his eyes. "I'm sorry," he whispered.

His sister's voice. Josh opened one eye. He heard his sister's voice.

He sat up. How'd she get down here? Veronica stepped in front of the cell.

"I don't know what to say to you." Her hands hung beside her hips, shaking, like a vibrating alarm.

Josh ran his hands through his hair, pressing his head against his palms. He let his hands fall onto his legs, exhaling. "I did what I thought was right."

She glared at him. "What am I supposed to tell Mom and Dad?"

"Nothing. I'm sure they already know everything."

She blinked, lowering her eyes to the concrete floor. "They'll have questions."

Josh curled his fingers around the cot frame. "Word will spread."

She looked at him, her earrings dangling. "Why'd you do it?"

"For you." Josh let the words sink in. "Our actions have consequences." He stood up and stepped toward Veronica. "I want you to make better choices. Go to college; don't get kicked out. Know which friends to keep and which ones to lose."

He shook his head. "Don't make the same mistakes I did."

"Find a drug dealer, buy drugs, then go into business with one?"

Her words stung like January air. Josh inhaled. "Yeah."

Veronica rested her hands on her bag, curling her fingers around the strap. "My bus leaves in half an hour."

Did she not care? He wouldn't see her at Thanksgiving. He wouldn't know her friends, know her boyfriends, how they treated her. He wouldn't see her graduate.

He would be fenced in, while the rest of the world moved on.

She turned, her sandals scratching the floor. She stepped back and looked at him. "I'll visit."

"I'd like that."

She studied him, her eyes deep in thought. She blinked, lifting her head. "Good luck."

"Thanks."

After several seconds she looked away and walked down the hall.

Lindy rolled the chair back, clicking a pen in and out. She lifted the tip, and scratched her head, yawning. She could have used another hour of sleep. Or another coffee. She stared at the empty cup on the desk. It wouldn't take long to make another cup.

Dew drippled down the office window. Fog blocked the view to the wheat stubble. Condensation covered the window trim. Warm, humid morning air flowed through the screen. Apparently rare for an August morning. It reminded her of Topeka summers.

Lindy stretched her legs, and used the arm rest to push herself off the chair. A layer of dirt on the window frame was turning into mud from the heavy dew. Evidence of the need for new windows. She'd thought about cleaning them, maybe she should, but Dave needed to replace them. They let drafts in, and after every windy day, she'd find dirt on the frames.

Lindy breathed in the fresh air, increasing her want for another coffee.

The rooster crowed; underneath the tree, chickens pecked

the ground. She'd rather take a nap than fiddle with Dave's finances. She usually liked numbers, but her brain couldn't concentrate.

Footsteps climbed up the stairs.

Lindy walked to the office door. Olivia stepped onto the second floor, turning toward her room.

"What are you doing inside on a work-day morning?"

Olivia shrugged.

"Did Dave say you could have off?" Lindy walked into the hallway. "Is there not much to do?"

"I wanted a different pair of pants."

Olivia turned, the tear behind her knee fully visible. Lindy followed her into her room. Bowls filled with crushed chips and popcorn kernels sat on her desk. Water bottles laid piled beside the overflowing trash can. A pack of beef jerky laid on her unmade bed. Lindy would've never thought Olivia's room could look like this. What did she do over the weekend?

Olivia threw a pair of pants on the bed. What happened to the girl Erick raised and loved?

Lindy walked to the desk and collected the bowls. "How have you been?" she asked, picking up the beef jerky.

"Fine." Olivia stood beside the bed, watching her.

"Have you talked to Josh at all?" Lindy straightened, setting the bowls on the desk.

"Yes."

She lifted the trash bag out of the trashcan. "I'm sure it's not easy on you," she tied the trash bag, "all of this."

Olivia picked up the pair of pants. "I need to go back to work."

"If there's anything..." How would she help? Lindy lowered her eyes to the rug underneath the bed.

"I won't ask you."

Lindy lifted her head.

Olivia waved the pants around. "You don't care about me except when it comes to Josh. You probably never liked him to begin with."

"It wasn't that, it's just that I hardly knew him."

"Because you never tried." Olivia arched her upper back, raising her voice. "You didn't want to know him, because that meant you'd have to get to know your own daughter."

"I know you. I watched you grow up."

"Hardly, I might as well have lost both my parents in Dad's accident." Olivia studied her, lowering her arms. "You blame me. That's why you don't love me. You can't forget what happened."

Lindy did blame her. She spent years resenting Olivia, not only about Erick's death.

"I did *everything* for you," Olivia shouted. "I needed you!"

Lindy swallowed the lump in her throat.

Olivia straightened her back, shaking her head. "Do you know how desperately I wanted my mom to love me?"

Olivia's braid draped over her shoulder. At the other side of the bed, she appeared taller than she was. Her shoulders appeared more muscular than Lindy remembered. A slid-up sleeve revealed her tan line. She'd grown into a woman in front of her eyes and she never noticed.

Lindy shook her head.

"I believed you. I believed that it was *my* fault." Olivia shook the pants, her grip creating a crease in the denim. "You don't know how much guilt I laid on myself," she shouted. "I killed my father. Because of me you became a widow."

"You didn't," Lindy yelled.

Olivia stared at her. Lindy swallowed. "You didn't kill him," she calmed her voice, shaking her head. "It wasn't just that."

"What then?" Olivia lowered the pants, "why would a mother not love her daughter?"

Lindy looked into Olivia's eyes. "I'm not your mother."

Olivia dropped the pants on the bed, glaring at Lindy.

CHAPTER TWENTY-SIX

Lindy ground the popcorn between her teeth. She pulled the blanket over her knees and brought the bowl to her chest.

"Was this not what you wanted?"

Lindy could still hear the anger in Erick's voice.

The rain dribbling against the diner window. *"What am I going to do?"* It was the first time she saw Erick cry. She should have comforted him. Instead, she hated that he would cry for *her* loss.

Lindy remembered the night it happened. She sat in the hallway, not because of Jenifer, but because of Erick. Afraid that if she didn't, something would happen between them. Everyone in the hallway heard the cries. The nurses looked up from their desk, glancing at the room. Everyone wondered the same thing.

She could still feel the cold, wooden arm rest against her forearms. For thirty-six hours Erick didn't leave *her* side. She never wanted the night to end the way it did. She stood underneath the doorway. Nurses scrambling around the room;

nurses suctioning fluids out of the baby. Doctors fussing over Jenifer.

Jenifer looked at her. Her eyes wide open, unaware of the people around her. Sweaty hair clung to her neck; her gown somewhat draped over her shoulder. The life draining from her, her pail arm flopped off the bed, pulling out the IV Jenifer's eyes never looked away. Lindy watched them, until the doctor shut them. She never wanted to step foot in that hospital again.

Lindy crunched popcorn between her teeth, squeezing her eyes shut.

Everything about that night, came back to her when Erick died. In fourteen years, the smell of the hospital hadn't changed.

Lindy tilted her head back, resting her head on the couch. *God, what have I done?*

The front door opened. *Please don't let it be Sam or Mary.*

"What's wrong," Dave asked.

Lindy lifted her head. He stood underneath the frame that separated the dining room from the living room.

Lindy shook her head. How could she tell him? A secret she should have told him a year ago. What if he left her? Grew angry at her. Told her the truth: that she was a wicked, selfish person. His family would shun her. They'd want nothing to do with her.

"Something's bothering you." He sat down, reaching for Lindy's hand.

"I can't tell you," Lindy bit her lip, "please don't make me."

Dave brought her to his chest and wrapped his arms around her. Lindy swallowed, blinking rapidly.

The judge sat down behind her table. Josh lowered his bottom, looking at the seat beneath him.

"No need to sit."

Josh looked at the judge.

"This won't take long."

He stood straight, folding his hands in front of him. He squared his shoulders, puffing his chest.

"I've reviewed your case several times." The judge folded her hands and looked at him. "I've never had anyone plead guilty to a charge against federal drug trafficking. It's a serious crime. It does not get handled lightly."

She breathed in, glancing at the papers. She shifted her shoulders and sat up straight.

"With the information you gave us about the members of the operation, and your clear record, I have decided on a shorter sentence."

Josh lifted his chin.

She looked at him. "You are to serve a four-year sentence in federal prison. At that time, you will be released on a two-year probation." She banged the gavel against the wood.

Josh winced, his eyes trailing toward the floorboards.

Four years. A six-year consequence for one summer of

wrong decisions. The same summer he fell in love. Where would she be in four years? Would she want anything to do with him?

"Why did you do it?"

Josh looked at the judge. "Excuse me?"

"Why did you plead guilty?" she asked.

She looked like a guest at the family dinner table. Her arms propped up on the table, awaiting a juicy answer.

Why would he choose four years in prison? He could have run, he could have continued what he was doing, he could have lost Veronica, he could have kept lying to Olivia. He could have taken his case to trial; pretended like he didn't deserve prison. Or he could serve his time and start fresh.

He lifted his shoulders, focusing his gaze at her. "Wouldn't you?" he asked.

The judge looked at him, thinking. She drew her shoulders back and straightened her posture. She looked at the papers, tapping her fingers against the edges. "In all my years as a judge, I have never had a case—" she looked at him "—or met a person, like you."

Josh nodded. The sheriff placed a hand on Josh's arm. Cold aluminum scraped his wrist bone. The cuffs clicked, locking one wrist at a time. Josh curled his fingers, itching to rub his wrist.

Would it be worth it? He had four years to plan the rest of his life. Where would he go? Back to Shallow River? Would he find Olivia? Or would he start in a new state, away from everyone and everything that brought him where he was.

The sheriff led him through the center of the room, out the wooden doors, into the hallway. The door clicked shut, echoing along the marble flooring. Wherever he went, he had a feeling he wouldn't be alone. God would be with him.

Lindy set the groceries on the counter. She tore a piece off the paper bag and used it to wipe the sweat off her neck. Immediately disgusted by her decision. The AC grazed her bare legs. She slid her flipflops off, allowing the floor to cool her feet. The weather station standing in front of the wall read 103 degrees.

She pulled out the condiments, setting them beside the watermelon. She walked toward the kitchen knives, lifting her hair, allowing the AC to dry her neck. *A thick slice of watermelon.* She couldn't think of anything better.

A flower bouquet sat beside the refrigerator in a shallow woven basket, filled with baby's breath, sunflowers and daisies. A card stuck above the flowers. Lindy stood in the middle of the kitchen. Who would give her flowers?

They were for her, right? She stepped closer. Why would Dave give her flowers, in August? She extended two fingers and pulled the card off the plastic stick. Roses. Lindy brought the card to her nose. The paper smelled like roses. She lifted the flap.

Husbands, love your wives, just as Christ loved the church and gave himself up for her. Ephesians 5:25

Dear Lindy, I know you're hurting. I know you don't want to tell me, but one day you will; when you're ready I'll be here. But know this: I love you. Nothing you say or do will change that. Above all, know that God loves you. If you can't confide in me, I pray you confide in him. Not for my sake, but for yours. You deserve to be at peace.

Forever yours, Dave.

Lindy reread the card. She glanced at the flowers, then read the card again. What did she do to deserve this? She squeezed the card. Nothing. She did nothing to deserve such love. Lindy listened, waiting for a door to open. Where was he? She wanted to thank him. To lay her head on his chest, hug him and never let go.

She brought the card to her chest. She needed to confess. To hear that everything was okay.

But it wasn't.

Lindy shook her head. It wasn't okay to resent one's daughter—Erick's daughter. It wasn't okay to hold Erick's mistakes against his child.

Nearly seventeen years ago. She should have moved on, forgotten about it, but she hadn't. She couldn't. Lindy inhaled, lowering herself to the floor. She sat crisscross in the middle of the kitchen. She just couldn't.

You need to.

Lindy's hands shook. She looked at the card. *Oh Erick, Jenifer*... she shook her head. "I'm sorry," she whispered. "I ruined your daughter."

"Lord, I have to tell you," Lindy raised her voice, "I know you're all-knowing. But I have to tell you," she breathed. "I'm sorry. I'm sorry I'm not the mom you want me to be, the mom she needs me to be."

"I can't move on. I can't do it."

Yes, you can.

"It hurt. Everything, it hurts too much."

Lindy pressed her fists against her chest, applying pressure until her breast bone hurt. Where was it? Where was everything that she hid from Olivia all these years?

Lindy secured the card between her fingers and pushed her fist off the floor. She walked through the living room, into their bedroom. She opened the closet, scanning the top shelf. The box. She grabbed it off the shelf and held it in front of her. Every bit of proof, the keepsakes she had, rested in that box. Every secret neatly tucked underneath the lid, stashed away in a corner, for no one to see.

She opened it. She removed her keepsakes and set them on the dresser. The rest didn't belong to her. Lindy breathed, gripping the box.

Let go.

"Lord, forgive me." She squeezed her eyes shut. "I'm sorry," she shook the box, "for everything."

Lindy listened to her heart rate slow down. A bird chirped outside the window. The late afternoon sun gleamed onto the wooden bedframe. She loosened her grip on the box.

"Help me move on."

Give to everyone what you owe them. She owed Olivia the truth. She needed to give to her what had always been hers.

Lindy walked out of the room and up the stairs, her bare feet tapping against the wood planks.

Olivia's room remained the same. The bed unmade, a red stained bowl with watermelon seeds sitting on the desk. Lindy wiped her palm on her shorts, breathing in. She did this. She pushed Olivia to this point.

It took seventeen years to bring Olivia to this point. How long would it take to bring her back? Only with God's help could Olivia be restored to her old self. Only with God's help could she forgive herself. To have a mother who loved her would help too.

Lindy set the box on the desk. She stretched out her chest, wiping her hands on her hips. This belonged to Olivia. She looked at the box. She kept it from her long enough.

Lindy exhaled, closing her eyes. "Help her, Lord. Help *my* daughter."

She breathed. "Help me," she whispered.

Chunks of compacted grass fell from the mower deck,

spreading over the shop floor. Olivia pounded the chisel around the knives. She should have taken the knives off before she started.

"I'm not your mother," the words echoed through her mind. How could her mom keep that from her? How could Dad have kept that from her?

Olivia pounded grass, as hard as a rock. She should have cleaned the mower a month ago.

The chisel missed the grass clump. It clunked against the metal, the knife slicing into Olivia's wrist. Blood flowed down her arm. She wrapped a hand around her wrist, biting her teeth, holding back a scream. She opened her fingers, peeking at the wound, exposing her flesh. She swallowed, vomit rising up her throat.

With her heels, she slid herself backward, away from the deck. The side of her shirt dampened, the warmth dribbling down her hips. She walked to the table and rolled off several feet of shop cloth, wrapping it around her wrist.

Her shirt stuck to her ribs. She needed to change—to shower. She wiped her hand on the shop cloth and walked out the door. She blinked, adjusting her eyes to the sunlight. The afternoon sun burned her neck, the heat bouncing off the gravel.

She left her boots beside the front door, and scanned the concrete for any fresh blood drops. When she didn't see any, she walked into the kitchen.

She opened the medicine cabinet, the shop cloth becoming

unraveled. Blood smeared the counter edge, and the top of the silverware drawer. She needed to change.

Olivia wrapped fresh paper towel around the wound, then secured it with gauze and a clip. For nearly seventeen years they let her believe a lie. They—Lindy—let her believe that her own mother didn't want her. She let her live with regret, with guilt.

If she would have known, would she have devoted the last two years to gaining Lindy's love? To caring for her, honoring her. She might have for her dad. But he lied to her. He died, taking his secret with him.

Olivia shut her bedroom door.

She should have told him to wait out the storm.

Olivia leaned against the door, biting her teeth. She should have never called him that night. She would still have a parent, someone who loved her. Who truly wanted her, truly cared about her. Someone who wouldn't leave her.

She opened her mouth, relaxing her muscles. But she didn't. She didn't have anyone.

T-shirts draped over the open dresser drawer. She should've wrapped plastic around her arm so she could shower. She sighed, wrapping her hand around the wound. The tight grip relieved the sting. She needed to sit, to close her eyes and drift away.

The chair creaked as she sat down. She leaned back, the back of the chair pressing against her shoulder blades. An aged shoe box sat in front of her. Who would give her old shoes? Olivia heaved herself forward, lifting the lid off the box. It was full of stuff. She scooted the chair forward and leaned over the box.

Photos, a Bible … a picture of her dad. Olivia smiled. Had her dad ever looked that young? She didn't remember him with a mustache. Olivia lifted the photo. A woman. The woman smiled from ear to ear, her bangs touching the top of her eyelashes. Smooth black hair draped over her shoulder. She looked beautiful. Did *she* look like that?

A birth certificate laid at the bottom of the box. Olivia flipped it open. Her original birth certificate. Jenifer Bell Bennet: the mother's name. She grazed her fingers over the document. Born at three thirty-seven a.m. in Stormont Vail Hospital. The same hospital she last saw her dad.

Olivia flipped the photo of the woman. Faded handwriting covered the white background. *Jenifer at family Thanksgiving dinner.* Olivia looked at the photo again. Was this her mom?

She shuffled through the pictures. A funeral pamphlet. Olivia's heart stopped. On the pamphlet was a collage of pictures displayed on a floral background. Every picture showed a woman full of life.

What would it have been like to know her? To be in that picture with her, bike riding beside her. To have two parents that loved her. To have a mother to confide in, a mother who wanted to hear about her daughter's heartaches. Would she have loved her?

Olivia set the photos and pamphlet on the desk. She picked up the Bible that nested in the corner of the box. An English Standard Version. Her dad's Bible.

The leather cracked at the edges. The first half of the book was taped onto the spine. Dozens of flags peaked out of the Bible, marking wrinkled pages. She remembered her dad reading at the dining table. The only light in the house was his battery-operated lantern. She had asked him once why he read at eleven p.m. He told her, "It's when I hear Him the clearest."

She never heard Him.

Olivia lifted the cover. Sticky notes stacked on the yellow stained first page. Prayers, thoughts, verses, one over the other, from years of study. An envelope stuck out of the Bible. It marked John fifteen. The thirteenth verse was highlighted in pink. *Greater love has no one than this, that someone lay down his life for his friends.*

Olivia opened the envelope and removed a handwritten letter. Her dad's handwriting. She couldn't remember the last time she saw something he wrote.

> *Dear Olivia,*
>
> *Whether you read this letter while I'm still alive or whether I've gone home, I hope it answers all your questions. If I'm still alive at the time you're reading this, I hope you will speak to me again. Either way, I pray that you won't allow this secret to harden your heart.*

You were conceived during a sinful act that I committed. I hurt Lindy; I was unfair to your mother. But you are the greatest gift God has ever given me. By His grace, my sinful act brought the greatest experience a man could ask for: to love his child.

Your birth mom's name was Jenifer Bell Bennet. She died shortly after your delivery. You may never understand why I kept her memory from you, I myself am not sure why I did it. Perhaps I thought it would save you from heartbreak, or it would bring you closer to Lindy. To confess a sin to one's daughter is not an easy task.

Whatever you're feeling right now, I pray that you bring it to Christ. If you haven't accepted him as your Lord and Savior then I hope you do. That you ask him into your heart. My prayer for you is that you know the unending joy and ever-flowing peace that comes from living a life with Christ. That you know what it is like to mess up, but still be loved. The love you feel from me could never measure up to the love Christ has for you.

Know that I am sorry for any pain this may have caused you. Don't store up hatred or anger toward anyone. A life of pain is worthless, especially when relief can easily be found in Christ. Whenever you read this, I pray there is someone who can tell you more, should you ever want to know the full story.

Sincerely, your dad.

The paper shook in Olivia's fingers. The words blurred. She looked above the letter, out the window in front of her. *That you know what it is like to mess up* ... she knew. Oh, how she knew. Dad didn't know, when he wrote this, how badly she'd mess up. He didn't know that her mistake would be the death of him. Olivia gripped the paper.

... but still be loved. She shook her head. No one could love her. The only person who knew didn't love her. Olivia breathed, lifting her chin.

God knew, he knew her guilty conscience.

Olivia looked at the open Bible, lowering the letter. A pink highlighter marked one verse on the entire page: *Greater love has no one than this, that someone lay down his life for his friends.* His friends. She dropped her head, her forehead inches from the Bible.

... still be loved. Olivia leaned back, hugging her elbows. She picked up the Bible. How many times had her dad read it? The same stories he used to read to her. Read over and over again. Some letters were faded; ripped pages were taped back together.

Read it.

She dropped it.

She couldn't. It didn't apply to her. She glared at the wall-papered wall.

A cry drifted up the stairs, through the AC vents. Another cry. Olivia bolted out of her seat, the cry becoming steady. She ran out of her room and down the stairs.

CHAPTER TWENTY-SEVEN

Towels were draped over the coffee table, falling onto the woven rug. The laundry basket was lying on its side in front of the couch. Olivia stepped onto the rug, closer to Lindy. Lindy hunched over the couch arm rest, hugging her stomach. Olivia reached out, then pulled her hand back, rubbing her arm. She stepped around Lindy, into the living room square. The late afternoon sun faded behind the clouds, darkening the room.

"Call the ambulance," Lindy cried. She tucked her chin against her chest, her hair grazing the arm rest.

Olivia patted her pockets. Where did she leave her phone? She swirled around, searching the side tables for Lindy's phone. Shouldn't she call Dave first? He'd want to know. Olivia looked underneath the pillows, lifted the towels, then threw them down. She jogged into the kitchen, scanning the countertop.

Lindy cried, groaning. Something hit the floor. Olivia ran into the living room. An end table was lying on its side, the lamp shade rolled across the wood floor. Lindy stood on her knees, arched over, her forehead touching the floor.

Olivia squatted beside her. "Where's your phone?"

Lindy shook her head. Where did she leave hers? Olivia stroked her jeans. Lindy hugged her ribs, whimpering. She needed help.

An engine rolled onto the farm. Dave. Olivia jumped up and ran out of the house, the screen door bouncing off the frame. The rocks jabbed her sock-covered feet. Dave's pickup shut off in front of the round top. Olivia leaped onto the slab.

"Dave, call the ambulance, Mom's hurt."

His eyes widened, searching her face. He stepped toward the house. "How hurt?"

"She's crunched on the floor, crying." The scorching concrete began burning her feet.

He walked past her, breaking into a jog. Olivia followed. She jumped onto the porch, catching the screen door before Dave let it slam shut. Inside the house, Lindy laid curled on the floor. Dave dropped to one knee and placed his hands on Lindy's back.

"What's wrong?"

"My stomach," she breathed, "it hurts."

"Olivia," Dave yelled, "call the ambulance."

"I don't have my phone."

He slid a phone out of his pocket. Mom cried. Dave shook his head. "This can't wait." He slid the phone back in his pocket and scooted his arms underneath Mom's body. He brought her to his chest and stood up. "The ambulance won't get here soon enough."

Olivia walked past him, into the dining room. "I'll start the Yukon."

She jogged out the door, toward the vehicle parked in front of the lawn.

She opened a rear passenger door, then ran around the hood. She opened the driver door, sat down in front of the wheel, and reached for the keys. The keys rattled in her hand. She used both hands to find the ignition key. This wasn't like her. She needed to calm down. She started the engine and slid her hands underneath her legs.

Dave stepped into the Yukon, setting Mom on the seat next to him. He closed the door. Lindy rested her head on his shoulder, holding her stomach. Olivia put the vehicle in drive. She turned onto the blacktop and glanced into the rearview mirror.

"She's running a fever."

"How fast can I go?" Olivia glanced at Dave.

Dave kept his focus on his wife. He squeezed her hand and kissed the top of her head. He leaned his head back, closing his eyes.

Mom rolled her forehead on Dave's chest, groaning.

Olivia pressed the pedal to the floor. The Yukan's speed increased to its fullest potential. If lights began flashing behind her, she'd keep going. On the hospital parking lot, she'd let the cop answer his own question.

The gurney rolled onto the concrete. Automatic doors staying open. Dave laid Mom on the mat; her knees bent. He shut the Yukon door, and placed a hand on the gurney's frame.

"Let go, sir," the EMS said.

They rolled the gurney over the door frame, into the air-conditioned hospital. They strode down the vinyl tile flooring, taking up the entire hallway.

Olivia trotted beside Dave, her arms waving back and forth. "Where are they taking her?"

"I don't know." Dave jogged up to the medical team. "What's wrong with her?"

"Sounds like an appendix eruption. She'll have to go to emergency surgery."

"When? Now?" Dave asked.

The doctor stopped in front of the two open wooden doors. He turned toward Dave and Olivia. "Yes, now. If we don't act quickly the infection will spread, which could be life threatening."

Nurses hollered behind the open doors. Someone answered a phone call.

Another dead parent? Olivia stared at the doctor.

"We'll let you know how she is as soon as the surgery's done." The doctor nodded, looked at them both and walked through the open doors.

Olivia brushed her thumbs against her palms. Dave breathed in, turning around. Nurses and CNAs walked through the room behind the doors. Some held clip boards while others wheeled carts across the floor.

Olivia's heart pounded in her chest. Someone touched her elbow.

"Let's go," Dave said. "We'll wait in the waiting room."

Olivia shook his fingers off her elbow.

"We can't stand here."

"I know."

She looked at Dave. Did he know? Did he know his wife's secret? Did he know that Olivia wouldn't really be losing another *parent*? Or was he thinking about himself? Was he thinking about Lindy? About life without her?

Gray highlights peaked through his dirty-blond hair. Wrinkles countered his eye lashes. His skin was cracked from days in the sun. Did it matter? Did it matter what anyone thought? God was in control. He would take Lindy's life, or He would heal her. Olivia looked down, walking past Dave. Without any consideration for the ones left behind. God was like that: doing what He wanted, when He wanted.

I pray that you won't let it harden your heart. Her Dad's letter came to her mind. How did he do it? How did he come to Christ after a life of sin?

Olivia found a window in the waiting room. She walked to it, starting to slide her hands into her pockets. The movement of her wrist tore at her open scar. She bit her teeth, lifting her arm to look at the bandage. She needed to change it.

Olivia sighed, lowering her arm. She needed to change a lot of things.

Dave sat down beside her, the chair cushion releasing air. Out of the corner of her eye she looked at him. He leaned his head against the wallpapered wall and closed his eyes, his hands folded between his legs. He was praying. She was certain.

What was it like? To have faith. Faith like her dad had, faith like Sam had, faith like Dave had? Would she view things differently? Would she find peace? Would God still take Lindy's life?

"Sir," a nurse walked up to Dave, "your vehicle needs to be moved."

Dave nodded and sat up straight.

"I'll do it." Olivia stepped back, turning away from the window.

Dave's family sat in the corner of the waiting room. Wyatt, the last person he would have expected to see, sat beside his sister. Wyatt scrolled through his phone, while John, and Great Grandma snacked on Lay's chips, Nate could hear Great Grandma chew from across the room. Mary, Grandma, and Sam whispered something to each other, while Dave looked out the window.

What was Dave thinking? Was he thinking about the unthinkable?

Nate thought of Olivia. Maybe he should have turned around and followed her to the farm. He wanted to know her thoughts, her feelings.

Nate stepped onto the waiting room carpet, away from the automatic doors. John nodded a hello, Great Grandma kept eating chips, Wyatt kept scrolling, and the women kept whispering. Nate walked up to Dave.

Dave looked up. Nate looked at him. He didn't need to speak; Dave knew why Nate came. He knew the words Nate wanted to say. Dave squeezed Nate's shoulder and shook it slightly. He lowered his arm and looked out the window.

"Where's Olivia?" he asked.

"I passed her on my way to town. She was headed back to the farm."

Dave crossed his arms over his chest, his thoughts appearing to change. "She hasn't been doing well lately. I don't think she should be alone."

"I can go get her if you want me to."

Dave looked at Nate. He pondered the idea, then shook his head. "She probably needs to work through it herself."

Dave shifted his feet, turning toward the waiting room. "Thank you for being here." He slapped Nate's shoulder. "You're family. You know that right?"

He felt more like family in Dave's family than he did in his own family. He didn't like that. He didn't like betraying his mom like that. He loved his parents. But too often their different opinions got in the way of their relationship. They had really liked Anna. The few dates they went on had given his parents hope that he would keep their conservative ways.

Dave waited for an answer.

"I know, Sir."

Dave nodded, released his shoulder, and walked to his family.

Sir. Another thing his parents had never taught him. But it just felt right. Like so many other little things that just felt "right." Things that his parents hadn't taught him, things his parents didn't approve of. Those *things* made him feel more like himself.

Great Grandma stood up, and reached out her hands, waving people toward her. "Come. Ve vill pray. It vill make the time go faster."

Everyone looked at Great Grandma. They lowered their heads; some started to fold their hands.

"No." Great Grandma waved her hands. "Together. Let's pray together. Come. Take my hand." She looked at her daughter, her granddaughter, and her great granddaughter.

Mary grasped Great Grandma's hand and reached for John's hand. Slowly they formed a circle. They left a gap between Dave and Sam. Sam looked at Nate, extending her hand toward him. She smiled at him. He knew the intent of that smile was to welcome him into their circle. But it was the first time he ever noticed her smile. It was true and sincere.

Nate stepped forward and placed his hand in hers.

Dave led them in prayer.

His heart ached for Dave, for Olivia. He wanted Olivia here with them, with him. Yet something felt right.

"…may Your peace fill our hearts," Dave prayed. "If it is Your will then we ask that You heal Lindy, yet not our will, but Your will be done. And Lord I ask, that wherever Olivia is, whatever she's doing, that You would heal her too. Help her through whatever she's feeling. Amen."

"Amen," Nate whispered.

Olivia sat on the chair in front of her desk. She looked out the dark window, staring at nothing. Her hair poked out of her braid; blood and dirt stained her shirt. The bandage she wore around her wrist was soaked with blood. What had she done?

Sam stepped toward Nate, stopping beside him. Nate felt Sam look at him.

Olivia rubbed a Bible page between her fingers. The Bible laid open at Psalm chapter six. It looked worn; the pages looked aged. Someone else's handwriting marked the side of the page. The chapter had two highlighted sentences: *I am worn out from my groaning. All night long I flood my bed with weeping, and drench my couch with tears.*

Was that how Olivia felt? Was there more to her sadness? More than a breakup; more than a mom in a hospital room.

An open box sat in front of the Bible. It housed pictures, a bracelet, a document, and some other items. Nate looked at Olivia. What was she hiding? Who was the girl behind those sober eyes?

He brushed his forearms and took a step closer. He should say something. She looked different than the girl he knew. She looked worn, beaten, abused.

Nate reached out a hand, wanting to touch her shoulder. He held his hand inches away from her. Unlike the time in the barn, she looked unapproachable. She didn't look up, she didn't move.

Nate lowered his hand.

"How is she?" Olivia spoke.

"She pulled through. You can see her whenever you want."

She nodded. She stopped rubbing the page, and folded her arms on the desk. Her upper back arched; her head lowered. Her head fell onto her arms; her body began to shake. Silent sobs came from her lips.

Nate placed both hands behind his head. He gripped his hair and bit his teeth. He ran his hands over his face and walked to the other end of the room. What could he say? What could he do?

He looked over his shoulder.

He desperately wanted to take her hands and force her to look at him. He wanted to wipe her tears away. He wanted to be enough. Enough to make this better—whatever this was.

Olivia whispered. Her body quit shaking.

Nate turned around.

Sam stepped closer, placing a hand on Olivia's shoulder. "What?" she asked.

"Help me." Olivia rolled her forehead on her arm. "Help me," she whispered. Her body started shaking "Save me," she said.

"Olivia." Sam hunched down beside her, and placed a hand on Olivia's knee. "Only Jesus can save you."

Olivia made a fist and punched the open Bible, her head resting on her elbow. Nate wanted to grab her wrist and force her to stop. He wanted her to look at him. He wanted to squeeze her shoulders until she stopped shaking.

She lifted her back, and dropped her head in her hands. "How?"

"By accepting him as your Lord and Savior and repenting of your sins."

Nate breathed, slipping his hands in his pockets.

Olivia wiped her cheeks. She looked out the window, into the darkness. "'To know what it is like to mess up and still be loved'," she quoted someone.

"Exactly," Sam said. "Ask Jesus into your heart and *feel* the love he has for you." Sam took Olivia's hands into hers. She forced Olivia to rest her hands on her lap and look at her.

"Pray with me." Sam squeezed her hands. "If you're ready then pray with me and ask the Lord to come into your heart. Not as the God you knew as a child, the God who existed in the distance, but the God that wants to live in your heart. The God you knew as a child has been waiting.

He wants you to open your heart and let Him in." Sam smiled. "Can you do that?" She shook Olivia's arms. "Are you ready to let him?"

Nate removed his hands from his pockets, folded his arms across his chest, and focused at the rug.

He heard Olivia whisper, "I am."

"Then do it. Open your heart. Forget your past. Start a new life."

Would she forget everything? Would she forget that he lied to her? Would she forget her boyfriend in prison? Would she live with a different light in her eyes? Instead of the heaviness he'd noticed the first time he saw her.

"Lord Jesus," Olivia cried. Nate glanced at her; her face glistened with moisture. "Come into my heart, forgive me for what I did. I'm sorry I ignored you. You never wanted me to blame myself. You control life and death. You took my dad's life. Not because of what I did, but because it was his time to go home. You forgave my dad. You took my mother's life, for reasons I don't understand." Olivia breathed. "I searched for love. I desperately wanted Lindy to love me; I begged Josh to stay, but only you Lord, can give the love that I long for. Only you can give me the peace that I need. Peace to let go, peace to start fresh. I give it all to you Lord. Take my life, take it, and lead me."

Nate opened his eyes. He couldn't remember closing them.

Sam's head hung on her neck. Her hair hung down in front of her shoulders. Both girls cried.

Nate wiped at the moisture on his cheek. He cleared his throat and straightened his back.

Olivia looked up. "Are you crying?" she asked, releasing Sam's hands.

Olivia wiped her cheeks.

Nate cleared his throat, shifting his feet. "No."

Olivia smiled. Her eyes, they looked different. Different from one prayer.

Nate wanted that. He wanted that peace.

CHAPTER TWENTY-EIGHT

"How do you feel? Do you need another pillow? Is this comfortable?" Mary's voice sounded through the thick wood door.

Olivia lifted her knuckles. She hovered them in front of the door. What would she say?

Across the hallway, nurses sat in a corner, typing, calling, talking. She needed to go in before they offered to help with something.

Olivia pushed the handle and opened the door. She smiled at Mary and Sam.

"Who's here?" Lindy asked.

Olivia pushed the door behind her and waited for it to click. "Good morning, Mom." Olivia walked past the nurse's cart and around the corner, toward Mom. "I stopped at the coffee shop on the way here." She extended the hot, paper cup.

Lindy nodded toward the food tray that stood beside the bed. "You can set it there for now. Thank you."

The food tray mainly held Mom's personal items. Ear

buds, her phone, a book, and a plastic jug of ice water stood around a cup of Jello.

"Have you not eaten anything?" Olivia asked.

Mom still wore the hospital gown. Her hair looked undone. The IV in her right arm wasn't hooked to anything. Mom was free to move off the shuffled bedsheets.

"Has Dave not been here to help you get dressed?" Olivia asked.

Mom smiled. "You're usually not this chatty. Where were you last night? I was waiting for you."

She felt Sam look at her. Olivia glanced at Sam. She walked around the plastic bedframe and sat down on the purple bench. The midmorning light shone through the window. Behind her someone mowed the hospital lawn. How would she tell Mom? Should she tell her everything? Should she tell her the truth? The ugly, broken truth. Should she voice the lowest moment in her entire life?

It was Jesus that helped her. If Sam hadn't been there, would she have accepted Him? Would she have confessed? Olivia looked at Sam. Sam stood up, stepping toward Mary. Sam had a light about her. Her blond hair helped, but it was deeper than that. The same light shone in Mary.

Olivia thought about Dave, about Granny and Grandma, about her dad. The light had always been there. Yet she had never noticed. Would that same light shine in her?

"Should we go? The nurses might not approve of so many guests."

Sam interrupted Olivia's thoughts.

Mary looked at Sam. "They wouldn't have allowed Olivia into the room if they didn't want us here."

Sam gave Mary a look. A look that told Mary everything she needed to know. How did that happen? How did mother and daughter form a bond where words weren't needed? How did mother and daughter become friends? Could that happen between Lindy and her? Could nearly seventeen years be forgotten? Could they start fresh after all this time?

Mary grabbed her purse off the desk behind her. "I suppose you might be right."

"Thanks again for stopping by. I'm sorry about…" Mom's eyes trailed down her gown.

"Nonsense." Mary pointed her nose at Mom. "You rest. Text me if you think of anything that needs to be done at the house."

Mary stepped forward. "Let us know when you get out." She smiled at Olivia, then at Mom. "Thank God everything turned out the way it did."

"God is good," Mom said.

"Yes. God is good."

The two women smiled at each other. Like sisters. Something Olivia had never seen with Dad's family.

"We'll talk to you later." Mary waved a hand and walked toward the door.

Sam looked back at Olivia. "Thank you," Olivia mouthed.

Sam smiled, nodded, and walked out the door.

The door clicked.

"Did you read the letter?" Mom looked at Olivia.

How did she know about it? Dad must have told her. They were husband and wife after all. If her birth mom wouldn't have died, would dad still have chosen Lindy? How often had that thought crossed Lindy's mind?

What would it feel like to have the man you love, not only kiss another woman, but to sleep with another woman? To share that kind of intimacy with another soul. Then to watch another woman carry his baby. They had not been married. They had not committed to one another. Yet, the love; the feelings; the trust; how could that *not* hurt?

Olivia sat on the edge of the bench; her hands folded on her lap. "I did."

Mom nodded, turning her face toward the black TV screen. "I figured."

"I'm sorry, Olivia."

Mom never said her name like that. She never said it like it meant something.

"I'm sorry too."

"No," Mom looked at her, "it's my turn to be sorry. I was a terrible mother. I don't deserve to be called your mom. More than that, I was a terrible Christian. But if you can, will you forgive me? I want to try. I want to be the mom you never had."

"I can't imagine what it was like. I can't imagine the hurt. I can't imagine losing a husband."

She remembered saying goodbye to Josh. That hurt, still did. But she hadn't been married to him. She hadn't shared a bed with him, she hadn't shared over a decade of memories with him.

"You never asked to be born. You never forced your dad to come home. You were a child—a child that grew up feeling guilt you never should have felt. I was out of line. What I did was more than unnecessary. Can you forgive me?"

She wouldn't have believed her heart could feel lighter than it had last night. But it did. She felt like the four-year-old child swinging on a warm spring day. She was that child. That same child felt loved then, that child felt loved now. Not because the words she heard, but because the words she had accepted. *Greater love has no one than this: to lay down one's life for one's friends.* Jesus laid down his life for her. It was *the Word* that brought Mom to say what she said, and mean them. Jesus did that.

"Yes. I forgive you."

Mom reached out a hand toward Olivia. Olivia placed her palm in Mom's. Mom squeezed her hand. "Thank you." Mom smiled.

A tear fell down Olivia's cheek.

Mom shook her hand. She sat up straight, releasing her hand. "Now, get up and comb my hair before Dave gets here." Mom looked at Olivia. "Please," she said, like a dog eyeing the food in his owner's hand.

Olivia smiled. "How would you like it done?" She looked around. "Where's a brush?"

"In the bag." Mom pointed to the duffle bag on the table. "I hope it's in there. Mary brought that bag last night."

Olivia shuffled through the bag. The mower drove past the window. Behind the mower, walked a boy with a trimmer in hand. She felt the sun through the glass. It warmed her shoulder. She stood in a hospital room, yet something felt like home.

"You're out late," Olivia said, looking across the pond. It looked the same way it had the night Josh brought her here.

"I had to check a sprinkler. I saw your pickup here; thought I'd stop by to see how you are doing."

Olivia looked at Nate.

"So, how are you doing?"

His hair remained freshly combed, his clothes still looked clean. It was strange for a Thursday, but it was a strange Thursday.

Olivia picked a leaf off the Elm beside her. She tore bits off, lifting her focus to Nate. "She's coming home later today. The doctors say after a few weeks she'll be back on her feet."

"I know that. I meant, how are *you* doing? A lot happened in the last few weeks. How are you feeling?"

Olivia breathed, dropping the leaf. A lot did happen. A lot Nate didn't know about, and probably never would. It didn't matter. That life was past her.

She watched the butterflies on the wildflowers. Purple and

yellow flowers dotted the ankle-high buffalo grass. On the hill cattle grazed. Some scratched their necks on the barbed fencing. She loved it here.

God worked in mysterious ways. She would never wish her father dead, but if life hadn't turned out the way it did, she wouldn't be here. She might have never accepted Jesus as her Savior. She wouldn't know the peace she knew now. Her dad's prayers might have never been answered.

"Good." Olivia looked at Nate. "I feel good. At peace. At home."

Nate smiled. His smile reached his eyes. It highlighted his square jaw and the fresh whiskers on his face. He scanned over the pond, lifting his shoulders.

"Will you visit him?"

Olivia turned and looked over the pond. "I . . ." she wanted to. But should she? Should she hold on to something that might not last? Should she spend her days waiting for him? What if he wouldn't want her four years from now? She'd be twenty-one—just about. Olivia sighed, "I don't know."

Nate nodded.

"Will you?" she asked.

He shrugged. "Probably."

He lifted his focus to the sky. Olivia followed his gaze. White summer clouds hovered in the baby blue sky. Birds flew overhead, landing in the trees. Flies buzzed around them; the midday air warmed her face.

"God's painting. Clear and bright," Nate said.

Olivia watched the sky. It told a story. It told of hope: a hope clear and bright. "God is good," she said.

Nate breathed. "He is."

ABOUT THE AUTHOR

Maria and her husband own and operate a farm in southwest Kansas, where she was born and raised. She is a mom of two small children. She loves to garden, raise farm animals, and spend time with her family. Follow her on Instagram or visit her at marialoewen.com.